LOVE ME NOT

This
Book
Belongs
to:

Sasha

Also by Nishawnda Nicole Ellis

Wives and Girlfriends

Love Me Not

Nishawnda Nicole Ellis

www.urbanbooks.net

Urban Books
1199 Straight Path
West Babylon, NY 11704

ISBN-13: 978-1-60162-032-3
ISBN-10: 1-60162-032-2

First Printing January 2008
Printed in the United States of America

10 9 8 7 6 5 4 3 2 1

*This is a work of fiction. Any references or similarities to actual events, real
people, living, or dead, or to real locales are intended to give the novel a sense of
reality. Any similarity to other names, characters, places, and incidents is entirely coincidental.*

Submit Wholesale Orders to:
Kensington Publishing Corp.
C/O Penguin Group (USA) Inc.
Attention: Order Processing
405 Murray Hill Parkway
East Rutherford, NJ 07073-2316
Phone: 1-800-526-0275
Fax: 1-800-227-9604

Acknowledgments

On a down day at a nowhere job, little did I know that a little letter to myself would ignite this fire to create an entire book!

I would like to thank my mom, Phyllis, and my dad, Charles, for making me the person I am today.

Mom, your touch of class is somewhere in this book. And don't worry, I made all this stuff up, it didn't really happen!

Daddy, your I-don't-worry-about-shit way of life is definitely in there. Thanks for everything you do.

To my grandmother, whose voice I hear in some of my characters—"Not a bit more than nothing!"—I don't know where my life would have been if you hadn't been in it.

To my sister, Tiffanie, for letting me know that you can do 101 things at the same time to get the job done, and be and do anything you want. And, yes, I had to use your Tanya alias. Sorry!

To my brother, Charles Jr., for having the biggest heart in the world, no matter how mean I can be to you. And, no, I won't charge you for a copy.

To my little sister, Charnai, who has the potential to be anything she wants to be. Even a writer like her big sis! Just kidding. Be you, because you are wonderful!

To the rest of my family, Reid and Ellis. Because of you I know what a family really is.

To the ladies—Kizzy, you got it going on, girl, no matter what you think. Krishona, be kind to your friends, not just the fellas. I love you anyway. Thanks for reading my book over and over again and letting me pick your brain over and over again. Don't worry, I will do the same for the next one! Ayana, your words of encouragement always move me in the right direction. Andrea, you are such an angel (AH HA)! Kenyetta, are you with us or what? Stop zoning! I love you all. You are my DAWGS!

To Jamila, for being one of my sane, but still crazy friends. To Christina, Yaneke, Zakiya and Adam, my Hampton road dogs, who didn't say to me, "Your major is nursing, not journalism. Leave that book alone!"

And last but not least, thank you, readers, who have supported this project and enjoyed this book as much as I have. I love you all, and I hope to have you laughing, crying, and kicking yourself in the you-know-what in the next book.

He loves me . . .

"That girl is poison, never trust a big butt and a smile, yeah hee."
Poison by BBD played over the loudspeakers at the YMCA
party. Sasha thought she was quite the cunning sixteen-year-
old. She'd managed to make up some effortless lie to her Aunt
Mimi about staying over at her best friend Lisa's house Friday
night, but she was really on Martin Luther King Boulevard at
the YMCA Halloween party hosted by BAD (Boston Against
Drugs). They always gave an event where inner city youth
could party instead of slinging dope on the streets, or getting
arrested or shot up from a neighborhood drive-by.

Sasha and her girls, Lisa, Tamieka, and Michelle were killing
it on the dance floor, sweating out their different-styled crimped
waves and French roll hairdos, while showing off their roger
rabbit, running man, and scissors-leg dance moves. They were
having a good time, flirting and driving the boys crazy. The
party was over by ten p.m. The girls hung around after the party
in the cool fall night, as if the MBTA bus didn't stop running
at twelve forty-five a.m.

Sasha didn't care what time she got in the house. She didn't have any real parents anyway. Six months ago, on her sixteenth birthday, her parents were killed in a car accident. Her mother, Eva Freeman, left the party to pick up her father, Raymond Freeman, who'd promised Sasha he wouldn't miss the event, even though he had to go out of town for a business trip earlier that Saturday morning.

As promised, he'd made it to Logan Airport at seven-thirty p.m. sharp so that he would only miss the first half of Sasha's special day. Unbeknownst to him though, he would break that promise and change Sasha's life forever.

There was nothing sweet for Sasha and her younger brother, Raymond Jr. after that. They went to live with her mother's younger sister, Melinda, and her daughter Tanya. They called her Aunt Mimi, and her men friends called her Mims. Aunt Mimi had Tanya when she was sixteen, and by the time her daughter was eighteen, she was ready to reclaim her life. When Sasha and Raymond were willed to her, she couldn't understand why they weren't given to their seventy-five-year-old grandmother, who was alive and kicking in Charleston, South Carolina. Aunt Mimi selfishly wanted to make up for old times, party, date, and release some sexual inhibitions she'd suppressed while raising Tanya as a single mother. Tanya, however, was like a big sister to her cousins and helped as much as she could when her mother was out acting boy crazy at thirty-four. So Sasha and Raymond were left to fend for themselves, and they did.

Raymond got in more trouble at fourteen than he ever did when his parents were alive. From boosting cars to selling weed and carrying guns, Raymond spent more time at the police station than at school. Like Tupac said, "Victim of the street, born to the penitentiary."

As for Sasha, green and gullible when it came to boys, she was buck wild, looking for love in all the wrong places, and smoking weed and drinking forty-ounce bottles of Olde English with her girls as they party-hopped every Friday and Saturday night. She thought she was the princess of deceit when it came to lying to her Aunt Mimi. Sasha really didn't think her aunt cared. She didn't think anyone cared for that matter, so why should she? She felt her parents abandoned her and Raymond by dying and leaving them with her young-ass-acting aunt. They were both hopelessly lost.

After negotiating with a willing patron going into the liquor store to score them four bottles of forty-ounce Olde English malt liquor, Sasha and her girls sat on the swings in Washington Park four blocks away from the YMCA. They drank, smoked marijuana, and cracked jokes.

Michelle looked at her pager. "Oh shit, and it's twelve thirty-eight! We're going to miss the twenty-eight!"(That was the bus that ran down Blue Hill Avenue from Roxbury to Mattapan, where Michelle lived). Michelle was two years older than her friends, so she got away with a coattail more than they did, and her mother didn't mind them all staying the night at her house when they went out.

The girls jumped out of their swings and raced for Blue Hill Avenue. They cut through Charlane Projects and high-stepped it to Martin Luther King Boulevard. A Black Ford Explorer pulled up alongside them as they were about to cross the street to Blue Hill Avenue. The driver rolled down his window, and a passenger in the back yelled out, "Hey, Lisa."

She turned around and it was Black, a fine-ass older dude from her high school. She went over to the car, and they chatted it up.

Impatient as Tamieka was she said, "Lisa, let's go. We're going to miss our bus."

Lisa turned around and shushed her.

The driver was in no rush either for them to take off; he was too busy admiring Sasha's apple-shaped butt in her black Levi's 501 jeans. "Hey, shorty," he said. "Come here."

Tamieka pushed up a gassed face like, *Oh, I know he ain't*

talking to me. Tamieka, the boss and momma of the crew, rolled her eyes like she was too good for any man dead, walking, or breathing.

"I wasn't talking to you," he said, "I was talking to your girl."

Sasha turned around and said, "Who me?"

The light-skinned brother smiled. "Yeah, you, come here."

Against her girls' warning, Sasha, always a sucker for a high yellow boy, especially one who was driving, walked over to the four-wheel driver. She figured he could definitely take her teenage behind somewhere.

"Where you on your way to, miss?"

"Home. The last bus stops in like two minutes."

"I don't know about your girls, but I would take you anywhere you wanna go."

Sasha blushed a little. A late bloomer, she thrived on any attention she got. She wasn't comfortable in her own skin yet and felt like she still had braces and hardly smiled. Boys always picked on her and called her "fish lips." So when she got her braces removed and went to middle school and then high school boys were then saying how sexy and juicy her lips were, she was confused about herself and couldn't help but feel insecure.

"I can't leave my friends," she said.

"What's your name, cutie?" The boy asked, noticing her thickness, her slanted eyes, and caramel cinnamon skin.

Cutie? "Sasha," she said without skipping a beat.

"Can I have your number, Sasha?"

"I don't see why not."

He gave her a pen, and she wrote down her number on piece of paper he found in his car. She gave it to him.

He smiled. "I think you missed your bus."

"No shit, Sherlock," a pissed-off Tamieka said. She had ears like a wolf.

Sasha walked away from the car, happy as a clam. She tried to keep the image of him in her head—his chinky brown eyes, low, cute fade, and huge dimples when he smiled. And his cologne, *Joop* (she recognized the fragrance) made her have nasty thoughts. Whew, she felt like she wanted to exhale.

Lisa gave Black her digits and joined her friends on the sidewalk so they could decide whether they were going to flag a cab and run their asses out of it before they paid the fare or do the unthinkable and call someone's momma to come and pick them up.

The driver asked, "Where you live, Sasha?"

Tamieka cut in, "Oh so now your ass done made us miss our bus and you think you're going to just take one of us home." She shook her head. "Nope, we came together, and we're leaving together."

"I was going to offer you all a ride, if you didn't mind squeezing in the back with Black." *Loud-ass bitch.*

"We can fit." Lisa walked back over to the car and hopped in. She wasn't going to let anyone else sit on Black's lap.

Michelle got in, and Sasha sat on her lap, and Tamieka sat next to the window.

The driver turned his music up loud and let "Doin' It" by LL Cool J bump through his BOSE speakers.

Sasha didn't know what to say to him. This was the first and only older boy who'd ever paid her any attention.

They pulled up to Michelle's house and hopped out of the car one by one like they were clowns getting out a tiny car. Sasha said, "Thank you," to the driver and turned around to catch up with her friends.

"You're welcome," he said.

The jeep was about to pull off, and Sasha realized she didn't even know dude's name. She turned around and shouted, "Hey, I don't even know your name."

The boy yelled out his window, "It's Montel."

From that night, Sasha and Montel talked on the phone for hours each day. He was eighteen and about to graduate from high school next year and go to college in North Carolina.

Montel showed Sasha a different world when it came to

how to treat a lady. He opened doors for her, picked her up from cheerleading practice, and drove her to her cashier job at CVS. He took her to the movies, the museum, and Good Times, a local Boston gaming room. He bought her anything she wanted, and she didn't want much, but he got it for her.

Montel's mother, Christina, was well off and spoiled him rotten. He had his own bank account, credit card, and brand-new car by the time he was fifteen. She was a corporate lawyer for Bingham Tucker & Gold, and very much into her career, as she was her community. That's why she refused to let her White co-workers buy up all the historical Victorian and colonial houses in Roxbury. She didn't follow her bourgeois sisters and move out to the suburbs. She planned to raise her a man in the heart of Boston. But fortunately for Montel (or unfortunately) his mother was hardly ever home.

Montel and Sasha met at his house to watch BET after school on days when Sasha didn't have cheerleading practice. Montel would sneak in some kisses, and Sasha didn't mind one bit.

"I can't wait to get up out of here," Montel said in frustration, as the sound of police sirens drowned out *Scarface*, the movie they were watching.

Sasha sighed at the thought as she lay across his chest. She didn't want him to go but understood his need to escape Boston. She wished she could runaway too.

"You going to come visit me if I send you a bus ticket?"

Sasha jumped up.

"Would I?" She straddled him and began French-kissing him.

Montel loved it when she took control. For all the six months they were seeing each other, he'd never pressured her for sex.

Even though Sasha was a little boy-crazy herself and used to feeling unloved, she was still a virgin. She didn't know how to let someone in, she couldn't trust anyone. Losing her parents froze her heart, but she was slowly letting Montel melt it.

They kissed, and Montel fondled her breasts. And she was

grinding her pelvis against his, as they dry-humped with their clothes on.

Montel was getting harder and harder. He knew they would have to stop soon, and he would need a cold shower.

This time Sasha didn't stop him.

What the hell. Montel put his hands underneath her shirt and caressed her breasts. Then he took off her shirt, unsnapped her bra, and began sucking on her breasts like a newborn baby.

Sasha still didn't stop him.

He turned her over on her back and unzipped her jeans then pulled them off. He slid his fingers through her pink Hanes briefs and into her kitty.

Sasha moaned and kissed him harder.

Montel pulled down his baggy jeans and rubbed his silk boxers against Sasha's Hanes. He couldn't believe she was going to let him.

He asked, "Are you sure?"

Sasha looked into his chinky eyes. She was a little scared, but for the first time in what seemed like an eternity, someone had gained her trust. She nodded her head. "Yes."

Montel didn't waste any time. He pulled out his "big willie," pulled down Sasha's briefs, and got down to business. Sasha was tight as a dead bolt, as if her vagina had a *Do Not Enter* sign in front of it.

Montel was quite endowed for a teenage boy. He kept trying to penetrate Sasha's vagina, but she would squirm in pain at entry.

She didn't scream or yell, she was trying to hang in there for her man. But then she began rethinking the whole idea. Her juices were drying up, and the pain of Montel trying to drive his big dick inside her was burning, like her skin was being dragged across the sidewalk. She gritted her teeth. "Shouldn't we be using a condom anyway?"

Montel couldn't go back to blue-ball land for losers. "Don't worry, baby, I won't bust inside you, I promise." *DAMN, THIS SHIT IS TIGHT. I AIN'T EVER LYING.*

The more he tried to do it, the less Sasha became interested. It just hurt too damn much. Finally, she said, "Montel, we need a condom."

Montel buried his head in her neck, sweating, exhausted, and out of breath from trying to do the impossible. He rolled over, disappointed as hell, but not defeated. He pulled his arm around her and kissed her on the lips, still breathing heavily.

"Next time," he said as he collapsed his head on the his pillow, worn the fuck out from not fucking.

Sasha didn't want to disappoint him, but his monster dick was killing her.

The next time became the next time, and the next time as their relationship carried on. When he left for school, he promised her that he would send for her to come and visit. He confessed, "I love you, Sasha." He had come to see her before he and his mother left for North Carolina that August.

Sasha couldn't even look at him. Another person that she loved was leaving her. She couldn't take it. She muttered, "I love you too," and started bawling and wailing in his arms on her Aunt Mimi's porch.

Montel tried to cheer her up.

"Hey, don't be getting all mushy on me. You know you about to go meet some other dude."

"I would never do that to you. Never." She didn't know if or when she would see him again. In her heart, she knew she wouldn't be able to replace him.

He hugged her for as long as he could and then pulled away from her. "Baby, don't cry. I will send for you, I promise." He brushed her long black shoulder-length hair with his hand.

She believed him but still didn't want him to go. "I love you, Montel."

He smiled at her and lifted her chin to kiss her one more time. "I know."

Sasha watched him as he jumped into his black Ford Explorer and took off. Her heart was burning a hole inside her chest. She had fallen so fast and so hard for him, she didn't know what she was going to do without him.

"Hello, Sasha, are you there?" Montel waved his hand in front of her face to snap her out of her trance-like state.

Sasha blinked in from her flashback to the time when she was so in love with this man. She had traveled so far from that girl she used to know. She was twenty-eight years old, graduate of both Florida A & M and Harvard University Medical School, a licensed obstetrician, home owner, and could buy just about anything she ever wanted. She traveled anywhere she pleased, like Cancun, Las Vegas, Paris, Italy, Hong Kong, and Egypt. She still had the same girlfriends, her family as she called them, and they were close as sisters could be. She wasn't married and had no kids but was in no rush either. She enjoyed dating and not being emotionally attached to anyone.

"Where did you go just now?"

Sasha gathered her composure and tried to force out those old feelings, but just the touch of Montel's hand against her skin made her quiver inside. *Why now? Why after all these years did he have to pop back in my life?*

Montel stared into Sasha's slanted brown eyes. Sasha wasn't that sixteen-year-old puppy he'd rescued. She was grown and calling the shots when it came to her relationships. She wasn't that cute and polite girl he'd met twelve years earlier.

Sasha tried to ignore the way his scent invaded her sense of smell and the way he licked his lips whenever he said her name, but something in her kept tugging her near him. She wanted to escape, jump out of his Range Rover, but couldn't.

"Sasha, can I call you some time?"

The right side of her brain wanted to say, "Hell, no. You broke my heart, muthafucka," but she went with the left side instead and said, "Maybe."

CHAPTER ONE

He Loves Me Not . . .

"Why haven't you called me, Sasha? Are you mad at me?" Jason asked, concern in his voice.

"No, I'm not mad. I just-I just ..." Sasha stuttered, caught off guard by this call. *I thought you were over, damn it. If you don't call someone, you're not interested.*

"You just what? Forgot about me? I mean, are you mad at me? What's the problem?" Jason rambled on and on about why she hadn't returned his call.

Sasha tuned him out. *How did I let him get this far?*

They had gone out a couple of times and it was all right, but as far as Sasha was concerned, he was no keeper, no soul mate, not even sexing material. She'd just wanted someone to talk with, to take her out, and maybe play for a while at the thought of him being the one.

Sasha's love life should have been titled "The Mis-education of Sasha Freeman." Her relationships began the same and ended the same—Meet them, date them, hump them, and leave them.

Chances were if you were trying to get too involved with her, you just bought yourself a deportation ticket because there was no "green card" to her heart.

After Montel, Sasha had met Chris, the one she gave up her virginity to, and the kind of guy you'd label as high-school sweetheart. She was attracted to his smile, the way he walked, and his kindheartedness. With him, she thought she was queen and could do anything, say anything, just act up and it would be okay. She wasn't in love with him. She'd liked him a lot and wanted to have sex, so she chose him. As a matter of fact, "What's Love Got to Do with It" was her theme song.

She'd fantasized about going to college and becoming a physician. She'd figured that as soon as she graduated, he'd be a thing of the past. Well, while in fantasy land, Chris cheated on her, and she sent him flying down her Aunt Mimi's flight of stairs with a "how-could-you" kick in his back. Was she hurt? Not exactly. More like appalled that he cheated on her before she got the chance to cheat on him.

Sasha flashed back into her telephone call with a still rambling Jason. "I'm not mad at you," she said in a silly voice. "I'm sorry I didn't return your call."

"Okay. Is the snow really deep outside? Because I was going to come over."

"Yeah, it's very deep out. You shouldn't come over."

"I could walk. It's not that far from here."

Walk? It's knee-deep in snow. Is he crazy?

"I could probably ride my bike."

"NO! Look, Jason I—"

"It's okay, Sasha. I'll call you back. You're not cheating on me, are you?"

"WHAT?"

"I'm just playing. I'll hit you back." Jason giggled and hung up.

What's going on around here? I stopped calling him a month ago. If he calls me back, I don't know what to do. What a bugaboo. Imag-

ine if I did give him some, Sasha thought. *No more picking up men at the gym.*

After hooking up the phone to the Internet so it would tie up the phone line, Sasha turned on the slow jams and walked into her bathroom. The shower was running, and the steam was fogging up the mirrors. She could see Damon's figure through the champagne-colored shower curtain. She thought, *Should I . . . ?*

Before she knew it, Damon had opened the shower curtain and swept her up into the shower in her lavender lace satin nightgown. She threw her arms around him and bounced into his arms, wrapping her legs around his waist and kissing him softly before he could open his mouth.

Damon tongued her back and began kissing her all over, ripping her nightgown off and throwing it over the curtain railing. He held her up with one hand and closed the shower curtain with the other.

Sasha wanted to burst when he cupped and sucked her nipples. Her wetness seeped from her "rooter" to her tooter as she felt his mercury rising.

They dreamt and melted in each other's arms as they made love for the rest of the night.

The next day it was still snowing outside, causing schools and stores to close. The hospital was open though, and Sasha had to be there in three hours.

Damon made her a vegetable and cheese omelet with toast. He knew exactly what a woman needed—pampering, good conversation, and great sex. If only he could stop being such a ladies' man, then he would've been a keeper.

But who was Sasha kidding though? She liked their arrangement. Damon wasn't boyfriend material. He had his own thing going on. He satisfied a hungry woman's belly, not a dying woman's last request. Sasha knew he was seeing other women, even though he swore up and down that she was his wifey. He didn't have to lie to her. Hell, she was seeing other men too. It's just that she wasn't that dishonest about it. From the beginning she'd told him she didn't want him to be her man, just a good friend. Her fuck buddy, in other words.

Well, that game got tiring quick, so she considered herself occupying time and space in an empty heart. She adored Damon, and what they had filled her needs for right now.

She worked almost fifty hours a week trying to advance her career as a obstetrician, so she really didn't have time for all the loving and nurturing a relationship needs. She figured his game was to show her off and make her think that she was his one and only. She could look into his eyes and swear all he saw in her was a pretty face. His feelings didn't run that deep. Instead, she thought he saw her as a commodity. *He just has to have a bad-ass girl*. So Sasha just played along with it for now.

By the next morning, the snowy road had turned into dirty, slushy mush, and huge piles of plowed snow. After working overnight, the first sight of daylight was kind of confusing. You think you're supposed to just be waking up, and then you realize you've been up for sixteen hours.

Sasha just wanted to reach the train station because she had forgotten her scarf and could feel the chill going down her neck. The cold wind smacked her in the face, re-awakening her. On days like these, she missed being in Florida, where she went to A & M, where it was warm in January and she didn't need a scarf and boots. Boston, on the other hand, was always cold in the winter. The hurricanes in Florida were ridiculous though, one of the reasons she'd returned home to Boston, the other being her family.

I wonder if Raymond made it home last night, she thought.

Sasha worried about her brother all the time. She tried not to mix business with family, but it never worked. She'd agreed to rent him her upstairs apartment in her two-family house in Jamaica Plain on the condition he not stay there too long. She loved her brother, but even more so when he was away. As kids they'd bickered like any other sister and brother, and he knew how to irritate her. But he promised not to do that any more, along with "a laundry list of life, according to Sasha Freeman." It'd been working out so far, since he hadn't brought any drama like he did after their parents passed away.

Raymond left his life of misdemeanors and would-be felonies after he met Coach Wood in high school, who was Raymond's father figure from then on, mentoring him to become a better man, showing him how to redirect his anger after losing his parents. Raymond tried to get as close to his hoop dreams as possible. Basketball seemed like his only way out. Dreams of a million-dollar house, a million-dollar car, and million-dollar girl seemed to be the only motivation for young men not interested in the academic path.

Raymond loved the game because it allowed him to escape whatever he was running from, the thought of all that fame and glory soothing any other bad feelings that crossed his mind. Eventually he realized the hoop life wasn't his heart, it was his safe point. Now he didn't completely have that dream any more, but he could see it through other's eyes and feel safe. Now the coach of a middle-school basketball team at the recreation center in Roxbury, he was hoping to do for some young lost boy what Coach Wood did for him.

By the time Sasha reached home, there was a policeman and an ambulance as well as her new VW Passat parked in front.

Her heart dropped. *I know I wasn't robbed . . . Raymond.* She rushed up the stairs to her apartment, following a trail of blood to the top, her heart pounding, and all kinds of thoughts running through her head.

It seemed like she'd run a marathon. Out of breath, she shouted, "Officer, I live here. What happened? Where's my brother?"

The officer replied in a snide voice, "So he's your brother, huh."

Sasha's face didn't hide her bewilderment. "Officer—"

He took his finger and pointed toward the back porch.

She walked slowly as though afraid to move. She didn't notice that her place was trashed, and the draft coming from a broken window. As she reached the back porch, three officers stood around her brother. There he sat, head bent to his knees, hands behind his neck and handcuffs around his wrists. The police had Sasha's brother shackled on her back porch, wearing just a t-shirt and jeans in the middle of winter!

Raymond looked up at her and said, "I tried to stop him."

One of the officers read Raymond his rights, "You have the right to remain silent, anything you say or do will be held against you in a court of law . . ."

"What the hell is going on? Why is my brother under arrest?" Out of control with anger, Sasha busted in between the two officers standing over her brother.

One officer grabbed her arm and manhandled her back off the porch into her dining room. "Ma'am, I'm going to have to ask you to restrain yourself. This is official police business." He pulled Sasha's arm behind her back.

"Get off me! Are you crazy?" Sasha didn't care if he was a policeman or not, she struggled, trying to get out of his tight grip. "I will have your badge for this." Her heart pounding, fists tightly balled like rocks, she was ready for war. "Get your hands off me!"

"Ma'am, you need to calm down."

Raymond jumped up while the officer was reading him his rights. He pushed through, using his torso, his arms cuffed behind his neck. "Get your fucking hands off my sister," he yelled, knocking back the officer reading his rights against the glass pane sliding porch doors.

The third officer, standing farthest from Raymond, unholstered his weapon, flicked off the safety, and aimed it at the back of Raymond's head.

A terrified Sasha saw him and screamed, "NOOOOOO!"

CHAPTER TWO

Sasha's voicemail message played: *Hello, you've reached Sasha. At the sound of the beep, talk to me. BEEEP.*

"Hey, Sasha, it's Jason. Said I would be calling you back. I will try again later." Jason hung up the phone, confused as to why Sasha's answering machine kept picking up on the first ring.

Two minutes later, he dialed her number again, and her voicemail message played again. *Hello, you've reached Sasha. At the sound of the beep, talk to me. BEEEP.*

"I'm calling you back. It's Jason again. Holla."

Maybe she's not there. Maybe she's with someone else. "Shut up!" Jason yelled at himself.

He dialed her number again another two minutes later, and her voicemail came on again. "Dang, girl, where you at? Is your phone off the hook or something?"

No, asshole, she's fucking the next man. "I said shut the fuck up." Jason yelled louder this time at himself. *Why isn't she answering?*

He dialed Sasha's number every two minutes for the next half hour and left message after message, but still no call back.

He kept looking at his clock on his digital cable box. What seemed like hours had only been minutes.

He picked up his dumbbells and started doing curls. His muscles glistened through his t-shirt. He got hot fast, started sweating, then he put down the dumbbells and took off his T-shirt. He dialed Sasha's number again. No answer. He looked at the time on the digital cable box then picked up his dumbbells and did another 100 reps in two minutes. He took off his sweat pants this time, because now he was drenched in sweat and feeling even hotter.

He repeated this routine, dialing her number, leaving a message, looking at the clock, and doing 100 reps of curls five more times.

She's fucking someone else. "Fuck you, fuck you! I told you to shut up!"

He recalled meeting Sasha for the first time at Gold's Gym. It was at the end of November.

Sasha ran and ran on the treadmill. She was up to running thirty minutes straight without walking, trying to get her body in tip-top bikini shape for her trip to Las Vegas for the All-Star Weekend with Tamieka in February. It was almost impossible to diet during the holiday season, so she tried to increase her exercise to combat what she was eating.

Jason noticed her while he was working out on the elliptical machine. He watched her butt bounce as she ran against the treadmill belt. He didn't want her to ever stop running.

Sasha did though, and she went into the ab room to work on her "ungetriddable" gut.

Jason, hoping she would notice him, followed her in there and parked himself right next to her on the ab roller machine.

Sasha did notice him, or rather, his six-pack abdomen. "Man, you must work out every single day to get those abs." Sasha really wanted to know how he did it and was hoping for some pointers. Personal trainers didn't work for her, since she wasn't a very good do-as-I-say kind of girl.

She noticed me. Jason smiled. "Not every day."

Always a sucker for a cute smile, bald head, cocoa-brown skin, and a hot-to-death body, Sasha flirted with him. "They don't look real. Can I touch them?"

Jason laughed a nervous laugh. *Baby, you can touch anything you want.* "Sure."

Sasha stopped doing her worthless crunches and took Jason up on his offer. Then she said, "Hey, you wanna go grab one of those fruit things over there and tell me your secret?" Sasha loved to play the damsel-in-distress, acting like she didn't know much to get what she wanted from men, and as always, it worked.

Jason was nervous. Now that he had Sasha's attention, he didn't know what to do. "So you come here often?"

Do I come here often? Oh, boy, he's going down. "No, I'm a temporary member on a fourteen-day trial thingy. So how often should I work out to get my abs to look like that?"

"I can show you better than I could tell you."

He does have a pair, Sasha reaffirmed to herself. "How about this Thursday same time?"

Jason agreed, and they exchanged numbers. They worked out together for the next two weeks.

Sasha's membership was ending, so she wanted to take Jason to dinner as a thank you for showing her how to flatten her belly.

Inside the gym, Jason was cool, but when Sasha took him outside of it, he acted like he was from another planet. She took him to the Outback Steakhouse in Quincy and tried to spark up a conversation with him. "So what do you like to do, other than work out?" she asked.

"That's just about it—work out, work, work out." Jason was off his rocker today. Unfortunately, he'd taken too much of his lithium.

"That's right. You're a computer engineer. Work long hours, I imagine. Do you design computer programs for independent companies?" Sasha was trying to show interest in his field of work, but she had no clue about it, except if something went haywire with a computer, Jason was the guy to call.

"Yeah, I do," he said, melancholy as blue note.

And that's how their so-called dinner date continued.

Sasha regretted giving him her home number but thought he seemed like such a nice, fun guy. Harmless even. But the know-all ab guy turned out to be a know-all nothing, so she thought better not to call him any more. Needless to say, she didn't renew her membership.

Jason was so upset that she hadn't called him, so he called her and called her, until finally he got a hold of her. He wasn't sure why she was avoiding him and thought they were having a good time.

Now she wasn't answering her phone after he told her he was going to call her back. *Fucking medicine!*

He hadn't taken his lithium since that dinner with Sasha weeks ago. He was so pissed at the pills for making him look like a drooling mental patient.

She's not into you. You are a loser. He threw one of his dumb-bells across the floor, and it hit the wall of his rented apartment, making a small hole. "I said shut the fuck up, damn it!"

Pouring with sweat, he sat down on his sofa and placed his head between his knees. He rubbed his sore, calloused hands across his bald head. He was so hot. He pulled off his boxers and flopped back on his sofa.

Trying to push out the voices, he imagined Sasha running on the treadmill next to the one he was running on. She winked at him, her breasts bouncing up and down in her tank top. Jason grabbed his penis and imagined burying his head in her bosom. He began to massage himself slowly as he envisioned Sasha licking her lips. More sweat dripped over his body as he moaned. He massaged faster and harder as he thought of how Sasha's ass jiggled in those tight workout black leggings as she ran. He wanted to fuck her so bad.

He massaged harder and faster as he thought of her naked on top of him, riding him, and he licked and bit her breasts as they bounced off his face.

"ARRGHH!" He was growling like a tiger and was about ready to pop when he imagined plowing into her harder and harder doggy-style, pulling her hair, giving it to her.

"AAAHHH!" he yelled, as cum shot out of his penis like a volcano. *You are so pathetic.*

Jason grabbed the phone and dialed Sasha's number again.

Hello, you've reached Sasha. At the sound of the beep, talk to me. BEEEP.

Jason smacked the phone against the TV. His naked body was egg-frying hot. He turned over his coffee table and picked up the digital cable box and threw it through the window, shattering the glass. He couldn't get the voices out of his head. *She's fucking someone else. Whore!*

The following morning Jason got dressed and ran out. He fought his way through the snow on foot down to the gym. When it wasn't open, he was livid.

He eyeballed a trash can on the street, picked it up like he was on steroids, and threw it through the glass door at the gym, sounding the alarm. He rushed in like he had "mutant" speed and ransacked the file cabinet. He found *F* for Sasha Freeman. He got her address and made it out before the police got there. He didn't care if the camera caught him on tape. He had to see her. She was his medicine.

He managed to make his way to Jamaica Plain from Quincy by train. The station was open from the snow storm. He came to Willow Street and walked until he found 222. He noticed Sasha's Volkswagen parked out front. *She's home.*

He rang the doorbell that matched her name, but no one

answered. *She's in there. I know it.* He rang and rang and rang. Still no answer.

He crept across the street, blowing hot breath into his hands. It was 16 degrees outside. He went up the street to an open coffee shop, where he hung around until he was asked to leave.

By nightfall there was still no Sasha. He knew she was home.

He had waited all night, too long, and now the sun would be rising soon. Jason was at the point of no return.

She's fucking the next man. Heated, he ran across the street to Sasha's car and kicked and kicked the rear windows until they smashed. He found a crowbar in her trunk after getting inside the car and ran for her front door like a savage, busting the glass in her front window and throwing himself through it.

Once inside her place he yelled, "SASHA!" He started swinging, smashing anything in sight. Her glass tables, her mirrors, her TV, her stereo, it was all coming down. Amped with rage, he couldn't stop himself.

Before he knew it, his body was thrown up against the wall. He swung the crowbar, missing his target. As the crowbar slipped out of his hand, punches rained on his jaw, his eyes, his ribs.

Jason yelled out in pain, "ARRGGH," as blood spilled from his bloody mouth.

As he fell to the floor, his attacker pounced on him like a bear.

Jason thought quickly. He remembered he had a jagged-edged knife in his boot, meant for Sasha if he found her with another man. He reached for it, but it wasn't there. He scanned the room with his good eye and saw it a few feet away from him.

As he rolled his body over, his attacker kept beating on him.

He crawled as fast as he could to get the knife. His attacker must have seen it too, because he was pulling on his leg, trying to prevent him from reaching it.

Jason kicked himself free and grabbed it. *Yes!* He scrambled to his feet and swung at his attacker with the knife.

His attacker jumped back then quickly punched him in his good eye.

The next thing Jason knew, his attacker managed to get the knife from him, and all he could feel was his flesh being ripped like paper. He fell to the ground, wounded.

"Freeze! Drop your weapon!" was the last thing Jason heard before losing consciousness.

CHAPTER THREE

The officer who wrangled Sasha managed to tackle Raymond before the other one could shoot him in the head.

Sasha was visibly scared and angry. She cried and wanted to beat the officers to a pulp. "You almost killed him! You almost killed my brother! You call yourself officers of the law? This is disgraceful!" She rushed out to the porch. "Why do you have my brother in handcuffs? Get him out of those things immediately! Get off of him now!"

"Well, ma'am," the officer who'd drawn his weapon said, "we were under the impression that he was the other perp."

"Was that before or after he informed you he lived here?" Sasha fumed, saliva spewing from her mouth.

"Look, we have a job to do—"

"And just what is that job? To harass the innocent and let the guilty walk? You thought, no way could a young black man live in a place like this. He must be a thief, selling dope, or one of those entertainers. Racist, racist, that is what you are."

"Look here, lady, we were just doing what we thought was right."

"That's the problem, officer. You were not thinking." Sasha

walked toward the door. "Look, here is his mail. Raymond Freeman, 222 Willow Street."

"Ma'am, we tried to identify him, but he had no identification."

"He didn't need any ID. His picture is right here on the wall."

"Ma'am—"

"Who's in charge here? You have completely acted out of bias and you have my only brother out here in below-zero weather with no coat for God knows how long!!!" Sasha pointed at the officer. "You didn't think, you reacted, and your reaction was he had to be part of the crime because of who you see!!!"

"Ma'am, if you don't calm down, I will have to—"

"You will have to what? Arrest me? In my own home? For what, speaking the truth? I wish a muthafucka would try that shit!"

Fucking nigger bitch. The officer reached for his handcuffs.

Sasha was so pissed, she didn't care if she was hauled off to jail. "Who's in charge? You didn't even offer him a blanket. If I have the last word, you will be doing crossing duty for the blind! I demand to speak to someone."

He walked toward her. "You are under—"

Just then a voice filled with bass cut in. "I'll take it from here, Bob." A tall man entered the porch and flashed his badge her way. "Ma'am, my name is Detective Perry, and I'm in charge here."

Sasha noticed his good looks but didn't let it interfere with her anger. "So you're responsible for my brother being left out in the cold? I would expect different from—"

Detective Perry said, "From what? One of your own? Look, lady, this is not a black-and-white issue. Officer Smith was just doing—"

"Yes, I know. His job. But his job is to protect and serve, not to leave people out in the cold."

"Look, lady, I just entered the scene and—"

"My name is Sasha Freeman."

"Well, Ms. Freeman, your brother's not going to be charged with anything."

"Charges?" Her eyebrows rose. "For what?"

"Well, he did assault the intruder, but I am sure no charges will be brought for that."

"Assault? He stopped the intruder from stealing everything, and from the looks of my apartment, he would have gotten away with it."

Raymond walked into the apartment, interrupting their heated debate. Sasha scurried to find a blanket in her ransacked home.

When she came back, she asked if he was okay. He didn't complain, dismissing his brush with death. Raymond was never the type to let someone know they got to him.

"I'm sorry for the mix up, Mr. Freeman," Detective Perry explained, "but the officer just wanted to make sure he covered all his bases."

Raymond nodded. "Whatever! I tried to stop him, Sash, but he had already gotten through the window and into the house."

"What happened, Ray?"

"I came home around five this morning and heard mad noise coming from your apartment. I knew you weren't home, so I used my key to check it out. He had already torn the place apart but didn't take anything. I snatched him up, and we fought. He pulled a knife. I managed to get it away and stabbed him."

"Don't worry about that. Detective Perry assured me there won't be any charges." Sasha shot the detective a look of death.

Detective Perry corrected her. "I didn't assure. I said it's not likely."

"Well, it's your job to make sure there's no charges. This is a clear-cut case of self-defense. The guy had no business in my place."

"Oh, so now we've moved from civil rights leader to judge, juror, and prosecutor," Detective Perry said sarcastically.

Sasha didn't appreciate his humor. "I am one phone call away from a lawyer."

"That kind of talk is hostile. Look, I told you, I'll do my best. In the meantime, I need you both to come down to the station to make a statement and press charges."

"What? Can't that wait? My place is a wreck, I just got home from work, and I am not in the mood."

"Oh well, that does it. She's not in the mood to make a statement. Let's stop the investigation. Everyone, go home." Detective Perry was back to being an asshole.

Sasha folded her arms. "Do I know you?"

"Excuse me?" Detective Perry said, his hands on his hips.

"I mean, you talk to me as if we were past acquaintances or you knew me or something."

"Ms. Freeman, I will do what I can, but I need you to make a statement."

"You need me, Detective Perry?" Sasha said, flirting.

He gave a smile covered with dimples, surrounded by a look of defeat. He couldn't win with her.

Sasha didn't know why he even tried. She wasn't blind. She'd noticed how handsome this man was, once she got past his arrogance. He was six-foot-one, nice body, absolutely gorgeous gluteus, and seemed to have himself together. The way he wore his trench leather jacket and flashed his badge made him very sexy to her. She loved a man in charge, not one who thought he was. One thing though, Sasha couldn't stand a man who loved himself more than anything or anyone else. She grabbed her coat.

Ray put a board over the broken window as the house was freezing, and Sasha turned on the heat and locked her doors, leaving the mess behind.

Sasha's angry thoughts consumed her for a second. *Out of all of the houses on the block, why rob mine? My car is parked right out*

front. Did the burglar not think anyone was home? What a moron!
I'm no expert, but if you're going to break into someone's house, don't
you think you should make sure no one is home?

As she walked behind Ray, the police cars began to scatter.
She noticed that her car had a huge dent on the side as if
someone had kicked it. Her rear windows were smashed, and
her lights were busted. She began thinking this was no random robbery. She looked toward the ambulance. A medium-
sized fellow stepped from the ambulance with his head down.
He wore a familiar coat, along with a familiar face.

As she bent to get into her brother's car, she overheard one
of the officers say, "The paramedics say it's just a flesh wound.
We can take him down to the station."

Sasha watched the officer as he handcuffed and pushed
Jason's head into the squad car.

Detective Perry noticed Sasha's facial expression and turned
towards her. "What's wrong?"

She was too embarrassed to say. *I can't believe Jason would do*
this. Is he crazy? Now she definitely wanted to go to the station
to find out what the hell was wrong with this man. Worried
she was caught up in some sort of drama, Sasha couldn't help
but wonder about Jason and how far he was willing to go.

CHAPTER FOUR

"Ms. Freeman, understand that we will try to do everything we can, but the extent of damage to your apartment might not be covered under the policy."

Sasha began to fix her face. The insurance man on the telephone was about to get blasted with words none too kind. "Mr. Tate, I pay every single month for that insurance policy, so I know you are not telling me you cannot fix any of the damages."

"Again, Ms. Freeman, we will have to get a look at the damages, total them up, and see what we can fix and what you have to pay."

"What I have to pay? I pay a premium that covers my entertainment center, including my DVD player, television, computer, fax machine, all my furniture, broken windows, and my jewelry, so you get someone out here immediately!"

"Ms. Freeman, we will do everything we can."

"I know that's right," she said, closing the conversation.

It wasn't bad enough she had to come home to this zoo, but for someone to tell her they couldn't do anything about it after all the money she paid for that policy wasn't the way to start off her week.

At the police station, Jason began apologizing to her for what he'd done. Sasha didn't care for an apology. The maniac wrecked her place. She pressed full charges against him and took out a restraining order. She even thought about getting a dog too. *A pit bull or Rottweiler will eat someone up. I don't even like dogs, but a woman has to do what a woman has to do.*

Her place was a mess, living room turned upside down, glass everywhere, pictures smashed, and her entertainment center was smoking from the busted TV and stereo system. How could she have known how crazy Jason was? She'd stopped calling him a month earlier. He wasn't her man. They didn't even sleep together. Yeah, they went out, but he wasn't anything special to her.

Sasha guessed that, to him, what they had was real. She should have said, "Fuck off." On second thought, he would have probably dumped her in a garbage can somewhere if she were that abrupt. Nonetheless, he wasn't wrapped too tight, and she was glad Raymond came home when he did. Sasha could only imagine what Jason would have done to her if she were home that morning.

He even smashed up her new VW Passat. Sasha had to call the insurance agency about that too. Lucky for her, her pride and joy was in the garage. *If he had touched my BMW 540, he wouldn't have made it to the police station. They would have had to read him his rights in a hospital bed.*

Jason told the police that he just wanted to talk to her.

Yeah right. If I'm not home, dumb ass, you don't go banging up my place.

He said he was upset that she didn't answer her phone when he called back.

Sasha checked her messages while at the police station: "Where are you, Sasha? I just want to talk, Sasha. Why you playin' games, Sasha?"

He was certifiable.

Sasha thought she should have known better when he was acting like he had been tranquilized at dinner that night. Jason must have thought she was with someone else for him to be tripping like this. He had no cause to get upset if she was with someone else because Jason and she had nothing. Still, she couldn't believe that she was caught up in this "fatal attraction" bullshit.

The doorbell rang.

"Girl, it is cold as shit out here," Lisa yelled from behind the door. Let me in!" She walked in shaking her head. "Girl, you told me he tore up shit, but damn, he beat you for your car too!" She looked around the place and picked up what was left of the picture of all four of them, Sasha, Lisa, Tamieka, and Michelle. The "ladies" were always into something that they couldn't get out of without drama. "Damn, homey, you don't got beef with us. Why'd you go mess up a perfect picture?" Lisa smiled and turned toward Sasha. "Well, at least you are all right. I didn't want to have to get 007 on his ass."

Lisa was Sasha's ace boon coon and always had her back through anything. They had seen each other through some hard times. Lisa and Sasha had been friends for almost fifteen years. Both used to get in so much trouble and turned out to be some fine, bad-ass-looking women. Lisa took the *D* out of diva, her short T-Boz blonde haircut suiting her round face. Her eyes were light brown and big like Popeye's, and her lips were as soft as Cottonelle. She was smart, witty, comical, and downright crazy. Whenever Lisa stepped in a room, all eyes centered on her God-given, down-to-her-roots butt. Shorty had back. She'd just got her degree and was a social worker for Children's Hospital. Her five-year-old daughter was her world. And for a single mother digging herself out of misery from a heartbreaking marriage, and who had been through so much in the past couple of years, Ms. Lisa had it going on.

Instead of following her friends' lead, Lisa didn't go to college right after high school. She could have done anything with her life, but instead, against her best friend Sasha's advice, she married this asshole from Jamaica named Jake. They'd met her senior year in high school at a football game. He was twenty-one and a big-time hustler in Boston.

In the beginning, of course, everything was beyond great. He was sweet, caring, attentive. He would buy her jewelry, clothes, expensive handbags, and sex her so good, she didn't know if she was coming or going. That was his game—treat her so good that she wouldn't dare leave him, even if he treated her bad later. And that's exactly what happened. He became possessive, claiming it was love, when really it was his insecurities. He didn't want Lisa doing anything but him, so that meant spending less time with her friends.

Jake and the ladies didn't get along. They'd feared for her and tried to talk some sense into her, but she wouldn't listen. He had her. Lisa used to boast that she was in love, explaining that his possessiveness indicated how much he really loved her.

After they'd graduated from high school, Jake knew her friends would try to talk her into leaving and going to college, and that's when he proposed. He was sexually dominating, never wanted to use a condom, and Lisa didn't protest. So it was no surprise when she popped up pregnant before they got married that summer. Needless to say, none of her friends was invited to the wedding.

Sasha truly believed he was the reason why Lisa didn't go off to college, even though Lisa claimed college just wasn't her thing. Lisa hid her reservations to her friends about the whole marriage, being pregnant, and being scared to death by complaining that she was tired and wanted someone to take care of her. After their wedding, Jake quickly whisked Lisa back to Jamaica, and she was heard from less and less.

The marriage didn't last too long. By the time Sasha returned home from her college freshman winter break, Lisa was home too. But not with Jake though, just an oversized belly, a couple of bruises, and a heart-breaking story.

Bottom line, Jake fucked up her life. His smooth drug operation was busted up by the FBI. On top of that he had another wife and child in Atlanta who were mules in his operation as well. That was how he worked; he would meet young girls, have them fall in love with him, marry them, then use them to smuggle his drugs in and out of Jamaica and across the U.S.

Lisa got locked up, too, for being an accessory and spent some months pregnant in a federal prison, all her rights stripped from her. Luckily, they realized she knew nothing, and couldn't help them bring any of Jake's partners down. At the time she was living lavishly in Jamaica with a big house, a Mercedes, diamonds, and a maid.

After the bust, afraid for her life, she couldn't go back to Jamaica. She ended up back in Boston, where she set up a nice home with the money saved from the daily allowance Jake gave her. It was supposed to be spent on needless things like clothing and jewelry.

Lisa may have been poor when she got married, but she knew how to handle money. She wasn't working while she was pregnant either because her little stash was more than enough to keep her living well for a while. She bought a house for her and her mother to live in Boston and thought life was going to get better.

One week after she delivered Jasmine, the IRS said she was living beyond her means. The house and everything in it was seized and eventually auctioned off, and Lisa was left homeless with a brand-new baby. Nonetheless, with no money, no man, and not a pot to piss in, Lisa made it and never complained. That was just who she was. She worked her way through college, earned her degree, and picked up the pieces to her life. She'd learned from her mistakes and grew to be an award-winning mother, sometimes overdoing it though—like right now, trying to be Sasha's mother.

Lisa went on about how Sasha's place looked like a tornado. Sasha began picking up things to shut her up. "Well, I called you to help me, not bitch over my place."

"I know, girl, but I'm saying, he really did a number on you."

Embarrassed, Sasha was ready to throw cheap shots. "Oh yeah, like Jake did on you."

"Oh, so now you want to get nasty with me? I'll just take my sorry ass out of here and let you clean this shit up yourself!"

That's how Lisa and she worked. They would go at it with each other.

Many people didn't understand Sasha and her friends, but that was okay, they weren't one of the ladies. Sasha persuaded Lisa to stay and help, something she was going to do anyway. She just wanted someone to beg her first.

The two took a break from cleaning up, and Lisa ran out to her car to get the bag of goodies she'd brought for her girl. When she returned, Sasha managed to find her tin shaker, two martini glasses, and a bowl to put ice cubes in. Lisa broke out the Smirnoff apple vodka and Puckers Sour Apple mix from a brown paper bag. They mixed, shook, and poured their home-style apple martinis. All that was missing was their other two friends and a joint. They improvised, though, and started their routine girl-time chit-chat.

"Girl, so what happened Sunday night?" Lisa asked. "You left the club with Montel?"

Sasha knew she was going to bring it up, because they hadn't spoken to each other since.

"You never came back. What? You left with that fool? What the hell is wrong with you, Sasha? That boy has stomped and devoured your heart, and you have the audacity to leave with him!" Lisa went on and on like that damn Energizer bunny. She wouldn't let up. She didn't understand what Sasha was feeling.

Sasha blocked Lisa out as she went back in her head to Sunday night.

The loud music couldn't drown out the four tighter-than-leather friends as they clamored on about one thing or another.

CHAPTER FIVE

Always a fiend for high fashion, Lisa was admiring Sasha's outfit. "Girl, that dress is killing 'em. Where'd you get those shoes, Sasha?"

"Arden B. You know that's my store." Sasha could afford Gucci, Prada, and Marc Jacobs too, but she was humble in the sense that she didn't always have to spend eleven hundred on an outfit that she'd only wear once.

"Well, I need to borrow that real soon."

"You know where to find me."

"I might have to call it an early night, ladies," Michelle informed them. "The kids return to school from winter break tomorrow." Michelle had two sons, Mitchell and Jamal Jr., named after her and her no-good husband, Jamal Sr.

Tamieka, always quite blunt, didn't take into account other people's feelings before she said something. "That's cool. It doesn't seem hopping in here tonight anyway."

Almost ready to call it a night after their third round of drinks and cutting it up on the dance floor to the latest R & B and hip-hop jams, the ladies hung out at the bar and finished their round.

The bartender planted another apple martini in front of Sasha as she finished up her last one. "This is from the gentleman at the end of the bar," the blonde full-figured bar maid told her.

Though not surprised, Sasha looked intrigued that she'd caught someone's attention. As she looked down the end of the bar, her heart began to jump to her chest when she saw him. *Fuck! It couldn't be.*

The ladies noticed the frightened look on her face.

"What's the matter?" Lisa asked.

Sasha couldn't speak. She just nodded her head in the direction of her admirer.

Tamieka, Lisa, and Michelle glanced down the end of the bar and, when they saw him, couldn't believe it either.

"What the fuck is he doing here?" Tamieka asked.

Clueless, Sasha shrugged her shoulders.

"Well, are you going to find out what he wants?" Michelle asked. She was always a romantic, even if her Romeo acted more like Snoop DOGG-fizzle my nizzle.

"I sure the fuck am," Sasha said, leaving her girls and making her way down the bar.

Lisa and Tamieka shook their heads like, *Oh no.*

As Sasha walked up to him, he stood up and smiled, his six-foot frame towering over her five-foot three-inch frame.

"Hello, Sasha."

"Hello, Montel."

The ladies looked at Sasha and Montel hug. They were surprised and couldn't believe it. Even more surprising to them was when they watched Sasha walk out the club with him after talking for like two minutes. They stood in amazement like, *How could she?*

In his black Range Rover, Montel and Sasha sat outside the nightclub, Ester's, as old feelings found their way to the surface. Montel found his opening, when Sasha gave him a maybe answer to the question, "Is it okay if I call you?"

As if nothing had changed, she laughed with him like she'd never hated his guts. Sasha wanted to forget about him, as if she ever could. After he treated her so bad, she still loved him. Why? "What's wrong with me?" she said to Montel. "Why do I even speak to you? I can't lie to myself. I do want to be friends with you and be a part of your life. It's just when I get close, I start to fall in love all over again." *Did I just say that out loud?* Sash could feel herself losing control and didn't know how to stop herself. She blamed it on the alcohol in her system. "What do you want from me?" she asked.

"Excuse me," Montel joked, "but that is no way to talk to … well, the love of your life."

But Sasha wasn't in the laughing mood and wished she could forget the last time she'd seen him, but the memory plagued her thoughts as if it were yesterday.

After Montel left her for college in North Carolina, Sasha occupied her time by seeing Chris. Even though it had been six months since she'd seen him, her feelings for him grew even more. They could talk on the phone for hours, running up a high phone bill. He wrote her letters saying how much he missed her and couldn't wait to see her. That they had unfinished business and he would send for her soon.

Sasha couldn't front. The thought of his yellow six-foot body on top of her turned her hot-seventeen ass to fire. She would be ready this time and more open, so to speak. She wanted him then and loved him then. And because he understood her like no one else, Sasha thought he was the one for her.

Determined to seal up their love and tired of waiting for him to send her a bus ticket as promised, Sasha managed to make her way to his campus in North Carolina during spring break of her junior year in high school. She signed up to go on a college tour sponsored by her church with other teenagers in her church and five adult chaperones. Her plan, once she got to his campus, was to sneak away during their tour of the school undetected, find Montel's dorm, and surprise him, because she was ready to do the do. Only, the surprise was on her.

When she got to his school, she found his dorm hall, recalling the address from all the letters he'd written. She managed to walk by the residence assistant and look for room 109. The hallway was smelly, like a typical boy's dorm. There were dudes in the hallway, girls in the hallway, radios playing. Sasha walked to the door. A nice-looking boy smiled at her as she knocked on the door. His smile suddenly turned to a surprised look, as if he recognized her and knew what she was about to walk into.

No one answered the door.

She began to walk away, until she heard laughter and a girl's voice. Sasha opened an unlocked door to find Montel and some fake-weaved chick lying on top of him like she was riding a prize horse. Montel had nothing on but his boxers and a wife-beater, but the girl still had on her North Carolina Central sweatshirt and thong. Sasha's first reaction was to snatch her up and throw her and her weave out the window.

Montel jumped up surprised as all hell. "Sasha? What? How the—yo, what's up, cuz?" He winked at her, like she'd go along with this lie.

Sasha gritted her teeth. "Cuz? Montel, what the fuck are you doing with this ho?"

Before Montel could respond, Weave-o-matic charged at Sasha and swung. They began to thump each other around inside his room.

Sasha grabbed a hold of the girl's weave and kept pulling for days, punching the girl in her face. "Fucking bitch, I'm going to kill you," Sasha yelled, slipping on one of Montel's sneakers and falling on her back.

Weave-o-matic was able to get on top of her. She wrapped her hands around Sasha's neck like she was choking a chicken.

Sasha kneed her between her legs then dug into her eye sockets with her freshly done acrylic French manicured nails.

"Ouch!" Weave-o-matic grabbed her face and screamed in pain. She bit Sasha on her arm like a puppy, leaving a permanent mark on her arm.

Sasha grabbed her weave again and held on to it like it was her lifeline and continued to punch and punch until the girl got off of her. In fact it was Montel who got her off as the R.A. came running down the hall.

The R.A grabbed Sasha by her bitten arm. "What the hell is going on around here?"

"Ouch! Damn it, that hurt?"

"Who are you?"

Rage in her voice, Sasha pointed to Montel. "Ask that muthafucka over there!"

Montel was speechless.

The girl who was Weave-o-matic no more was bleeding, and what was left of her fake hair was hanging on by a thread, exposing her braided hair underneath. "I'ma fuck you up." She rushed for Sasha, but Montel held her back.

Sasha stood without fear, ready to kick some more ass. "Come on, bitch, I would like to see you try it."

The RA shook his head and held on to Sasha's arm, dragging her out like she was an outsider. "You don't belong here."

Weave-o-matic yelled, "That's right, bitch. You better leave."

She noticed Montel didn't come after her. She couldn't believe it. She didn't want to believe it.

When the RA got to his desk and tried to call security, Sasha broke free of his grip and ran out of the dorm.

"Come back here!"

"Fuck you, bitch! Fuck y'all!" Sasha ran as fast as she could. Her words couldn't describe how angry she was. She'd promised herself she would never let anyone do that to her again.

Montel called Sasha when she got back to Boston and tried to explain, but she wasn't having it. His lies hurt her. Before, he had Sasha filling out college applications in North Carolina, so they could be together. Now he admitted that he'd been seeing that girl since starting school but still loved her.

Feeling betrayed and desperately wanting to get over him,

she resumed her relationship with Chris, who ended up being her first, and the rest is history.

Montel got kicked out of school because of the fight in his room, and the girl was talking about she was pregnant with Montel's baby.

Historically Black colleges do not play when it comes to matters like that. They are very strict about freshmen engaging in sexual activity, drugs, and violence. The girl was lying about the pregnancy, however, and last Sasha had heard, Montel had moved to New York to pursue a music career.

During that time Montel still wrote Sasha apologizing, claiming he and the girl were just kicking it and that she meant nothing to him. He even invited her to come to one of his shows, but she resisted.

Sasha moved and went off to college, then med school, and didn't hear from Montel anymore. Montel became the blueprint for all her relationships to follow, and getting close to someone was just not what she liked to do.

Montel smiled as he remembered what they had. "I'm so sorry I hurt you. I would do anything to make it up to you, if you would give me a chance. You say that you still love me. I still love you too. I never stopped. At least, can we be friends?"

His words sounded so sincere, and that smile and those eyes made Sasha doubt all she knew. She'd let her anger go a very long time ago, and just sitting there with him made her forgive him even more. Montel said everything Sasha wanted to hear, and she believed him again, accepting his apology for all the wrongs he'd done to her. In the back of her mind she hoped things would work out and was willing to give him another chance to make things right.

Meanwhile back in the club, Tamieka was about to get her own surprise. Her boyfriend Linc came looking for her at the club after she stood him up for dinner.

Lisa spotted him first. "Hey *T*, isn't that Linc?"

Tamieka turned around because she just knew Lisa was hallucinating, but to her embarrassment she wasn't.

Linc spotted her and walked up to her at the bar. "Hello, ladies."

Lisa and Michelle said, "Hello."

"T, can I speak to you outside for a minute?"

Tamieka sipped on her apple martini. After what seemed like a long time, she put down her glass and said to the ladies, "I will be right back."

Linc followed her outside the club, and they got into it on the sidewalk.

"What the fuck are you doing here?"

"You don't know how to call if you are not going to show up?"

Honestly, Tamieka forgot they had plans, and that's why she didn't call him. Linc wasn't at the top of her priority list, and he knew it. "Damn, I forgot. I'm sorry," Tamieka said, trying to sound sincere.

"You forgot? What do you mean, you forgot?"

"Look, this is not the time for this. We can talk more about it when I get home. I will see you there." Acting like she didn't have a care in the world, Tamieka walked away and left Linc standing there.

The ladies were surprised to see her back so soon.

"We thought you left like Sasha did with that fool."

Tamieka rolled her eyes. "Linc can kiss my ass, coming in here like he's running things. He ain't running shit!"

The DJ announced, "Tamieka Williams, your ride is at the front."

Linc had snuck back in the club and told the DJ to announce that over the loud speakers.

T almost threw up, but she wasn't moved, ordering another martini and sipping it slowly.

"You're not going out there?" Michelle asked.

T continued to sip her drink. "Does a bitty have lips?"

The DJ thought the whole thing was hilarious, so he announced over the speaker, "Tamieka, you know you wrong. How can you leave a brother outside waiting in the cold?"

The ladies all laughed, and the whole club was laughing at Linc.

T never went out there to see him. In fact, they stayed until around two in the morning, despite Michelle's earlier protest about not getting home too late.

When they got outside the club, a fuming Linc was parked out front waiting for T.

Even though, T swore up and down she wasn't leaving with him, she got in the car with him, and they drove off.

Laughter seeped out of the broken boarded up window inside Sasha's house as Lisa told her the story about Linc and T.

"T shouldn't treat Linc that way," Sasha said in Linc's defense.

"Try telling her that. T doesn't care. All the heartbreak she's been through, she needs a punching bag."

"Whatever!"

"What are you going to do about Montel?" Lisa asked. "You can't be serious about hooking back up with him."

"Damn! Will you shut your trap? It's too early in the afternoon to be overbearing. I know you didn't come over here to beat my head in about Montel!"

"Sash, I'm saying you could do—"

"I could do what? Better? Man, Lisa, you don't even know what you're talking about. Like it's any of your business, but nothing happened between Montel and me. We were in the car talking until five a.m."

"Talking and bumping like nobody's business. Ha, ha!"

They both laughed.

Sasha was defensive about Montel because she didn't know what to expect from "being friends" with him. She'd convinced herself, though, that she was ready for whatever happened next between them and couldn't care less if her friends approved or not. Deep down, she still loved him and owed it to herself to find out if he could mend her broken heart again.

CHAPTER SIX

Tamieka lay on her bed wondering what she had done. Questioning what went on last night. What had been going on for the past five years. It wasn't like she didn't love Linc. It was just the way he looked at her or called her name, as if she were the most beautiful and desirable woman in the world.

Linc was a caring, sensitive man. He loved to do things for her. They met while T was visiting her family in Atlanta. After a year, he quit his blue-collar job in Atlanta and moved to Boston, leaving his family and friends to share his life with her. His salary was much less than T's, but he pulled in extra money at the barbershop he'd bought after selling his home in Atlanta.

You'd think that'd be enough for her to marry him after damn near eight proposals. The last request T received for her hand in marriage was from another guy who almost ruined her. Maybe that's why her feelings for Linc were so in check. She didn't want to be hurt again.

She was completely devastated when she'd learned that

Richard, her ex, was in love with another woman. T just knew that she would be with him forever. When he left, her whole world crumbled. Wedding invitations had to be sent back, money was spent to cancel halls, churches, flowers, everything. If it weren't for that high-paying salary, T would have been left broke. That wedding cost a fortune, not just financially, but emotionally as well. She had her entire future centered on that man. He was the reason she'd moved back to Boston, instead of starting a life in Chicago, where she wanted to live after finishing college.

T hadn't seen Ricky for five long years and went through hell without him. After he left her, she found out she was pregnant, but couldn't get a hold of him to tell him. All the stress of her hotel business going under and losing the one man she'd loved since high school took a toll on her body. She lost the baby. The timing just wasn't right for that angel to enter T's life. Ever since then, she'd been working out hard at the gym, thinking that the next time her body would be able to take anything.

T picked herself up after about a year of rejected feelings of love and managed to save her business, but not her personal feelings of disgust in men. Then Linc came along and turned her world around. It would almost be a fairytale, if she could get her depressed heart to feel anything true for him.

Meanwhile the years piled on. She and Linc now shared a life together in a false world, tainted by the reality that their relationship would never work.

"Tamieka," Linc shouted, "breakfast is served! I know you're probably hungover from last night, so I warmed you up some ginger ale."

"Oh, that's it," T said in disgust. "I thought I smelled eggs and bacon. It's just enough to make you nauseous."

"I made that for me. I thought you were sick from—"

"From what? Amaretto sours, or you behaving like a stalker last night?" T said with an attitude.

A surprised look of bewilderment crossed Linc's face. "T, I only went to the club because you said you were meeting me for dinner at Uno's."

"Linc, if I stood you up, have some dignity and go home. Don't come looking for me!" T sucked her teeth and rolled her eyes.

"Is it your time of the month, or is it just a bad time?"

"No, Linc, I always have time for you to annoy me."

"That's more like it, I knew you loved me. T, it would just take time, like five years."

Tamieka got out of bed and moved towards him like she wanted to fight. "I know you're not trying to be the funnyman in this, because I have got—"

"Oh yes, I know. Plenty of other things to do with your time than hang around a little man."

What has gotten into him?

"You know what, T, you're right. I'll just leave you alone for an hour, come back and maybe love you, but right now I just can't stand you!" Linc said, reaching his boiling point.

Has Linc finally gotten the picture? Did a light bulb come on inside his head? Does he finally realize that he's the fall guy and, in a blink of disgust, wants nothing to do with me? T watched her words. "Maybe that's for the best right now."

Linc picked up his pride with a look of despair. He didn't want to hurt T. He just wanted her to stop bashing him. All he wanted was to love her and hope that one day she could return the favor. He got fed up for a minute and thought his abrupt approach would make her appreciate him more. He was wrong. "I'll try to call you later. I have a very busy schedule, and I don't know when I'll have free time," he said, sounding defeated.

"That's okay, honey," she said, helping him out of the door. "Call me when you get a chance."

Linc thought about saying I love you, but decided not to, and instead kissed her on the cheek and left.

For a minute, T thought Linc was serious. The thought of him standing up to her did turn her on.

The following Saturday night, it was ladies' night out, and Lisa, Sasha, and Tamieka were on their way from happy hour to pick up Michelle to go to a concert hosted by the local radio station Hot 97.7.

Lisa had only been in her shoes for less than two hours, and the walk alone from the pub to the car was murder on her feet. "Remind me never ever wear pumps or anything with heels to a show," she said in agony.

"No one told you to wear that shit." Tamieka scolded Lisa like she was a two-year-old. Those two were always arguing. "You're twenty-eight years old, not nineteen. Can we please act like we know? Always trying to be Ms. Cute."

"T, now don't start with me, 'cause I might have to dig into your business, and I know no one is interested in that shit."

"Don't start with me, Lisa. It's bad enough I have to deal with Linc's sorry ass. I came out tonight to have fun."

"Whatever. Hey, Sash, why you so quiet?"

Sasha rolled her eyes as she drove down the avenue. "Who said I was picking up Michelle? I am sick of this nonsense. We all have cars. Why can't you guys meet me somewhere? I have to come all the—"

"Would you stop complaining? You're like a bitch on wheels sometimes," Lisa declared. "What happen? Montel didn't call you?"

"Wait a minute," T said, "did I miss a couple of days?"

Here we go all over again, Sasha began thinking. *I'll have to explain to her why I'm speaking to Montel, she'll give me her unneeded two cents, and we'll start arguing before we reach the show.*

"Sash, you didn't tell me you was messing with Montel. After the way he treated you? I thought you learned your lesson."

"Oh, did you say something back there, T? I couldn't hear you. The music is up too loud." Sasha turned up the music.

"You heard me, bitch. Why are you putting yourself through this shit again?"

"Okay, T, now you wonder why I didn't tell you. I knew what you were going to say because I have said it to myself. Montel and I are just friends, damn!"

"Just friends, huh? Then you shouldn't be upset that he didn't call you." T rolled her eyes and crossed her arms. "Look, all I'm saying is that you're doing so well without him and you've been down this road one hundred times, so you know what's at the end of it."

"Thanks, but no thanks. I know what I'm doing. I'm an adult. Montel and I are just trying to fit each other into one another's life."

"Sash, what you need to realize is that there will never be a 'Montel and I.' Just you and your idea of what love is, until you figure out you've been duped again by the same asshole," T said, trying to talk some sense into her.

Sasha shouted over the music in frustration. "T, you are getting on my nerves now. Just drop it . . . before I drop you off at the bus station."

"You're always quick to tell someone about what's wrong in their life, but you can't stand it if someone says something to you."

"Whatever!" Sasha shouted.

"You know what? You can drop me off at a bus station." T shook her head in anger. At least I know I been taken for a ride. Sash, you act simple sometimes, like you don't know what's really going on. Like with Jason. Come on, you're a freaking physician."

Sasha pulled over to the side of the road, pumping her breaks. "That's it, bitch. Get out. Take the bus. You're not riding with us."

Lisa jumped in, "Chill out, Sash, chill out. T, this is supposed to be ladies' night out."

"So what? I don't care. You can't tell me shit. I know what I'm doing, and if it doesn't work out, I'm one day wiser than the day before. Why do you care anyway? The real problem is not Montel and me. What's bugging you is that Ricky left you at the altar, and you hate any man who is not groveling or picking up the broken pieces of your heart." Sasha pulled out and pressed on the gas hard, her tires peeling.

BEEEEEEEEP!

Sasha cut off a not-so-happy driver, who politely gave her the finger as she looked in her rearview mirror.

"Oh now you're silent back there? This conversation is not about me, it's about you and your unresolved feelings of man hating. You talk all this crap about other people's lives, but disregard the fucked-up shit going on in your life."

Lisa held onto the dashboard. "Sash, slow down. T must have hit home because you are tripping."

"Whatever. She needs to mind her own fucking business."

T, hurt by Sasha's comments, still tried to reason with her. "I am just trying to look out for you."

"I'm a grown-ass woman. If I can't look out for myself, then shame on me, right?"

"Whatever. You're tripping, Sash, and that's all you'll hear out of me." T began to drink her Hennessy and coke.

When they pulled into Michelle's driveway, Sasha honked the horn as usual.

Michelle ran to the door and yelled, "Just a minute please, young ladies." She turned away from the door and ran back upstairs to her house.

"You kids, it's time to get in the bed. Mommy has to go out for a little while."

Mitchell, her oldest son, said, "Mommy, you have to go to work again?"

"No, baby, Mommy needs to go out with her friends."

"Oh, okay. I guess mommies need time off too."

"Yes, they do, Mitchell," she said, tucking him in. She kissed his forehead and jumped down from the bottom bunk to kiss her youngest, Jamal Jr.

He jumped up and said, "Have a good time, Mommy, and bring me something back."

"You, Jamal, can have anything, okay, baby?" She kissed him and pulled the covers over him. Then she blew a kiss and turned off the light, just leaving a dim glow from their night light.

Michelle rushed downstairs and left a little money for her mother for taking care of the kids. She knew her mother would watch them at no price, but she always felt like she had to give her something. That was just who Michelle was. No matter what direction her life was headed in, she always gave much and expected little. Life had left her with a feeling of gratitude. Even though money wasn't always in the bank, or men weren't always treating her the way she deserved, she could hold her own.

Michelle was angelic in a way. Her very presence just seemed to make you feel protected and looked after. She was the oldest out of all of the ladies, so of course, they looked to her for advice and guidance, but her life was always in turmoil. Her husband had recently left her, and she worked two jobs, while trying to finish college. Luckily, her husband left her at a time when school and after-school programs kept the kids busy. Otherwise, Michelle didn't know what she would do, even though her mother and sisters were a big help.

Of course, she had the ladies too. Michelle was always there for them. Being the voice of reason and reality, she let you know how things really were, but it never worked for her. She could always tell you what was wrong with your life but could never analyze herself truthfully. She remained in fantasyland when it came to her husband, who eventually left her for another woman.

Michelle knew of Jamal's extracurricular activities before they even got married. She tried to provide a home for her children, so on the outside it looked good. As if her life was meant for television, Michelle played her part in the marriage and pretended that everything was okay. She knew her friends were aware what was going on, but she continued to delude herself, pretending that her family life was picture-perfect.

Her parents were the same way. She grew up with them together, but not. You would think that would have prepared her. In the end, her parents divorced and moved on to separate lives, after Michelle moved out of their home at nineteen.

Now she seemed to be following the same path, but who could fault her for trying to make it work? She had a big forgiving heart, not realizing that she needed to forgive herself and love herself before her heart could do anything else.

The ladies tried to reason with her, but no one could be the voice of reality, but her.

Michelle ran out of the house and waved for Sasha to stop blowing the horn. Smiling, she hopped into the back seat with Tamieka. "What's up, ladies? You know I have to go to the ATM, right."

Sasha yelled, "Oh for crying out loud, you're just stepped in here and you are already making demands."

"I didn't have time before. Anyways, I need to go. What's the attitude for, Sasha?"

Lisa answered, "T and Sash got into it over Montel."

Sasha interrupted, "Yes, Lisa, go on. Tell the whole story."

"Damn, do you want to drop us off somewhere, Sash, so you can handle your rage?" Lisa asked.

Sasha didn't respond and continued to drive straight to the club without stopping. As she pulled into the parking lot where the show was being held, her attention drifted to something else.

Michelle told her, "You didn't go to the ATM. I guess that means you're paying my way, Ms. *MD*."

While getting out of the car, Sasha said, "Stop your whining. There's one inside the place."

Tamieka hadn't said a word since the argument. She looked like she wanted to apologize, but before she could, she noticed Sasha walking up to this tall, light-skinned brother, who hugged her and gave her a kiss on her lips.

A disgusted Tamieka said, "I thought this was ladies' night out."

Sasha heard her and ignored her as thoughts of why Montel was there filled her head. After all he hadn't called her like he said he would. He knew she was going to the concert from their last conversation in his jeep.

As Sasha remained hugging him like he was hers, she couldn't shake the feeling that something wasn't right.

CHAPTER SEVEN

Montel didn't have a real excuse for not calling Sasha. "I've been trying to get a hold of you all week," he explained.

Sasha didn't believe him. "So why didn't you? All this technology, cell phone, e-mail, house phone, pagers, voicemail, and you couldn't use one?"

"I'm sorry. Where are your seats?"

T wasn't giving Sasha any space to be led on by Montel. "We're in the front row, floor tickets. I imagine you're in the nosebleed seats where you belong."

Montel never liked T from the day he met her, and she felt the same about him. He smiled. "How about I meet you after the show right here by your car?"

Sasha wanted to finish their conversation. "Yeah, after the show meet me here."

He hugged her again, and then she skipped off to catch up with the ladies, who already were making their way inside the building.

T had hurried them along, sick to her stomach from watching her friend be made an ass of.

Jay-Z, DMX, Mary J. Blige, Lil' Kim, Missy Elliot and Busta Rhymes gave a rocking, sold-out show, and the crowd was amped.

Tamieka was drunk off the Hennessy from before and the Budweiser beer they sold inside the Fleet Center. Lawd knows what she was going to say to Linc, feeling as nice as she was.

After the show, Michelle met Allan Iverson as she was going to the bathroom. Lisa was still after DMX. The ladies didn't think she was serious though. Sasha had backstage passes, so they were chilling out with the celebrities for a while after the show.

Sasha left the ladies backstage to meet Montel by her car. Almost an hour had passed and still no sign of him. She was heated with anger. As the steam began to seep out of out ears, she noticed a tall gentleman walking her way. He was smooth from the way he walked, and his leather trench coat wasn't fastened up, showing off his Sean Jean tailored suit. Sasha watched him as he came closer and closer to her car. As he came from out of the shadows, she frowned. It was Detective Perry.

"Ms. Freeman, I thought that was you. Are you waiting for someone?"

Damn was he following me or something? "Hello, Detective Perry. No, I'm not waiting for anyone. What are you doing here?"

"Just making sure everything is running smoothly, no altercations." He leaned against her car.

Sure you are. He's dressed to impress, not arrest. Sasha didn't like him around. "I don't mean to be rude, but—"

"But what, Ms. Freeman. Are you waiting for someone?"

Astonished at his directness, Sasha responded, "Look, Detective Perry, I appreciate—"

"Please, Sasha, call me *Michael*."

"Oh, so now we're on a first-name basis? I never said you could call me Sasha." She didn't crack a smile.

"I figured, all we've gone through . . ." He smiled and winked at her.

"Are you serious? Your character is wearing on me, and my patience is limited. Shouldn't you be giving someone a ticket or something?"

He laughed. "I believe, if I let you, you would insult me at any given moment."

"Well, you are starting to catch on finally." Sasha still wasn't smiling.

"Yes, I am, Sasha. I am indeed."

"Did you want something, or have something to tell me, because if you don't—"

"Ms. Freeman, I came to tell you that Jason would not be bothering you any more."

"Thank you for that information."

"I'm not finished." Michael put up his hands, gesturing for Sasha to wait and listen. "He's in the hospital. Apparently, he tried to commit suicide by running his car off the road."

"What!" *I knew he was off, but not that off.*

"He's critical. They don't know if he's going to make it or not."

"That's not good. What hospital is he in?"

"Why? You're not going to see him, are you?"

"I don't know. A part of me feels he got what was coming to him, but another part of me feels he didn't deserve that. He obviously needs psychological help. I just want to send him a card, or see if I can refer him to a good psychologist."

Michael looked surprised. "The man trashes your apartment, and you want to make sure he's all right. I guess I figured you wrong, Sasha. You're not a man-eater."

"Excuse me. You need to stop talking to me as if you know me. I haven't even begun to say what I think of you, so back off. I just want to do the right thing."

"If that's all, I must say good night to you. I'll see you around, Sasha. Stay out of trouble." He walked away.

Who the hell does he think he is? He has the audacity to criticize me? Is he crazy? Detective Perry or Michael, whoever the hell he thinks he is, better stay far away from me. How dare he call me a man-eater? If he only knew I was sitting out in the cold for a man who would never come.

Sasha got out of the car and began to walk inside the place to retrieve her friends. As she was walking, she heard someone yelling her name.

"Sasha!" Montel hollered. "I've been looking for you."

"Montel, maybe you should have looked by my car where I said I was going to meet you."

"I did, but I saw you talking to some guy."

"Okay, so when he walked away, why didn't you come over? Or better yet, why didn't you meet me an hour ago like you said you would?"

Montel began his excuse, but it was all too familiar to her. She tried not to let him get to her, but he could so easily. Sasha couldn't show him she cared, but he was the only guy who brought mush out of her. She would turn into a simple girl who needed direction. Sasha so wished she could block him out.

Someone save me, please, before I believe everything he says and leave with him instead of the girls.

Meanwhile inside the Fleet Center, Lisa put T up to helping her find and meet DMX. T was drunk enough to walk up to one of the bodyguards and ask, but before she could, her attention went to the left. She felt someone watching her, and a second later wished she didn't look. There he was, all dazzled up, and some groupie on his arm, Richard Dwight Masters, aka Ricky. She hadn't seen him since he was supposed to meet her at the altar years ago. Her temperature climbed.

Before Lisa knew it, T left her to execute some unfinished business with her ex-fiancé. Loudly and without apology, she got in his face, mad as hell. "Where the fuck have you been for the past five years, you low-life, broke-ass muthafucka!"

Ricky stood there and didn't answer her.

T got more irate. "You didn't have the balls to tell me you didn't want to marry me, sending your weak-ass brother to tell me? What kind of man does that?"

Ricky knew that if he opened his mouth, T would start throwing blows. Five foot, nine inches, and stacked like pancakes, T was no joke when it came to beefing, but Ricky's girl didn't know that.

She was decked out in a black fur shawl that partly hung over her Bebe blue halter dress that favored her cleavage and revealed her toned dark brown legs. Her long red acrylic nails made their way to T's face, and she sucked her teeth, rolled her fake blue contact eyes, flipped her long blond weave with the other hand, and fixed her red-painted lips to say, "Who the fuck is—?"

BAAM!

Before she could finish her sentence, T landed a rock-solid punch to the woman's face, and she fell back, holding it. Two security guards grabbed T quickly before she could do anymore damage.

Realizing T was contained, Ricky all of a sudden had the balls to speak, "T, you always acting crazy. How could you hit my wife?"

Both T's and Lisa's mouths dropped.

T broke free from both security guards like she had Wonder Woman strength and charged at him. "Your what?"

The two full-sized security guards caught her before she ripped Ricky a new one and quickly hauled her out kicking and screaming, "You married a tramp-looking, no-class hooker?"

Lisa fled the scene and went to find Sasha outside for help. She knew Michelle was off talking to Jamal on her cell phone. He'd been calling her the whole time she was inside the concert, begging for another chance. Lisa left that alone because she wanted to meet DMX, and now because of her, T was going to get arrested.

* * *

As Sasha tried to resist Montel's perfect excuses, Lisa came out of the concert looking for her. Sasha spotted her and flagged her as she came running over.

She blew out of one breath, "What's up, Montel?" and with the other she began, "Sash, there is drama up in there. We were all backstage, and guess who came out of the woodwork?"

"Who, damn it?"

"Ricky. You know Richard. Stand-me-up-at-the-altar Richard."

Sasha's mouth dropped. "Where's T?"

"She's being escorted out by security as we speak."

"What happened?"

"We were backstage, and I wanted to meet DMX, so T and I were looking for him. Michelle had gone off somewhere. You know how she wonders off. Anyways, we found DMX, but there was mad security around him like he wasn't going to talk to the fans. I thought that was odd because he always—"

"Lisa, damn it, would you get to the part about Ricky?"

Lisa told her what happened with Ricky's wife.

"Where's T now?"

"Security has her. I think they're trying to haul her off to jail for disorderly conduct. After all, she was drunk in a public place."

"Where's Michelle?"

"Shit if I know. Probably looking for us, or on that cell phone talking too never mind you don't need to know that."

"Lisa, who is Michelle having a conversation with?"

"Probably her kids, yeah."

Sasha's voice heightened. "At damn near twelve a.m.? Come on, Lisa, spill it."

Just then security brought T out to put her in a squad car, when Sasha saw a familiar face giving orders to the officers. She ran over to Detective Perry, hoping that their last encounter wouldn't affect his next decision. "Michael, can I talk to you for a minute please?" She batted her eyes.

"Not now, Sasha, I have to—"

"I know. That's my friend you're about to arrest. She doesn't need to go to jail, she just needs to go home and sleep it off."

"Oh, so now you want a favor from me. A minute ago you shooed me away like some pest. Is that how you treat all your men?"

Michael had the most audacious mouth. He would say just about anything to make Sasha feel like a bad person. It wasn't her fault Jason was crazy or that guys just couldn't get enough of her. *Who are you to criticize? I'm sure with your looks and arrogance you have a trail of broken hearts lined up at your door.* "Michael," she said, trying to get past his comment, "this is not about me, this is about my friend. She didn't mean any harm. Her emotions just got the best of her. Don't haul her off to jail like some criminal."

"Sasha, look, I wish I could help you, but I can't."

Sasha bit her lip and put on her sad face. "I know you can help me, Michael. You're in charge, right?"

"Yeah, I am in charge but—"

"But what? You can't let her go with a warning? I'll make sure she gets home safely. You can even follow me."

Detective Perry began thinking it over. He signaled the officer to let T go, and then turned to her and said, "You're right, this isn't about you, so don't even think for a minute that your charms work on me. I'll let her go with a warning, but the person she assaulted is probably going to press charges."

"Oh, I wouldn't worry about that, Michael. Besides, I know you can make sure that doesn't happen." Sasha winked at him.

As she walked away with her arm around T, Michael Perry saw her differently. The image of her being some self-righteous "manizer" began to fade. He never dismissed her beauty, but was well aware of the trouble she could bring. He stopped staring at her rump in those fitted leather pants, and began to move the crowd away from the scene.

"Thanks, Sash," T said, "I want to apologize about before."

Sasha removed her arm from around T's neck. "Girl, you

know I know how you are. It's a given. You don't want to see me hurt, I know, but I have to figure Montel out for myself. Kind of like you and Ricky. You finally let him have it. How did it feel?"

"It felt like a stone was lifted off my heart. He didn't even say anything. And that chick he was with was so ugly. She reminded me of 'RuPaul meets the gremlins.' "

They laughed.

"If that is the girl he left me for, I have to wonder what the hell is wrong with him. I look too good tonight for any man not to notice." T rocked her hips.

They both laughed again.

When Michelle reappeared after talking things out with Jamal, they all got into the car.

Sasha stopped and thought about how she left Montel hanging. "Hey, Lisa, where did Montel go?"

"Girl, he left a long time ago . . . when you were talking to the police. He didn't need to stand around me. He knows I can't stand his ass."

They laughed as Sasha pulled away.

Sasha thought. *Is he mad? Is he going to call me later?* She couldn't think, not with Lisa filling Michelle in about T and Ricky.

T had a smile on her face from cheek to cheek. She seemed content with the fact that she told Ricky off. It hurt like hell seeing him with another woman, his wife at that. A good thing she was drunk. If not, tears would have been falling from her maple-walnut face.

In the back of T's mind, she hoped no one got wind of this story though. T was a successful owner of a chain of small hotels in Cape Cod. Her business associates wouldn't appreciate seeing her knocking someone out like she was a title contender. T didn't care too much about that. She was just happy to have some sort of closure with Ricky.

Sasha dropped everyone off, and since she lived the farthest, she planned to stay at T's house, but when she saw Linc's car in the driveway, she changed her mind.

On her way home, she checked her messages: *"What's up, beautiful? I haven't seen you all week. I hope you got your place fixed. If you need any help, call me."*

That was Damon.

Sasha didn't mean to ignore him. It'd just been a crazy week. *What's wrong with me? I better give him a call. My body needs relaxation.*

As Sasha pulled up to her driveway, the thought hit her. Montel still didn't call. She promised herself to stop stressing him. They'd agreed to be friends. *That's it. He doesn't have to call me all the time. Shit, he hasn't called me at all actually. I will get it together one of these days, but today is not the day.*

As Sasha's garage door opened, she drove inside to park the car. As the garage door began to close, she turned around quickly because she noticed someone ducking under the garage door before it closed completely.

As he came out of the darkness, he grabbed her waist close to his body. "Where have you been, woman?" He began to kiss her, undoing her waist-length black mink coat and fondling her breast.

As Sasha kissed him back, the light in the garage timed out and went dark.

Damon lifted Sasha up around his waist and tapped her ass. "I missed you. Where have you been hiding?"

She licked his lips. "Fuck me," she said to him, passion filling her stare.

Without hesitation, Damon reached in his pocket for a condom, dropped his pants, and slid it on, while Sasha quickly unbuttoned her leather pants and scrapped them off. Then he turned her around.

As she placed her hands on her BMW hood and bent over for Damon's heat, he mounted her, putting his hard dick inside her moist, warm pussy. He thrust into her deep, slapping her firm, juicy ass, and pulling her hair. "Whose pussy is this?"

Sasha laughed inside to herself. *Mine, nigga. Now shut up and fuck me.*

CHAPTER EIGHT

The weather was getting warmer, and things were fresh and new. It was spring time in Boston, and the temperature wasn't too hot or cold. It was the right time for new things, new people, new ideas, new events, new fashion, and most of all, new beginnings.

Sasha picked out the largest lobster in the grocery store for Damon to eat. She was planning a special goodbye dinner for him because she was ready to get serious with Montel. Her heart had finally healed, and she felt confident about their relationship. They had fallen back in love, and now she just wanted to be with him.

When she met Damon it was a sexual attraction. Sasha needed a no strings attached type of relationship. But after that wore off, because she done dropped the panties and was tired of picking them up with this same person, who she probably didn't have anything in common with, she realized that was it. Her needs were met, and Damon didn't suit her purpose any more.

The last couple of months, most of her time had been spent with Montel. He called her a week after the concert and they met for lunch at her job. The next week, they caught a show at the Comedy Connection. He started meeting her at her house after work, day or night. Sasha even flew with him to Los Angeles to promote this music group he was writing songs for. Their relationship started to grow again. He said things that made sense. He confessed to her that he wasn't ready to really commit to her when they were younger, and he'd be damned if he ever lost her again.

Finally, Sasha knew where she stood with him. He confessed it took him all this time to realize she was the one for him and couldn't deny it any more. He was tired of living a lie. Feelings came back as if they had never left.

Sasha believed their relationship was more mature now and together they could handle anything. She wanted to take her and Montel's relationship to the next level. They had even toyed with the idea of marriage and having children. She almost didn't want to jinx it though because sometimes she felt it couldn't be real, he was so right for her. She was enthralled with their relationship though and wouldn't have it any other way.

After picking out the lobsters for Damon's special meal, she walked toward the checkout counter in the supermarket. Thoughts of the upcoming evening began to swirl in her head. She had the scene all planned out. She'd tell Damon what was up, and that would be that. He had left messages that she returned days later. They saw each other less and less because, between work and Montel, she had very little time.

Time spent with the girls also had diminished. They hadn't hung out in a long time. Either one of them couldn't make a gathering or something. Their lives were going in all directions. Sasha missed them, though. She spoke to Lisa and Tamieka less. Michelle had drifted away from all of them at the time too. Sasha felt it was selfish of her, the way she neglected her friends now that she was with Montel. She wanted everyone to be as happy as they were though and definitely wanted to get up with the ladies soon.

The checkout counter line was always long, so Sasha picked up an *Essence* magazine to peruse. As her attention began to point elsewhere, she noticed a little boy waving at her. It was Michelle's little boy, Jamal Jr., with Michelle in fact.

I know she saw me, so why didn't she say hello? Sasha waved. "Michelle, hellooooooo." She walked up to her. "Hey, girl, are you going to walk by like you didn't see me?"

Michelle turned to Sasha. "Oh, I didn't see you. How have you been?"

How have I been? How have you been?

Michelle looked worn out. Her hair wasn't together, and she wore no makeup, except for the day-old eyeliner and mascara. She had socks over her lint-covered leggings and wore a dirty t-shirt that was too small. Surprisingly the kids looked clean. They wore jackets and boots, and their jeans looked washed and ironed.

What was Michelle's excuse?

Sasha did hear through the grapevine that she and Jamal had gotten back together, but was he stressing her out that much? She tried to avoid saying anything, but knew deep down inside she had to address this hot issue.

"Well, Chelle, I'm trying to make dinner for this man, Damon. You remember him, right?"

"Oh that guy you sleep with from time to time?"

Sasha's face turned to ice. "What? Chelle, what's that all about? I know I haven't spoken to you in a minute, but you don't have to be rude."

"Look, Sash, I know you and our friends don't approve of Jamal and me, but you don't have to talk behind my back about it."

"Talking behind your back? What? Are we in high school?"

"If you have comments about Jamal and me getting back together, you should keep them to yourself. Your life is not so perfect. Just because you have a successful career as an obstetrician and own your home and what not doesn't make you better than anybody else."

"Wait a minute, Chelle," Sasha said, feeling defensive, "you're going down the wrong road. I never said anything about you and Jamal, and if I did, it would be to you. Don't get things twisted."

Michelle rolled her eyes.

"This is why you've been avoiding me? You think I'm going to give you grief about Jamal? Let me tell you something, Michelle. Yes, I heard you were back with Jamal, but that's your business. I'm not the one to criticize, but he did some foul shit. That is your life though, if you feel me or anyone else is being harsh, I apologize, but you know that shit isn't cool. Once again, I'm in no position to criticize. Let me refresh your memory, though. We all give each other a hard time about everything. I'm still your girl. Anytime you need something I'm there. If you feel I give you a hard time about Jamal, it's because I care what happens to you, and I know you know you can do better. But, like always, no one listens. We can't run each other's lives. You guys are always putting in your two cents about Montel or any other dude."

She gently rubbed Michelle's arm with concern and said, "Come on, Michelle, I know you weren't avoiding me for that petty nonsense. What's up, Michelle, for real?"

Michelle broke down and confessed, "I just needed time to myself to figure things out. Jamal and I have been married for a long time, and I just want to give that a chance and see what our next move is. You guys don't understand. Every time I bring up his name, all I hear is, 'That good-for-nothing piece of shit.' I need to form my own opinion about him for myself. You just don't understand."

Sasha knew where Michelle was coming from. She and Montel spent so much quiet time together that she had no time for anything else. But Sasha believed you needed that time to yourself to figure how things are going to go without your friends dogging your man out.

"Michelle, I do understand what you're going through. I myself have been spending a lot of time with Montel exclusively. It has gotten to the point where I don't know what is going on with the ladies."

"Well, Lisa has a new man, and T is on speaking terms with Ricky."

"In other words, they're fucking," they said simultaneously.

"She's crazy," Sasha said.

"See, there you go."

"My bad." Sasha slapped Michelle on her shoulder playfully. "Oh please, Michelle, I know you were saying the same thing."

They both laughed.

"Michelle, I'm throwing a party for Raymond. He passed the fireman test."

"Oh, that's good. Is that what he wants to do with his life?"

"I think he wants to teach, but he's having issues. And he needs a stable income until he goes back to school and stuff. The party's not until next month, but I thought I'd tell you now. You can still put a call through. You don't have to act like a stranger and shit. We're your family, no matter what man is in your life. Don't you ever forget that."

Michelle dropped her head. "I know y'all try to have my back, but I am grown and can take care of myself."

"I know, Chelle. Just keep your head up, okay. I'll talk to you soon."

Sasha left Michelle in the market. Even though she understood where Michelle was coming from, she couldn't stand to see her like that. She could do better, and Michelle knew it. Sasha hoped Michelle would stop living in fantasyland.

If that wasn't bad enough, T was talking to Ricky again. Now she definitely had to get up with the ladies real soon.

Later that evening, of course, Sasha was running late. She had to let the steak marinate, boil the lobster, and cut up a ton of vegetables. She felt like she had to do something nice for Damon, because their season had ended and she wanted to start things off right with Montel.

As she finished preparing dinner, Sasha reiterated to herself she was doing the right thing. *Never, under any circumstances, try to make your booty call your man. It never works. I wasn't trying to play house with him or daydreaming about a future. The most daydreaming I did was about the night before or the upcoming night.* She had to give up her lifeline and upgrade to a better one.

As the food sizzled, she freshened up into one of her relaxing Victoria's Secret leopard baby doll negligee and matching robe. Looking edible was called for tonight.

It was almost time. She left the oven on, so the food would be warm, started a fire, and turned the slow music volume on low. She waited by the fire in her "ready to get some" gear and sipped on her Moet.

The doorbell rang.

He's early. She sprayed her cucumber melon body mist on her neck, belly, and between her legs. Her hair was down, she wore natural shaded make up, and her feet were bare. She opened the door, looking sexy as hell to find Detective Perry at her door.

CHAPTER NINE

"What are you doing here? I'm expecting company." Detective Perry said with a smirk, "Well, I know we've only known each other for a few months, and I am handsome, but we should keep it formal." He passed by her into her apartment, trying not to let her see his facial expression. He was turned on by her.

"Well, just invite your rude ass in, why don't ya? Look, I'm expecting someone, so you need to make your way back out this door." Not in the mood for his bullshit tonight, Sasha pointed towards the door.

"What's the matter, Sasha? Afraid you might get caught in your man trap?"

"Listen here, inflatable boy, I don't need or want your comments today. State your purpose and leave. I don't care what you think. You don't count. You're just some nosy, smart-mouth, second-class detective who has nothing better to do than harass women you can't have." *Oh no, where did that come from? Did I say that out loud? I can't let him get to me.*

The detective was silent for the first time since they met.

He looked chipped, like Sasha hit a soft spot. "Look, Sasha, I came over to tell you . . . well, would you like to change first?"

"What? No! Can you make this quick?"

"That depends on your cooperation."

"What?"

"Is Raymond at home?"

"Raymond? What do you want with him?"

"Apparently, there've been some charges against him, and I need to take him downtown. Since I know him, it would be best if I came to get him."

"What charges? Ray hasn't done anything. Look, Michael," Sasha said, beginning to flirt, "I'm sure Ray-Ray has nothing to do with this, whatever the charge is."

"I know you want to protect your brother, but Tina Lewis is filing an assault charge against Raymond. And now there is a warrant for his arrest."

"Who? That scank trick? She's trifling. Her word isn't worth a penny."

"That may be, but she has bruises and black eyes that arouse attention, and the attention is pointing Raymond's way."

"Tina's a liar. She's mad because Ray and her are finished and he moved on. Let me tell you, Ray-Ray cut her loose two months ago when he caught her cheating with his friend Marcus. After that he met Tasha. They've been kicking it since, and Tasha is pregnant. Ray and her are now trying to do right by their baby. Anyways, Tina hates on Tasha, because Tina still be messing with Marcus, who is Tasha's cousin's man. Did I lose you, Michael?"

"No, I know what you're saying, but regardless, Ray shouldn't be putting a hand on Tina."

"Okay, you're not listening. Tina is a liar." Sasha folded her arms. "Ray and Tasha are in New York telling her parents about the baby, so as soon as he gets in, I will have him go to the station and make a statement."

"How do I know you're not making this up?"

"Why would I lie?"

Duh. "To protect your brother," he said quickly.

"Look, he's not here. You can check, but you can't stay."

"I know you're expecting someone."

"Right. So see your way out please."

"I hope, for your brother's sake, what you're saying is true. Ray could be in a lot of trouble if this isn't straightened out."

"Yeah, I got this, DT. Can you go now?"

"I'll go, but I'll be back if need be. And try to have some clothes on next time."

Sasha swung at him, but he blocked her fist and pulled her close to him. Michael's mouth began to open as he came closer to her face, and Sasha closed her eyes and puckered her lips.

"Next time don't overuse the body mist. You could give a brother an allergy attack."

Sasha sucked her teeth and pulled away. For a second Michael caught her attention, but she should have known better.

Just as Sasha made her way to blow out the candles, the doorbell rang. Damon was fifty minutes late. *Now, he really wasn't getting any.*

Sasha opened it and said with an attitude, "Well, Damon, nice of you to join me."

Damon scooped her up and kissed her softly. "How's my baby doing?"

"Damon, you're late, which means I have an attitude."

"Well, I hope your attitude changes, because I've been missing you all week."

"Whatever. Sit down. We have to talk." Sasha showed him to the dining room table then went into the kitchen to warm up the food.

She served him like a king and then sat down next to him at her table.

"Damon, I know where you and I are heading."

"You know I'm not ready for anything serious. In fact, I'm

seeing someone right now, and I wanted to tell you that we could still kick it."

Sasha couldn't believe what she was hearing. *The nerve . . .*

"I know you always wanted me to be honest, so I'm being honest. Before, there was no one else, we were just kicking it. Now I feel like I need to let you know about the other woman."

"Whoa, whoa, Damon! This isn't how things are supposed to go. I have to let you know that—"

"I'm saying you and me can still kick it. I'm not giving up our late nights for no one. I care about you, and I want things to be open between us."

So much for feeling special.

Damon rambled on about his new revelation of how he was enjoying their platonic relationship. He had no clue that Sasha wasn't down for it any more. She was the network canceling this show. He wasn't going to diss her. *We can still kick it? Translation: we can still fuck! Oh, hell no. That episode is over. No reruns.*

Sasha sipped her Moet and tried to pick and choose her words as Damon scuffed down his meal.

"You like the food?"

Damon just nodded.

"Well, baby, it seems we both have gone shopping."

"What do you mean?"

"I'm seeing someone else as well."

Damon stopped eating.

Sasha snickered. "Only difference is I want to get serious. With him, of course. Because like you said, you're not ready for anything serious. So here's the deal—This is our last night together. We can't continue late evenings or early mornings. I'm glad you met someone because I can't be with you like that any more."

Damon began to drink his wine. "So you're saying no more whipped cream and handcuffs?"

"Not unless you're eating a pie or being arrested." Sasha burst out laughing.

Damon stood up. "That's not funny, Sasha. Damn, that's fucked up." He walked away from the table.

She followed him and playfully put her hands on his back. "Come on, Damon, you knew our situation. Don't front. There was no relationship here, just physical satisfaction. We're not moving in together, getting engaged, or having any children. You know this was fun. You were what I needed at the time. Now my needs have changed, but yours haven't. It's time to let go and move on. We've exhausted the possibilities."

Damon turned around to face her.

"I know you were trying to gas a sister's head up, but I knew from the start what we were to each other."

He put his arms around Sasha and kissed her lips. "Does he kiss you like this, touch you like this, or even hold you like this?" He began to kiss her neck, then chest, navel and thighs. "Answer me, Sasha." He picked her up.

She tried to resist that tingle between her thighs. "Damon," she said softly.

He shushed her as her legs wrapped around his waist.

Sasha bit his lips. "Damon, baby, I lust you, but I love him. In time, when you meet the one, you'll know the difference and want love any day over lust."

Damon tried to let her words sink in, but he continued to kiss her body. They now lay naked, wrapped in each other's arms, giving into lust.

Afterwards, Sasha got a blanket and blew out the candles. She knew that this was it. She and Damon couldn't give way to each other's physical desire any longer.

Damon left the next morning, knowing what "last night" meant, and Sasha slept late, closing the world out and feeling settled because she knew what she wanted.

CHAPTER TEN

Sasha hadn't seen a Saturday free of work in a month, so she was looking forward to this day. Since she and the ladies had lost touch, they were going to spend this weekend together. Just the girls.

It was Memorial Day weekend, and May had hit an all-time high of eighty-eight degrees. Such a weekend couldn't go unnoticed. Of course, Sasha would have loved to spend the weekend with Montel, but she and Montel had been spending all their time possible together. Sasha felt they needed a break.

She still couldn't believe she'd opened up her heart again. She was stripped bare and let Montel see all of her. She got rid of all her old flames and threw out her phone book and all her sheets, tossing pictures and everything else from past relationships to the attic. Out of sight and out of mind.

Sasha was in love, not puppy teenage love, but real love, the kind of love that Mary J. Blige sang about. A love that was so unbelievably true. Sasha thought she'd found her soul mate in Montel, and he was everything she wanted in a man—intelligent, handsome, funny, devoted, strong, and easy to talk to. He knew what he wanted out of life and did it. Sasha loved their connection and felt incomplete without it.

The plan for ladies' weekend was to dedicate Saturday morning to being pampered at a spa—nails, feet, body massage, the whole nine. After that, shopping. Then Lisa and Michelle would pick up the kids from swimming lessons at the YMCA, and they would trot off to the Cape, where T was accommodating them in one of her cottages on the Vineyard.

Sasha rented a Suburban, so they could all leave together for the Cape.

Sasha was all too familiar with lesson one—when rolling with females, leave together, because females will make you late.

The whole weekend was dedicated to hanging out like the ladies used to.

Sasha heard about T and Michelle's "turn-backs," but knew little about this new man Lisa was seeing. She didn't know his name but heard he was really nice to Lisa's daughter. This could only mean he planned to stick around. Sasha only hoped he had good intentions.

Montel rolled over and silenced the beeping alarm clock. "Baby, don't you got that thing to do today with your friends?"

He listens to me all the time. Sasha let out a yawn. She'd been up since six a.m., thinking about how happy she was, and about her plans for the day.

Montel had been spending the night at her house for the last eight Fridays. She loved being around him, and she just knew he couldn't get enough of her.

"What? You trying to get rid of me?" Sasha shifted her pelvis his way, wearing nothing but a tank top and panties.

"Never that, boo. I'm just wondering if I'm going to get fed today, or do I have to starve? You know I like the way you do it up in the kitchen, so why not hook a brother up, baby?" Montel began to kiss her forehead, then neck as he let out a sensual grunt. "See, that's the sweetness I'm talking about. What's up?"

Sasha moved her eyes downward, signaling Montel to follow. In a sexy voice, Sasha said, "That's what's up, baby. Don't stop what you were doing. Finish."

Montel scooped her up into his arms, and Sasha straddled him.

"Come on," he said, "you know there's more to us than that. In time you won't be able to get enough of me."

Her mind understood what he was trying to say, but her desire within just couldn't.

He gently pushed her off him and got up, and she followed. He led her by the hand toward the stairway to go downstairs toward the kitchen.

Sasha jumped on his back, wrestling him to the floor, but her five-foot, three-inch frame couldn't hold him.

Montel pulled back, landing on the bed with her under him. Then he turned around as he lay on top of Sasha's body and began to kiss her.

Sasha's hormones raced as she spread her legs wide and ready.

Then Montel stopped.

Is he serious? Sasha had to get up before she got evil. She felt like a horny teenage boy pleading to get some virgin girl to do it with him.

"You always playing, Sasha. You can't wrestle me. You too little. Give it up."

Maybe this is his way of foreplay. She mashed his face playfully. "Whatever. Be stingy if you want to. I don't know why you always over here on Friday night. What happened? The wife kicked you out again?"

Montel rolled his eyes. "Yeah, she decided to replace me with your man, you know, that Black cop, that bad boy wannabe."

Sasha was confused. She knew he wasn't talking about Michael. *That inbred was the farthest man from my mind.* "Oh, so now you got jokes, stingy?"

"Yeah, okay. You know you're mine, and you know you want me over here, no matter what we do."

That was the truth, but Sasha couldn't let him know that. She was still a bad ass. "Why you worried about Michael? You trying to mark your turf?"

"You didn't hear me. I'm not worried. I got you." Montel began to hum, "The Roots" featuring Erykah Badu, "*If you are worried 'bout where I been or who I saw, baby, don't worry, you know that I got you.* He began to kiss her lips.

"Don't finish what you can't start."

Montel snapped, "What? Is that all you about?"

"You know what, you are becoming way too sensitive about this. How old are you now? Look, you can't sit there and tell me you don't want to, because I see it in your eyes. You're teasing me. Why, I don't know. Yeah, we talked about it and talked about it, and so forth. We're both adults, and ain't neither one of us virgins. There's been plenty opportunity, and we've known each other for years. What's the problem? You sleeping with someone else?"

Montel stood silent for a minute. Then he pulled Sasha next to him and sat her on his lap, like he was Santa Claus about to grant her Christmas wish. "Look, Sash, what we have is very special to me, and I don't want anything to go wrong. When we're together like that I want it to be special, because I've wanted to be with you for a long time. I'm waiting until the time is right. It's not just about sex when it comes to you. I love you, you know that. And, no, there's no one in my life but you. You're the only one who could hold me down. That's why I'm waiting. You're that special."

Sasha wasn't getting it. That speech could only last for so long until her mind started clicking to what was really going on here. But she took it in, just like she took in all that he'd said. Sasha felt like when you're in love, things make sense, and if they didn't yet, then they will soon. You just don't worry about it. She didn't want to admit it to herself, though, or maybe she didn't know it, but the truth was, Montel had her snowed. Blinded by what she felt was love, she was ready to do anything for this man. Her shutters were closed, and her head was buried deep under Montel's hypnotic snow bank. They were in love, and that's just how it went.

Sasha kissed his forehead and said playfully, "Since you ain't heating up things upstairs, how about you satisfy my other hunger?"

Montel smiled as he carried her downstairs like she was his child. He hugged her close, while she wrapped her legs and arms around him so he couldn't let go, burying her head in his shoulder.

After eggs, bacon, home fries, and toast, Montel ran Sasha's bath water. He filled it up with bubbles and even scrubbed her back.

Sasha smiled. "Keep this up and I might not need to go to the spa."

He giggled, she giggled, and that was that.

CHAPTER ELEVEN

Montel blew Sasha a kiss and drove her BMW from the car rental place. She drove off in the white Suburban she'd rented to meet the ladies. The events were set in motion for the day.

Sasha met up with the ladies and enjoyed manicures and pedicures later that Saturday morning. Sasha wore her hair pulled back in a ponytail, Lisa had her blondie shortcut done the day before, T wore her hair down, and Michelle had synthetic braids.

Gossip in the spa amongst them began as always, with Lisa bringing up some issues. "Hey, Sasha. What's up with Ray-Ray's girl, Tina? I saw her at my clinic the other day for battered women."

"Oh, please. That ho wasn't battered. Well, not by Ray anyways. She's tripping because Ray-Ray's with Tasha, and they're about to have a baby. So she's acting a fool, you know, kind of like how T was at the show." Sasha may have been a physician, but when it came to hanging it out with her girls, she was just another girl from the block.

They started laughing.

"Whatever." T said. "When a man stomps on a woman's heart, he should expect repercussions."

"T, I'm saying, to take it so far as to getting the law involved, that is some crazy crap," Sasha told her.

"Well, nothing's worse than a woman scorned. Everyone knows that. And don't let no other woman get involved. She's in for torture," T replied.

"Don't remind me. I wanted to kill that girl I found with Montel back then."

"Why? Didn't you already beat that bitch's ass?" T asked.

Lisa started laughing. "You bringing back memories, girl."

T said, "Sash always bringing up old shit and finding some way to talk about Montel too." She and Michelle gave each other dap, while they hollered.

"Don't hate. Montel and I are in love," Sasha said seriously.

They started laughing.

T said, "You know where love takes you. Stop fronting. Forget love. Get the money, the house, the cars, and the ding-a-ling."

"T, you really don't believe that, do you?" Sasha asked.

"Anyway, those days were good to me, when we were younger. We were naïve, no clue to the real world. Just me, myself, and some good sex, and a bottle of deuce-deuce Olde English to go with it," T said.

"You stupid, T," Lisa cut in. "I wouldn't trade them days for no one. But we were stupid, fighting over dudes. I never fought over any man, though."

"Yeah, right." T stared at Lisa like, *Yes, I'm talking to you.* "We all used to be hood rats—baggy clothes, triple goosed down, skullies, carrying army knives in our boots, rolling ten deep to the movies, rolling with the fellas. We thought we were the bomb. BIG BOOTY CREW in the house." T did the "Bankhead Bounce" with her shoulders.

"True, but I never got into a beef over a dude," Lisa declared.

"Me neither," Sasha said. "It wasn't worth it. I knew he was to blame, and I was going to handle him."

T and Michelle looked at each other like, *Yeah, right.*

They all started laughing.

T said, "Sasha, what about KeKe and Mika, the twins you fought over Chris's corny ass. Lisa, what about Hilda, that big giant from the bricks?"

"Oh yeah," Lisa said. "That wasn't my fault she came charging. I didn't know Malik was messing with her."

"He was messing with you both," T said.

Sasha corrected them, "Nah, Hilda liked him, and he wasn't interested."

"So she thought beating my ass would make him not want me?" Lisa asked. "Little did she know, he had my back and stomped his size eight in her ass for messing with me."

"Yeah, Malik was cool," Sasha said.

When he was gunned down years ago, it took Lisa a long time to get over his death. Till this day, they all will never figure out why dudes still are killing each other over their block, or their respect, or whatever. If you didn't live that life, then you couldn't understand.

The ladies fell silent for a moment, remembering all too well their teenage love life and the pain of loss at an early age.

Trying to change the subject, Sasha said, "Well, Lisa, keep a heads up on that Tina chick. Make sure her story is legit because I know Raymond didn't have anything to do with that."

"I'm way ahead of you, Sash. I already signed her up under my counsel."

"Yeah. 'Cause you a nosy gal, Lisa."

"Whatever. I don't gossip, I just share information."

They started laughing again. The ladies were back on.

Michelle said, "It's messed up how far sistas are willing to go these days over some dude. Back then we were ready to fight, but nowadays chicks are on some other type mess. It's one thing to be messing with someone's boyfriend, but breaking up happy homes, blackmailing men for money, even sex . . . Do this, or I will tell your wife. Do this, or she will get a phone call. I know that's how it was with Jamal."

Silence took over.

Michelle never gave up any info on Jamal and her, not to all of them at once anyways. She kept her life private when it came to Jamal.

No one knew what to say. This was such a sensitive topic.

Sasha took the bait. "Jamal's girls would blackmail him to stay with them?"

"Yeah, this last one, Tammy. He told me she would beat him out of his check or force him to have sex with her, or she would tell me that they were having an affair."

You believe that bullshit. Sasha couldn't believe her ears. Michelle had gone completely deaf, dumb, and blind. She was under his spell. A man like Jamal didn't have to be forced to have sex. He was a dog. Secondly, he had to come up with an excuse as to why he was giving this chick money. *Blackmail, my ass. This, I am sure, wasn't Jamal's first affair that Michelle knew about, so why would he give a flying fuck if she knew or not.* Sasha knew that Jamal knew exactly what to say to Michelle to get that door back open. *Maybe if I egged Michelle on she would realize how stupid this sounded out loud.*

Sasha said, "So that's why he left you for her?"

Michelle spoke with enthusiasm, like she had Sasha sucked into this story. "Yeah, he didn't want to hurt me or the kids, and he couldn't afford or stand this blackmail anymore, so he thought it would be best to leave me and finish what he started with her, so she couldn't blackmail him anymore."

Sasha tried to hold in her laughter. "So he left you because he didn't want to be blackmailed any more?"

Hip to all his bullshit, Lisa and T turned away, trying not to focus on Michelle.

"Yeah," Michelle said, looking for sympathy.

T broke in with, "Well, I guess it worked because he's back at home blackmail free."

Lisa quickly changed the focus. "Women don't play now. We get the money and half on everything you own, chump." She slapped T's hand. "As you get older, things change, needs change. Forget about fighting to keep a man. You can have him. Just send all the other assets my way."

They all started laughing again.

T said, "Linc pays for everything, and he is over."

Sasha reminded her, "But T, Linc hasn't done you wrong."

"So what? He's a man, and a man eventually turns back into a little boy, because he always has been. Afterwards the moon comes out, and he turns into a vampire, out to suck all he can out of you."

T's stark view of relationships had Sasha scared. She'd been through some hard times with men, but the number Ricky had done on T was frightening. She hated men, even the good ones like Linc.

Sasha chose her words carefully. "Well, T, it's been five years, and Linc hasn't showed his colors yet. I think you've seen all there is to see."

"Nah, he hasn't shown them. He wants me all to himself, so he tries to butter me up so I'll give into him. But I won't . . . ever. Love is wasted on men. When you love to be loved, you are punished. When you love to get what you want, you come out smelling like roses."

Again, T and Lisa gave each other dap.

T just didn't know how good she had it. Love was loving her, she just didn't know it.

Sasha didn't want to hear anymore of T's distorted ideas about love, so she changed the subject. "Lisa, I heard you got a new friend."

"Yeah." Lisa smiled. "He treats me well these days."

"*D*, that's his name?"

"That's what I call him, *D* honey, *D* money, and *D* dick."

They laughed.

"Damn, Lisa, he got any friends?" T asked. "I gots to have one of those."

Sasha looked at her. "Don't you have enough on your plate?"

"Sasha is all content with milk dud, and Michelle, well, she's married, so I need a smile too," T said, pleading her case.

"What about Ricky?" Lisa asked.

"Yeah," Sasha said.

"Ricky who? I'm just stringing him along, like he did me, breaking him off a piece to get back at that bitch wife and teach them both a lesson. Teach that wifey of his how it feels to be polishing a knob that is diving head first in another woman's pootang."

They all laughed, except Michelle. Of course, she didn't agree with T's antics.

"Do you ever think about how that affects his home? I mean, that woman is constantly checking messages, phone bills, and laundry. She's practically glued to his side any and everywhere they go because she can't trust him. That isn't funny, T. The only thing that teaches you is how not to trust men or yourself. You become a spy on his every move, checking body parts, smelling his penis, and smelling his clothes. You start to wonder if his disinterest in sex or him coming so quick is due to the stress of work or whether he was being satisfied somewhere else on a regular basis."

"Damn, Michelle," T cut in, "I'm not worried about her 'cause she wasn't worried about me when I was at the altar and they was in Tijuana somewhere sipping on Pina Coladas. As far as trust, you wouldn't need to play spy if you did trust him. All that shit you talking is to each his own. Meaning, if you don't trust Jamal, deal with it. Either let him go, or live this crazy life that you are living."

Michelle stood up.

The Chinese lady said, "Wait. I'm not done with your toes. You pay now."

Michelle didn't even hear her. She needed some air.

T had said what they all were thinking, but Lisa and Sasha didn't want to hurt Michelle's feelings.

Lisa and Sasha looked at T like, *Damn, did you have to say it?*

T felt bad and afterwards paid the lady for both her and Michelle's pedicures. She tried to redeem herself with Michelle outside.

The funny thing was that T used to be in that same situation. She'd played detective with Ricky. Come to think of it, they all had the trust issue one time or another with men. T knew of Ricky's activities but chose to ignore them. She followed along with him, hanging on his every word.

She'd forced the issue of marriage, and he went along with it, until the day of the ceremony. Knowing he didn't want to get married, T convinced herself he did and finally realized it when she didn't have a groom meeting her at the altar. She'd been in a relationship where love was one-sided. She'd loved him, but he only loved himself. She was the giver, and he was the taker.

Now she was taking it all, while Linc continued to give it all away. That's how those relationships worked. At one point in time you expect the tables to turn, so you either just accept it or grow enough strength to move on.

T had thought that she'd moved past Ricky, but slowly and steadily she was being sucked back in, no matter what she said her real motives were.

T and Michelle made up, and they proceeded to the mall, where shopping was like second nature to Sasha.

After spending what Sasha thought was chump change, Michelle and Lisa picked up their kids, they loaded the car, and off they were to what looked like a promising getaway.

CHAPTER TWELVE

Lisa's daughter, Jasmine, loved the pool. Meanwhile little Jamal and Mitchell were dunking each other's heads under the water. The chlorine water darkened their chocolate bodies and made their skin ashy.

The sun beamed all day as the kids enjoyed the water and the ladies relaxed, chilling like they didn't have a care in the world. Then as the day turned dim, Lisa and Michelle prepared the kids for dinner and then bed.

T had been drinking already, getting an early start for the evening.

This was a good idea, Sasha thought.

The kids enjoyed this outing so much, a thought fell through Sasha's head about kids. She imagined having at least three, but first she would need a donor. She and Montel had talked about kids. He wanted a boy, of course, but Sasha was more partial to little girls.

While Sasha continued to daydream about having children, Michelle made potato salad, and T started the grill.

It would be getting dark soon, so they wanted to hurry up and feed the kids and put them to sleep, so the party could begin. It was time to break out the wineglasses, cards, and what not.

T brought some smokes. Sasha tried to resist, but thought, *What the hell. I'll just drink some vinegar in case the job comes up with a surprise urine test.*

The first time Sasha ever puffed the magic dragon was with her cousin Tanya and her girls. She was around sixteen then and remembered not knowing what the hell she was doing, so getting high didn't feel like getting high until the second time around.

T started rolling the blunt, Sasha started mixing the daiquiris, and Lisa popped open the Moet. Next thing, they started drinking and running their mouths as usual.

They decided to play "questions," a drinking game where you would ask anyone a question, but you couldn't answer. That person would have to ask a different question and so on, until someone messed up and answered a question. Then they'd have to drink.

They played until they got dizzy. After the alcohol took over, other questions that weren't part of the game arose.

"So, Sash, you and Monty haven't hit the sheets yet?" T asked. "What's up with that?"

"We just haven't had a chance. A relationship can be based on more than just sex, you know."

T busted out laughing. "Who you kidding, Sash? Sex is like food to you. Shit, it's like food to anyone who isn't fronting. We pretend it's the men who want it all the time, but it's really us. We're just holding out." T shook her head. "So let me understand something—Montel is holding out? Are you sure he's a man? Because I know you, and you aren't holding anything out. You want it bad. What's the issue?"

Sasha ignored her.

T then tried to get under Sasha's skin. "Oh, his thing is too small?"

"Yo, T, chill. Montel and I are each other's business. That's why I can't tell you guys nothing. You always up a sister's back."

"Whatever. You be acting the same way when shit doesn't sound right."

"What? There can't be a relationship without sex?"

"Yeah. Maybe when you're a virgin or just young, like in elementary or middle school. Besides, even kids nowadays are having sex at that age anyway."

"See what I mean, T. Kids that young shouldn't be having sex. Where are their parents?"

"Oh, don't get high and mighty on me. You been sexing since high school. Stop trying to change the subject. I'm talking about two adults."

"T, you been sexing since you were twelve. And?"

"I'm saying, open your eyes. Montel and you aren't virgins, so what the hell is up with that?"

"There comes a time in everyone's life when you just have to mind your own business. We have come to an age where things are better left unsaid. Montel and I are Montel and I, and that's it." Sasha started to sound like she really believed the shit she was shuffling to her friends.

"All I am saying is, if you two are so much in love, what's the issue? Something doesn't sound right, and that's all I'm going to say about that."

Sasha wanted to get in T's business. "T, what's up with Ricky? So you're giving it up on a regular basis now?"

T smiled. "T and Ricky's business is their business."

Michelle sucked her teeth.

Lisa said, "Let it go, ladies. Please just let it go."

The alcohol really began to take its effect, and the weed was enlightening Sasha's thoughts, smoke filling the air while Mary J. Blige's *My Life* CD played.

"Sasha, you always listening to this shit. When you gonna let it go? Play some Erykah Badu or something upbeat, not this 'I'm-going-down' crap." T twisted her lips. "Always listening to old shit."

As the evening went on, it was evident they were drunk because T began barking like a "pit bitch," and Lisa began groping her throat and fiddling in her hair.

Michelle was quiet, as if she wasn't even with them.

As the liquid courage took over, Sasha began talking shit. "Yo, why is it that men can't handle being with one woman? If we started that shit, we'd be whores." Sasha giggled. "Oops, too late!" She covered her mouth to contain her laughter.

They all started laughing.

"I understand if it's a hit-and-go relationship, like me and Damon was. We had an understanding. But men still feel the need to be about other women, like that shit just comes naturally."

"I know, girl," T stormed in. "Linc doesn't understand that I have wings and I have to fly out of the coop. He just wouldn't understand. That's why I have to keep things from him."

"You're saying Linc can't handle it, but you couldn't handle it when Ricky was messing around either," Sasha said, playing devil's advocate.

"It's just like you to throw shit in my face—"

"All I'm saying—"

"You say too much, Sash. Just keep your critical opinion to yourself. Yes, I knew about Ricky's flings, but I could handle it. It didn't matter because he was bringing it all home to me. Those bitches just got dick. Ricky really loved me. I just overdid it by the whole marriage thing. I shouldn't have pushed for it."

"Hold up," Lisa said. "Are you saying it was cool for Ricky to leave you standing at the altar because you pushed him into the marriage?"

"No, Lisa, I'm saying I understand why he did what he did. I pushed him into another woman's arms. The way our relationship worked was, I knew where we stood with each other at all times. I was happy with him, and if he fooled around with some other chick, it was all good, as long as I didn't find out about it. Somewhere down the road the rules changed, and I wanted him for myself. I thought marriage would do that, so I let influences about the brass ring get into my head and into my relationship. But the truth was, I was happy how things were. You see, Lisa, men are going to be men, no matter what, good or bad, dogs, players, whatever. They get away with what you let them. Our relationship was no questions asked. The moment I tried to change that, he made the decision to leave. Don't get me wrong, Lisa, I was hurt a lot from that, and I learned a lot, but I'm not mad at him any more. I know, to you guys, it may seem like I hate men, but I don't. Linc lets me get away with whatever he desires. I'm not happy with him. I never will be, because he isn't Ricky, and that's what I'm used to. He's my passion, my soul mate."

Sasha's head spun. "T, you're losing me. A minute ago you couldn't stand men, let alone Ricky. Now you're saying he's your soul mate. What the hell is that about? You beat my head in about Montel, but then you forgive Ricky, like that shit never happened. You sound like you want to get back with him. I think you've had too much to drink."

"See, Sash, that's why on some topics, especially men, we have to be silent or fake the front, because none of us understands what the other one is going through. No matter how much we whine about our problems, we run right back to them. So what does it matter? I know what I'm saying, Sash. Just like no one can tell you shit about Montel, or Michelle about Jamal. And we all told you, Lisa, not to marry that fool Jake. We don't listen."

"So what you saying?" Sasha asked. "We aren't true friends? We're faking with each other?"

"No, Sasha, I'm saying it's *your* life. Only you can decide how to live it. Choices you make are your choices, no matter what influences brought you to that decision. If push comes to shove, we are true friends, because no matter what nigga has done us wrong, we stick together like family. And that's how it should be. Yes, we judge each other, but we only do that from our view. That's something that can't be helped."

"I understand what you're saying, T, and I agree. You still need to mind your business about Montel and me." She smiled.

"You crazy, girl."

Lisa broke in with, "Oh, I think I need a hug."

"You stupid too, Lisa," T told her.

Michelle had been silent the whole time. It took Sasha six champagne glasses and three rotations of blunts to realize that Michelle hadn't even smoked or had that many wine sips.

"Michelle, what's up?" Sasha asked. "You aren't drinking tonight?"

Michelle held on to her cup, as if she didn't want anyone to notice she hadn't been drinking.

"What's wrong, Chelle?" Lisa asked.

"Well, I—see, I was going to tell you guys, but, well anyways, the reason I'm not partaking in the intoxication process is because I'm pregnant."

A dead silence filled the room. No congratulations or nothing, just silence.

Just then the CD began to skip, and Lisa got up quickly to stop it.

Sasha had to be the one to get Michelle to replay that one. "How far along are you?"

"Just a couple of weeks. I found out last week."

A long pause fell through for the next question. "Well, are you keeping it?" Lisa asked.

"Of course."

T cleared her throat. "I will say it again, influences or not, we make our own choices, and Michelle you just made the biggest mistake. How long are you going to let Jamal get his way? He continues to knock you up, and you play house, and then he dips out on you for some other woman."

"T, it's her life. You just said—"

"I know what I said, Sash. I just hate to see you like this, Michelle."

"At least I'm not fucking someone else's husband. Shit, if you were to get pregnant, it would be a bastard child. Oops, then again, you probably wouldn't know who the father was."

T rushed at her with a fist, and Michelle fell back, just avoiding T's fist.

Sasha grabbed one of T's arms, and Lisa grabbed the other.

Michelle stood up. "Look at you, T, ready to swing at me. For what? I'm telling the truth that you can't handle. Yes, we make choices, and your choices definitely aren't any better than mine. How dare you judge me?"

T kept silent, trying to hold back angry words.

"The truth is, T, you're a hypocrite. You can't stand that I'm on my third child and you have nothing but empty arms."

Even that blow was too low for friendship.

Sasha let T's arm go. Then Lisa tried to hold T back, but she couldn't.

T darted up and pushed Michelle to the floor. They tussled and tussled.

Lisa tried hard to break them up.

After a few smacks and kicks, Sasha helped Lisa hold T back.

Michelle stood up. "None of you are my true friends. All you do is judge me and tell me how fucked up my life is, but when the topic hits your way, your lips get tight. Fuck y'all." She ran out and slammed the door to her bedroom.

Everything happened too fast for everyone to grasp. They were drunk, and it was time for them all to go nighty night. None of them said anything, and they went to bed hoping that it would blow over the next morning.

CHAPTER THIRTEEN

Sasha dropped Lisa and her daughter Jasmine off first. Lisa said she had to be home in time to straighten up because *D* was coming over that night. She spoke softly and quietly to him on her cell phone on the way from the Cape.

T was silent, and Michelle rode in the back with her two boys. After Sasha dropped everyone off, she checked her messages. To her surprise, there was nothing from Montel. A familiar voice clogged her voicemail though: "*Sash, we need to talk. Sash, you were supposed to handle this. Sash, you're really playing with fire and I don't want to be the bad guy in this, but you have to do what we discussed.*"

Seven damn messages from that Detective Perry. Is he straight stalking me?

Sasha figured this would blow over, but it wasn't happening. She made another mental note to stop putting off telling Ray about the warrant. She knew he was busy with just the idea alone of being a father and didn't want to burden him, but the other alternative didn't compare.

Sasha had been paging Montel for like an hour. She tried to get used to the idea of paging someone this day and age of the cell phone because Montel insisted that was the best way to get in contact with him. He didn't have a home number but did have a cell phone number and claimed he barely checked his messages, or answered it for that matter. He didn't even know how to text message on his phone. Imagine that. He was supposed to meet her at the rental place at two p.m. so she could drop off this truck and go home. She missed him and wanted to spend some quality time. *Damn it! Where the hell is he?*

She waited until about three p.m. and then caught a cab home. By now she was seriously pissed. Not only had Montel not returned her pages, but he also left her high and dry at the car rental place. *If he doesn't have his ass at my house when I get home it will be on. If he's not dead, then I'm gonna kill him.*

As the cab pulled up to her house, Sasha gave the driver a twenty. He didn't even ask if she wanted change. *Bastard! Men were just bastards!* Sasha felt that they just took women for all they got, and women just let them. *Fuck that!* At this point, the way she was feeling, Montel could drop all her keys to her house and cars in her mailbox, 'cause this shit was about to be over.

As Sasha walked up the stairs, Raymond and Tasha were on their way out. She was so concerned about Montel that she forgot to tell him about Tina. As she shuffled through her bag to look for her keys, the door opened.

Montel had the audacity to ask, "Where you been?"

Sasha stood in the doorway with her head tilted and a look of confusion on her face. Her words went out of control. "Where the fuck were you? I've been at that damn rental place for an hour waiting on you and my fucking car, and you have the balls to ask me where have I been?"

Montel put his hands up in a motion to stop her, but Sasha kept going.

Waving her arms, she said, "Hello, earth to Montel, where the fuck were you? Don't even think you are going to tell me you didn't get my pages, because your pager is right here." She snatched it off his waist. "Here. Right here. Now what? And what do you have to say for yourself?"

Before Montel could open his mouth, Sasha added, "You're tired, you're tired, and you're trifling. How are you going to leave me high and dry? No concern for me at all. You disgust me. Get out of my way. Get out of my house. Give me my keys. Scram. Run along now, doggy."

Sasha threw his pager at him and pushed past him into the house, going on and on. She threw her overnight bag on the sofa and slouched in the chair.

Montel slammed the door, threw the keys she gave to him across the floor, and began to gather his things, not saying a word.

Sasha stared him like he was crazy. *I know he wasn't pissed with me.*

After he finished gathering his things, he made his way out the door.

"You don't have anything to say for yourself?"

Without a word, he came close to her as if he wanted to kiss her. He leaned in and with one hand braced himself on the sofa, and with the other pushed the button to the answering machine on the table behind the sofa, playing the seven messages that Michael left Sasha. Then he left and closed the door behind him.

Sasha stood there in shock. *I know he can't think there's anything going on with Michael and me.* True, he left plenty of messages, but they were about Ray, not her and not him. How could he get that confused? She was convinced he must've been jealous, thinking Sasha had something else going on the side. Maybe he was just as insecure about her as she was about him. *Wow! Maybe we weren't from different planets.*

She knew she could straighten this out with him, if she talked to him. She would just leave him a sweet message, and that would be that. She dialed his cell phone and waited for the prompt to leave a message.

"Hey, baby, it's me. I'm really sorry about going off on you today. I was real pissed with you because I thought . . . well, it doesn't matter. I was wrong. And about Michael, he's a detective working on a case with Raymond, that's it. There is no he and I. If you don't believe me, come down to the station with Raymond and me when he makes his statement. This was all a big misunderstanding, and I don't want to lose you over something silly like this. Call me. I love you. Bye." *That should do it. He'll be back by the early morning*.

As she relaxed and tried to unwind in her empty home, she took a bath and fantasized about all the things she was going to do to Montel when he came home. She would tie him up and put a blindfold over his eyes, strip him and cover him with heated baby oil. After that, she would place each of her breasts against his mouth, one by one. Then she would sit on his penis with just her thongs on and lick his body from head to toe. Then she would get up and leave him there for a couple of minutes until he started moaning and begging for her to come back. *Oooh weeee!* The thought gave her chills up her spine.

After nine o'clock hit, Sasha started reading a book. As eleven o'clock hit, she got her clothes ready for work. When one in the morning hit, she realized no one was calling. Certainly not Montel. *Did he get my message? Is he still angry?* She wished she knew the answer. Her night of possibilities was over.

Great. This was a perfect day. Michelle isn't talking to the ladies, Michael is on my back, Raymond is probably in jail because I didn't tell him about Tina, and Montel is pissed over some bullshit.

Sasha shut off her light and pulled the covers up, thanking the Lord for this day and asking for another chance tomorrow.

By the end of the week, with no Montel, Sasha found herself in a stupor. She was a love-sick fool who felt her chance at happiness had slipped through her fingers. This was all just a misunderstanding. She figured if she could only speak to him, this could be straightened out. She was a mess.

Sasha tried to speak to Lisa about it, but she was off somewhere with D. She called T, who was chasing Ricky and dodging Linc. As for Michelle, she needed time to cool off, to realize the ladies were still her girls.

Work was the only thing keeping her afloat. In the past week, she'd worked fifty-five hours at the hospital and the clinic for women's health, delivering sixteen babies, performing twenty-eight pap smears, and counseling a dozen women, mostly young, on safe sex and breast cancer.

Coming home to an empty house wasn't something she looked forward to every night, so she slept in the hospital most of the time. She had her calls forwarded, but still no Montel.

Sasha was only left wondering, Damn, how long you can stay mad at someone? And for nothing. Montel, of course, was blowing this out of proportion. The question was why? Her imagination began to take over. Where is he? Who is he with? If this was what she was like without him for a week, imagine forever. She needed some help.

Sasha finally made it home one evening. The smell of his cologne had finally left, his things were gone. She couldn't bear to look at the picture they took while they were in L.A. *Was he just busy? Did he get my message? What am I going to do if this is it?* If she wasn't so perplexed by his absence, she would have cried every night.

After watching a dozen movies, she began to search for her phone book and realized she had thrown it away. She knew Damon's number by heart, but couldn't bear to call. She was lonely, a place she hadn't been in a long time.

Sure, she didn't have fulfilling love-blown relationships in the past, but she had some sort of outlet. She had the girls, flings, the regulars. Sasha traded it all in for Montel, a man whom she'd loved for so long. She believed in sacrifices, and she believed that he was worth it. Her life seemed better when she was with him. She had fallen into the "you-need-a-man-in-your-life-to-have-a-life syndrome" and didn't know how to pull herself out.

After two weeks, Sasha realized Montel wasn't going to call. She guessed it was over, time for her to try move on.

After countless attempts for Detective Perry to catch up with Raymond, Sasha finally arranged a meeting between the two. They agreed that he didn't have to come down to the station. Michael was pulling all the strings. He called in a couple of favors from his old buddy the mayor, who'd been running Boston for the last fifteen years.

Sasha got up early to fix up the place. She made brunch, and got dressed, just going through the motions, not even realizing that her appearance wasn't the same. She didn't feel like herself and felt really vulnerable and sensitive.

Raymond came downstairs and offered to help, but she was already finished.

"How long is this going to take? I have a game with the little ones, and Tasha has an appointment with that doctor you referred her to."

She stepped back and looked at her brother in a whole new light. He had grown up so fast, taking on all his responsibilities, and living up to the man she knew he could be. She felt so proud, like she was the mommy. At least one of them was going to be happy.

"Ray Ray, I haven't been around you much lately, but you sure have changed. Besides this little incident, you haven't brought any drama to my house yet. You really are becoming a man. I can't call you Ray Ray any more. It's Raymond, right?"

Raymond giggled and put his arm around his sister. "Yeah, I know. I am the shit."

They laughed.

"Are you all right, Sash? You aren't going to start getting emotional, are you?"

"No, Raymond, I'm just in awe of you right now. One minute you are little Ray, the next, you are about to be a dad."

"I know, right. Don't worry though. I'm going to make sure my son has his shit together. I'm going to teach him about being a man, a better man than me. I'm going to show him the world is at his feet. He just has to learn how to play the game." Raymond's face just lit up talking about his future son.

"Hey, Ray, how you know it's going to be a boy? What if it's a girl?"

"I want her to be just like you."

Sasha almost cried.

"Ay, you, don't get all girly on me now."

"I am just in a weird place right now, and I don't feel like myself."

"Yeah, that nigga got you bugging. Stop playing yourself, Sasha. You know what needs to be done. Cut him loose."

"I know, but it's hard when you have your mind set on something, and it doesn't turn out the way you hoped after you put all your energy and all your emotion into it."

"I know what you're saying, but just like basketball, if you don't win, you either play again or take up a new sport."

"Whatever. I just have to figure this one out on my own."

"Yo, what time is this guy going to get here? I have things to do."

"He said two, and it's two now, so it shouldn't be long."

"He needs to hurry up."

"Do you have your story straight? You know what you're going to tell him?"

"Yeah. I saw Tina that night, we talked, I told her it was over, she flipped, started hitting me. I pushed her, and she started crying, yelling names—"

"Wait a minute, Ray, you pushed her?"

"Yeah, to get her off of me. Not in a violent way, but in a get-off-me way."

"How hard did she fall?"

"I don't know. Once I pushed her, I walked out of there. She was yelling shit as I was leaving."

"Damn! You pushed her. She could use that if she wanted to."

"Yeah, I know. But I'm telling you, if we get the lawyers involved, she'll back off."

"I hope so."

The doorbell rang. It was Michael.

They went over what needed to be said. Michael told them he would let them know and Raymond needed to get in touch with a lawyer, just in case she wanted to take this thing further.

Raymond thanked Michael for coming. And they held onto a couple of laughs as they drank and ate.

The conversation, Sasha noticed, was turning into men against women, so she had to defend herself.

Michael said, "Some sisters today are so trifling, and I just don't want to be bothered."

Raymond gave him dap.

"Excuse me, *brothers* are trifling as well. It depends on who you're messing with."

"Whatever. You women think us men speak a different language than you, but the truth is, we have feelings like you and don't want to get hurt like you, so we avoid being who you want us to be." Michael looked Sasha dead in the eye.

"Well, you need to stop hiding, so we all can get together and have a good time, you know. The way I feel right now, all men can kiss my ass."

Michael said quickly, "Hey don't they already do that?"

Ray and Michael laughed.

"If you must know, Detective, I too get done wrong. I'm not always the bad girl, as you would like to believe."

Michael smiled. "I understand you more than you think, but you, just like every other woman looking for love, are searching in the wrong place. Your ideal man is just that, an ideal. Stop loving with your mind, and start loving with your heart."

Sasha asked, "Where did that come from?"

"I tend to get deep about these things. I was divorced about seven years ago. I married my high school sweetheart because of what I thought she was instead of what I felt about her. Now I know what's what. And on that note, if you will excuse me, I must use your bathroom please."

"You know where it is." Sasha pointed to the hallway.

As Michael got up, Raymond looked at Sasha in a weird way. "What's going on here?"

"Nothing."

"Yeah, whatever. I'm out. You two love birds are going to have to do without me."

"We aren't any lovebirds."

"What-ever," Raymond said, walking out the door.

Michael came back with a look of surprise to find they were alone. They didn't say a word. No insults, and no sarcasm. They just sat there.

"I better get going," he said.

"I'm sure duty calls or something. Hey, thanks a lot for what you did today. I guess I figured you wrong. You're not such a bad guy. Decent even."

"I guess I come down hard on you sometimes."

"Sometimes? Try *all the time*, with the exception of today."

"True. I don't know. You just spark something in me that I can't control."

Sasha seemed a little confused.

"I mean . . . never mind. I'll talk to you later."

As he opened the door, she reached for his arm to tell him to stay. Sasha didn't know whether it was loneliness or desperation, but she wanted him to stay.

Before she could get the words out of her mouth, the door opened, and Montel appeared in her doorway.

CHAPTER FOURTEEN

"Yeah right, Ms. Sasha," Montel said in disgust as he rolled his chinky eyes at her and walked away.

Of course Sasha dashed after him.

"Wait, Montel. It's not what you think."

She grabbed his arm, but he snatched it away.

"Would you just listen to me? What did you come by for?"

Montel turned around and said to her with a look of craziness in his eyes, "What did I come by for?"

Before Sasha could explain, Michael came onto the scene, like he was coming to her rescue. The same damn manner he'd used when the cops had Ray handcuffed on her porch.

"Excuse me, I'm Detective Perry." He extended his hand for Montel to shake.

Montel looked at his hand like, *Whatever*.

"I don't know what you thought, but I'm here working on a case for Raymond, Sasha's brother. We're through here, Sasha. I'll be in touch with Raymond and you when I hear from the D.A.'s office. Take care. Oh, and nice to meet you, Montel." Michael walked away, but gave Sasha a disapproving look as he kept going. He couldn't believe she was chasing this man.

Well, whatever Michael thought, it didn't matter. Montel was here, and Sasha just knew he wanted to work things out.

"Montel, it's not what you think. I know it seems like Detective Perry is always around and that's because there is always drama. I told you about the dude who wrecked my place, and I also told you about the charges being brought up on Ray, so I don't understand where this attitude is coming from. Talk to me. I know you didn't come all the way over here to pout."

"No, Sasha, I didn't come over here to pout, I came to see you. I missed you. It seems every time I come around, am not around, that cop cat is. You say there's nothing going on with him, but he acts like there is."

"What are you talking about?"

"Sash, I know men, and that man is into you, so I don't want him around you if Ray isn't present."

"Montel, you're being barbaric. You can't forbid me to see anyone."

"I'm not forbidding you, I'm just telling you I don't like it. And if you cared about me at all, you would understand."

"I do care about you, baby. I love you. When you were gone, I thought it was over. You didn't call, didn't return my messages."

"I needed some time to think. That shit that went down with us was crazy, and I felt out of control. I didn't realize how deep my feelings ran for you. I can't stand the thought of you with some other man." He put his hands on her shoulders and stared into her eyes. "I don't know what I would do if you were."

Sasha put her arms around Montel's waist and buried her face into his chest. "You won't have to worry about that. I only love you."

Montel pressed his head on the top of hers. "I'm glad to hear it because you are my world."

They just stood there in each other's arms like time stopped for them.

Montel really loves me. He just needed time. Sasha kept saying that in her head over and over again, so it would stick and she would believe in it. *He loves me.*

"Dr. Freeman, we're ready for you in 1420," Nurse Morgan said with urgency.

Sasha quickly raced into the room to deliver another newborn that day. She ripped off the plastic cover to open the sterile delivery table instruments, careful not to contaminate anything. The summer months were here, and with the heat came the baby boom.

"We're going to have a baby," she said to the laboring mother.

Sasha gowned her sterile paper blue apron, put on her face mask, and then donned her sterile gloves. "Okay, Eryln, on the next contraction, I want you to push as hard as you can."

Too out of breath to speak, Eryln nodded, sweat dripping from her forehead down to her cheek.

Sasha poured normal saline in a blue basin and checked that all her equipment was readily available and working properly as she waited for the next contraction. She gently massaged Eryln's perineum, stretching it to make room for the impending delivery. So far, no tears, her perineum was intact.

Sasha could see the baby's head crowning. "Excellent, Eryln. I can see the top of your baby's head." She looked to Nurse Morgan. "How's the baby's heart rate?"

The nurse referred to her fetal monitor strip. "A couple of decelerations, but returning to baseline quickly after each contraction."

"Excellent." Sasha was almost sure Eryln's delivery would be normal, but in the back of her mind, always expected the unplanned emergency.

"ARRRGHH!" Eryln screamed out in pain. The next contraction was here.

"Push, Eryln, push," Nurse Morgan urged, helping Eryln's husband, Jeff, hold Eryln's legs as she tucked her chin to her chest and pushed for dear life.

Eryln, exhausted from being in labor for seventy hours, had an epidural twelve hours ago when she reached four centimeters dilated. This was the couple's first baby, and they were expecting a girl and planned to name her Skylar.

Eryln wanted to deliver like yesterday and continued to push like there was no tomorrow. Despite the pressure she felt as she could feel her baby's passing through her pelvis and emerging through her burning vagina and perineum, she pushed down hard, taking one short breath, then back to chin to chest for another hard push during her contraction. Her epidural was wearing off, and she could feel everything. She cried out in pain as tears and sweat soaked her face like a raging river. Her body smelled of salt and funk from her laboring.

"Push, baby, push," Jeff shouted.

The head was almost out.

"Almost there, Eryln," Sasha encouraged her. "Almost there. Push."

The head was out now. Sasha steadied her hand around the baby's face, rotating it firmly. "One more big push!"

Eryln screamed out in pain, "ARRGH!" and her baby girl was born.

Summer time was always busy in the maternity unit. Sasha didn't blame her patients though. Sometimes, she felt she would have loved to have the summer off.

For her these past couple of months had gotten crazier. She saw less of Montel, when she thought they were supposed to be growing. He was trying to get this new group off the ground and was traveling more.

Sasha delivered more newborns that summer than she did in her entire first year of being an obstetrician.

Lisa, Tamieka, Tasha, and Ray were throwing her this surprise birthday party they didn't think Sasha knew about, and she was real excited about that.

Sasha called Michelle, who was still was keeping herself distant from the ladies, but she didn't return her calls. She dropped off little gifts for the boys, but she wasn't around. Sasha really needed to know what was going on with her. How was the baby doing? Which hospital? Which doctor? She had to make sure she was all right. They'd always stuck together, and the way she was shutting out the ladies couldn't be healthy for her or the baby. Sasha made it a point to see how she was doing.

At the end of the day, Sasha had called in a number of favors to find out who Michelle's obstetrician was. She finally got the necessary info. Coincidentally, Michelle's doctor worked out of the same hospital as she did. Her name was Dr. Matilda Roebuck, one of Sasha's instructors in medical school, and a real bitch. A stickler for the rules, she and Sasha didn't see eye to eye and were always getting into debates about ethics and patient rights. You name it, and they didn't agree on it. That was the past though, and Sasha hoped she would've calmed down by now.

On her way home, she stopped by Dr. Roebuck's office. "Matilda the Hun" wasn't there, but her secretary was. Her secretary happened to be Tamela Meeks, a friend of her cousin Tanya, so of course, Sasha used this edge.

"Hey, girl. Whazzup? How you been?"

Tammy rose to hug her. "Oh, I'm fine. Are you a doctor yet?"

"Yeah, girl. I finished my residency last year." Sasha was a chameleon, switching up her manner and the way she talked in a heartbeat to adapt to her environment.

"Oh that is so wonderful. Do you need a secretary?"

"Tammy, you're crazy. Don't you work for what's-her-name?"

Tammy gave her a look. "Exactly! I can't stand that heifer." *This was even better.*

"Have you spoken to Tanya, Sash?"

"No, I haven't, but I plan to soon."

"Yeah, we kind of lost touch when she got married, but we'll hook up soon."

"Hey, Tammy, could you do me a favor? I need to look at my friend's file. You remember Michelle?"

"Oh yeah. I seen her in here. She's having another baby?" Tammy asked, concerned.

"Yeah, I know. I just want to see how she's doing. We haven't spoken in a minute, and I'm worried about her."

"Say no more. Dr Roebuck is going to be out of the office for at least another hour. She's delivering, so help yourself."

"Thanks, Tammy. I'm going to be just a minute."

"That's fine. I'm going to get a soda anyway."

"All right. If I don't see you, take care."

"You too, Sasha."

Sasha looked in the *E* section of Dr. Roebuck's files and came across Edwards, Michelle. She looked through the folder, and everything seemed to be in order.

Damn! She's almost six months pregnant. She didn't look that big that weekend. What are these other tests? Michelle needs to take better care of herself. I don't care what's going on, I'm going over there today to let her know the deal. You'd think she was highly experienced in this and would know what she's doing.

Just when she was about to put the file down, she noticed another slip of paper that read CONFIDENTIAL. It was an HIV test, and to Sasha's horror, it read positive. Sasha thought she was going to collapse or cry. She quickly tucked that slip back in the file, dashed out, closed the door, and just made it out when Dr. Roebuck came into the office.

"Freeman, what are you doing in my office?"

Sasha was quick on her feet. "I came to see you."

"Did you not notice I wasn't here? Why are you coming out of my office?"

"I didn't see anyone, so I figured you were in your office. I checked and you weren't there, and here you are."

"Is there something you want to tell me, Dr. Freeman?"

Sasha shrugged. "No."

"Then why are you here?"

"Oh yeah, that's right, I was looking for some advice about a patient."

"Advice? You've never come to me about advice, so why now?"

"You know you're right, Dr. Roebuck. I never have, and now I know why. You ask too many questions, and I never get an answer, so what's the point, I mean, really?" Sasha gave her the same look she gave her when she was her instructor. *Bitch!*

Dr. Roebuck looked at her funny, as though she knew Sasha was up to something, but Sasha stared her down and kept going out of the door, out of her office, praying that she'd make it out of the woods.

Sasha didn't know how she was feeling on her way to Michelle's house. Not only did she violate her friend's right to privacy and put her own job on the line, she also thought that she'd failed her as a friend. They all did. Who knew what she was going through right now?

Sasha began to cry as she thought about all the fun they'd had as kids, and then Michelle's kids, and then Michelle's unborn child, and then Jamal, that low-down, dirtball bastard. How could he do this? If Sasha felt this way, she could only imagine how Michelle was feeling.

She reached her house door and tried to get what she was going to say to her straight as she rang the doorbell.

Michelle answered the door with a surprised look on her face.

Sasha just hugged her tight. "Michelle, I missed you so much. Don't send me away."

"Sasha, what the hell is wrong with you?"

She wiped her tear before she could see it. "Nothing. I'm just all emotional. My period is coming."

"Don't be talking about periods around here. I won't see one for a long time."

Sasha laughed. "So how have you been? I call you, but you don't call me back. Whazzup with that?"

"I just needed time to think."

"I know. You don't owe me or anyone else an excuse, and I just missed you, that's all. We all missed you."

"I missed you guys too. So what you been up to?"

"Montel and I are still kicking it. Ray's girl, Tasha, is twenty-four weeks pregnant. I haven't heard anything about that crazy Tina girl. Hopefully she dropped the charges. And the ladies are planning me a surprise party that I'm not supposed to know about."

"I see. How are the ladies?"

Just then Sasha's cell phone rang. "Hello."

"Sash, it's me. Linc done found out about Ricky, and shit is just a mess. Where are you?"

"Michelle's. Why don't you come through?"

Michelle heard T through the phone and grabbed it from Sasha. "Yeah, why don't you bring your stank ass over here?" Michelle said in a playful way.

Sasha then called Lisa up for reinforcements, and the ladies were back on.

The four of them stood outside on Michelle's porch, getting everything out.

Michelle apologized to T for saying what she did, and T apologized to Michelle for hitting her.

T really felt bad. "If anything was to happen to your baby, I would just kill myself."

"Okay, so this one will be your godchild then. How about that?"

The thought left T speechless, and they just hugged each other.

Sasha had her own thoughts going through her head. *One day T might have to take that baby in.* Sasha tried not to be sad, not wanting to let on that she knew. She kept the happy front going. "So, T, what up with Linc? He's mad?"

"Of course, he's mad, but more so hurt," T said, feeling guilty for causing Linc's pain.

"You mean to tell me you care about Linc's feelings?" Sasha said playfully.

"Yes, I do. But I don't want to be with him, I want to be with Ricky."

"Oh no, here we go again," Michelle said.

Lisa said, "Well, you've had them both for months. Now you have to choose. You know what kind of men they both are. The question is, Who are you going to be happy with? Are you going to be happy with Linc, a man who loves you unconditionally? Or are you going to be happy with Ricky, a man who is obligated to another woman?"

"Well, that isn't a hard choice. Ricky is the man for me. He and I fit together. Linc and I don't make sense. He needs someone . . . well, like you, Michelle, soft, motherly, homebody type, angelic. I'm rough around the edges and I like it rough around the edges. I need that drama in my life."

Sasha asked her, "So what are you going to do?"

"I'm going to tell Linc the truth and take it from there."

"Well, all the power to you." Sasha patted T on the back.

They all stood out there, talking for a while. Sasha's advice on the situation would be to let Ricky go, but you can't advise a woman in love. No one can.

Sasha just stood back and took a good look at her friends. She loved and accepted them no matter what.

An exhausted Sasha went home to an empty house that day. Montel still wasn't back from his trip. She checked her answering machine. No new messages. *Oh well.*

There were many nights she wished he were there with her, but what was the use? She still wasn't getting any and was becoming used to that too. She hadn't hit a dry spell in a very long, long time. She guessed it did her mind some good. She began to see that sex wasn't everything in a relationship.

She reached the top of her stairs and opened her bedroom door. To her surprise, dim candle lights flickered in her room, and rose petals covered her bed. As she stepped in, the door closed behind her. One hand from behind grabbed her waist, the other hand brushed her cheek with a single rose.

She turned around and saw Montel, dressed in nothing and ready to press on her soft body. "I thought—"

Montel placed his hand against her lips, shushing her. He kissed her and led her to the bathroom, where he undressed her and gave her a bath.

As he turned the radio on, he dried her body, lifted her to his waist, and they fell on the rose-covered bed, his naked body pressing against her damp skin. He kissed her lips, chin, and neck. He gently grabbed her breasts and placed them in his mouth one by one, sucking them and biting them like juicy plums. He continued licking her up and down as he turned her onto her stomach and licked down her spine to Jagged Edge's "I Just Got to Be."

Montel took a petal and swept it across her vagina, causing Sasha to giggle a little. Then he started to lick, suck, and lick and suck.

His tongue and lips felt so warm, Sasha was about to explode.

He stopped and stared her dead in the face. "Do you like that?"

Sasha just nodded. She couldn't even speak. She rose to her knees to meet him at the edge of the bed.

He rose to his knees and was still a little taller than her on his knees.

Sasha began to kiss him everywhere, wrestling him down to the bed. She crept up to him slowly and licked him down his chest and navel, to his penis. She used her mouth and tongue and hands sucked and massaged his mister. She came up for air and sat on top of him as she licked his navel, causing him to moan.

He grabbed her hair, the tips of his fingers touching her roots. She licked his nipples then sucked on his neck.

When she reached his lips, he said to her, "I love you, Sasha."

She gave him a sexy smile as he rolled her over to be on top.

Still grabbing her hair, he entered her. Her legs were past her ears.

As he thrust slowly, she moaned every time. She rolled him over and rode him first frontward then backwards.

His hands grabbed her breasts, and she could feel the explosion coming.

She yelled out a load moan as she reached ecstasy.

Tears were coming out of his eyes as she sat on his lap and they both moved in the same motion, her legs locked around his waist and her hands holding his back in a bear hug.

He buried his face in her neck and moaned, and moaned, and moaned. When he reached his point, he lay back with Sasha on top of him.

Sasha kissed him. "I love you, Montel."

And they fell asleep in each other's arms.

CHAPTER FIFTEEN

Sasha was on cloud nine at work the next morning. She and Montel finally made love. He was worth waiting for. It was so beautiful, she wanted to cry. She just knew everything would be uphill from now on. By the end of the workweek she was even more excited because, come this time next week, she'd be starting a two-week vacation. If this wasn't heaven, then she didn't know what was. Montel claimed he was taking her to L.A. again, since they'd had such a good time there before, and she couldn't wait.

Sasha made her board rounds. All her maternity patients were doing fine, no deliveries, surprisingly, and just two more hours left until freedom. She was going to use all the time she had to spend with Montel. Since they'd made love, she figured they could do it all the time and wanted to do the do again and again.

Sasha's surprise birthday party was tomorrow night. She had a lot of things to do today, so four o'clock needed to hit like right now. She began to make out her to-do list in her office. *Hmm, let's see, I need a new outfit for tomorrow, some shoes, some new earrings, some lingerie, some bath oils, some whipped cream, some cherries. Oops, my list is turning into a sexing list.*

Her phone rang.

Don't they know I'm trying to get out of here like now? She answered the phone giddy as hell, "Yes."

"Hello, Freeman. This is Dr. Roebuck. I know you were in my files last week. I'm taking this up with the hospital board."

Sasha cleared her throat. "Excuse me. I don't know what you're talking about."

"My secretary told me. You have a lot of explaining to do. I'm setting up a meeting with the board today." She hung up.

What the hell is going on around here? I know Tammy wouldn't tell Cruela Deville anything.

She rushed out of her office and down to her accusers. Dr. Roebuck wasn't there, but Tammy was.

"Hey, girl. Whazzup?"

"What's up?" Sasha said in amazement. "What's up is, you told Dr. Frankenstein I was in her office—Duh!"

"Oh, well, she figured it out for herself. I just reinforced it. No big deal."

"No big deal? I could lose my license."

"For what?"

"Haven't you ever heard of patient confidentiality . . . HIPAA?"

"What? Michelle is your friend. By the way, how is she doing?"

"Tammy, you're not with it. Don't you know anything about patient rights? Michelle is not my patient, so I can't look in her chart. Now if she happened to tell me something as a friend, then that is fine."

"Oh, I see. Well, I'm sure it will work itself out. How is her hubby Jamal doing?"

"Why are you so interested in Michelle? You guys only met once when we were kids. You don't even know Jamal?"

Just then a conversation came to mind. *Tammy the blackmailer.* "Wait a minute, Tammy, I know you're not the Tammy who's having an affair with Michelle's husband?"

"Damn! Jamal told her? He's so stupid."

"Tammy, you're fucking someone else's husband. Don't you even give a damn?"

"Frankly, I don't. That's on him. If the home was happy—"

"Don't give me that if-the-home-was-happy shit. If you were happy with yourself, you wouldn't be . . . Oh, never mind, it's pointless. You're nasty, and you better watch yourself."

"What's that supposed to mean?"

"It means Jamal has—" Sasha stopped herself.

"Jamal has what? A family?"

"Yes, he has a family, and you're not a part of it."

"Whatever, Sasha. You just don't understand the circumstances around it."

"I don't want to know. But I'll tell you one thing—You keep your mouth shut about me being in this office, and I won't tell Michelle where you work. She'd choke you if she knew. And to think you can just sit there and sign her in for her doctor visits, while in the back of your mind you reminisce about sucking her husband's dick. You are sick, Tammy. Just trifling."

"Whatever. You just keep your end of the bargain."

Sasha slammed the office door. Not only was she keeping a secret about Michelle's test, but now she had to be quiet about this Tammy shit too. She just wanted to see if Michelle was okay. *Damn it! I'm too nosy!*

Sasha walked back to her office, and to her surprise, the chief resident was waiting for her.

"Look, Dr. Cooper, I can explain."

"No need, Dr. Freeman. You'll have your say at the boards. For now it's best for you to take an extended vacation until this matter is cleared up."

Her heart dropped. "Am I being fired?"

"No, but this matter needs to be cleared up. Until then, I think it would be best that you—"

"That I what? Leave the premises immediately? You haven't even heard my side of the story, and you are ready to throw me out of here."

"Dr. Freeman, I already told you, no one is throwing you out."

"Whatever. You're taking sides. Dr. Roebuck has hated me since med school, and now she's trying to ruin me. I can't believe this. You're taking sides. Her case is bull."

"You'll have your chance to defend yourself at the boards."

"Defend myself? I shouldn't have to. Whatever. I'm out of here!" Sasha left the chief resident standing outside her office and slammed the door behind her.

Sasha didn't even pack up her things, because she knew she would be back. *I'm not going to let some two-bit old hag tell me what I can and cannot do. Talk about patient confidentiality. She had her patient's husband's mistress signing her in, taking down all her information. This fucking hospital hasn't heard the last of me!* She dashed out of there.

Well, she got the vacation she always wanted. Who knew when she would work again? Sasha was glad she'd saved up, or else she would've been in a shitload of trouble.

The thought of Montel soothed her. She had to call him, since only he knew how to comfort her.

By the time she got to her house, she found a frail Tasha on her doorstep.

"What's wrong, Tasha? Where's Raymond?"

"They took him."

"Who took him?"

"I don't know." Tears started pouring down Tasha's face.

"What's going on?"

"The police. Tina didn't drop the charges. That detective called and tried to warn us, tried to have Ray's lawyer present. It just all happened so fast."

Sasha grabbed her arm and ran inside her house. "Come on."

Michael had left her several messages telling her to hurry down to the station before it got too late and she wouldn't be able to get Raymond out until Monday. That message was at two p.m., and it was now four-thirty p.m.

Sasha called the station, but Michael wasn't around.

The desk clerk told her, "No one is going to be bailed out tonight, and the judges will be gone by the time you get here."

Sasha yelled at him, "We'll see about that!" Her thoughts raced. *Who do I know with connections? Tanya . . . she would know.*

She called Tanya, her cousin, who was also a lawyer. It took several rings for her to answer.

"Tanya," she said.

"Sash, is that you? What's up, girlfriend? Why haven't I heard from you?"

"There's no time for that. I need your help. Raymond's in jail, and they're talking about no bail," Sasha ranted like a mad-woman to her cousin. "And I want him out fucking tonight. You have to help me."

"Calm down, Sash. I'll see what I can do. Meet me at the courthouse in twenty minutes."

Sasha grabbed a crying Tasha by the arm, got in her car, and sped off. By the time Sasha got to the courthouse, which looked closed, Tanya was waiting for her there.

Sasha's cousin, Tanya, didn't play. Dressed to the nines, of course, she wore a skirt suit that fit her hourglass frame, white blouse, pumps, and had her hair pinned up. She had her glasses on, French manicured nails, and her makeup was flawless. She walked down that hall with Sasha as if she were running the place, her light-skinned face turning back and forth as she tried to explain the situation.

They walked down the hall fast and stopped in front of the D.A.'s office.

"All right, Sash, my field is entertainment law, as you know. Luckily, I know the D.A. She's a real bitch, but she likes it when I invite her to the celebrity parties. Right now as it stands, Tina dropped the charges, but the D.A. wanted to take it fur-ther and is continuing this case in the name of the so-called people. Translation: She's running for some office and needs votes. The important thing today is to get Ray out. Since he's my cousin, that shouldn't be a problem. Your problem is going to be getting these charges dropped. I have no idea how that's going to play, but here's a card to a very good attorney, second only to Johnnie Cochran. He could've gotten Charlie Manson off. He's sweet on my mother, so he will take this case, but he normally doesn't deal with itty-bitty cases like this. He's very expensive, but that shouldn't be a problem for you, *doctor*, right?" Tanya was talking a mile a minute, as lawyers did.

Sasha quickly said, "Right." She didn't want to embarrass herself by discussing what went on earlier, so she played along.

"Okay, Sash, here goes nothing. Oh, and, remember, let me do all the talking." Tanya entered the room. "Devonia, how are you today, girl?"

They hugged like they were old sorority sisters.

"This is my cousin, Sasha Freeman."

"What kind of name is Sasha?"

Sasha gave a look but kept her mouth shut. This wasn't about her.

"All right, let's get down to business. Devonia, you have Raymond Freeman in custody, and we want him out. What is it going to take?"

"Tanya, you get right down to business. It'll take a signed confession and a plea of guilty."

Sasha sucked her teeth, and Devonia looked at her, seemingly offended.

Tanya tried to buddy her up. "Ha, ha! Really, what is it going to take, *D*?"

"Given the magnitude of this case, I plan to take it all the way. Now, I can release him, but I'm starting right up with indictment charges, so you better move fast on this one. I can get the judge to set the bail for around five thousand."

Sasha couldn't hold it in any longer. "Are you serious?"

"Ms. Freeman, I'm very serious. Your brother is going down, and so is that Detective Perry. He handled this case all wrong. If I left it up to him, justice would never be served."

"Oh, that's a bunch of bologna. Detective Perry is a good cop, and the only place my brother is going is home to take care of his family, so you better back off, sister." Sasha was sick of playing nice with a woman obviously out for her brother's blood.

Tanya gave Sasha that look.

"Will you excuse us?" She grabbed Sasha by the arm and pulled her outside Devonia's office. "Look, Sasha, I told you I'm an entertainment lawyer, and although I may look like I belong on TV, I'm not any entertainer and neither are you. So wait out here."

Fifteen minutes later, Tanya came out. "Ray will be released. His hearing is on Monday. Here's Martin's card. Call him tonight. You almost blew it back there."

"I don't care. Raymond hasn't done a damn thing."

"That's up to the judge to decide."

"How much is bail?"

"I don't know. Let's go down to the clerk's office and find out."

Raymond's bail was five thousand. His retainer would probably be more for this scum-ball lawyer, and Sasha's stash was about to dwindle away very quickly.

After they left the courthouse, Ray thanked Tanya for her help, as did Sasha.

"Not a problem, but you can call a sister and let her know what's going on with y'all." Tanya missed her cousins and still worried about them even thought they were adults.

"I know, Tanya. I will definitely keep in touch."

Sasha drove everyone back to the house. She wanted to scream. Her day was hell. She called Montel, and it took him three pages to call her back.

"What's wrong, Sasha? You sound upset."

"I just had a hell of a day, you know. Where are you?"

"I'm in Montreal with the group. I won't be back until late tonight. I'll call you tomorrow. Get some rest, sweetheart."

Sasha thought, *Great. My man couldn't comfort me, and I couldn't go shopping, since I didn't know where my next meal was coming from.*

Sasha ran her bath water, soaked for an hour, and went to bed. *Well, tomorrow is my party. Yes, tomorrow will be a better day.*

Sasha woke up on her twenty-ninth birthday feeling yesterday's heat. She decided to go shopping anyways. After all, it was her birthday. She picked up a nice outfit for the party with some matching shoes, got her hair, nails, and toes done. She was ready for the evening. She didn't know how her friends intended to get her to this party, but as long as she got there, she didn't care.

Lisa called her and told her they were going out tonight to some club and for her to be ready at nine o'clock. Sasha said okay, as if she didn't know about this party. Ray and Tasha had already left.

Sasha wondered if Montel knew about this party. She hoped so, or else who would be her date? Anyway, T came to pick her up, and off they went.

As Sasha walked into this so-called club, she noticed the luxury vehicles in the parking lot, BMW's, Lexus, Jeeps, and Benzes, and figured that they'd invited some high-society folks. *Oh, my party is about to be ignorant off the hook.* Sasha didn't see Montel's car out there though.

When she hit the door, everyone yelled, "Surprise!" and Sasha played along, feigning surprise.

The party was jumping. Cousin Tanya and Aunt Mimi were there, T invited Ricky, Michelle and Jamal were there, as well as a few buddies from Sasha's job. Some friends she knew from high school were there also. Her college roommate, Marian, was there with her husband David. Even some of her parents' friends were there.

Sasha felt nice to know that she was loved. After the way the previous day went, she needed this real bad. She escaped to the bathroom and found Lisa in there.

"Hey, girl. Surprise!" Lisa said.

"Thank you, girl. Is Montel here?"

"Ray told him about it and for him to be here. That fine-ass detective is here though."

"Where? Tell me where, so I can avoid him."

"Why would you want to do that?"

"I'm just kidding. Actually, I need to talk to him about Ray, but if Montel is here, I don't want to be around him. Montel claims Michael wants me, but I don't think so. Just to keep the peace, I want to keep my distance, you know."

"You really love him, don't you?"

"Yeah, I do, Lisa, I really do. Where is this *D* you're always talking about? Can we finally meet?"

"Yeah. He seemed to disappear right after you came in."

"Well, go find him, girl. I have to meet the man who put a smile on your face."

When they left the bathroom. Sasha searched for Montel and tried to avoid Michael. She saw a familiar face through the crowd. *No, it couldn't be.*

"Damon, what are you doing here? Who told you about my party? Oh, that's really nice of you to come. How have you been?" She hugged him before he had a chance to answer any of her questions.

"Oh, I'm fine. Look, honestly, Sash, I didn't know. Believe me on that one."

"What are you talking about, Damon?"

Just then, Lisa came over. "Oh there you are, and I've been looking all over for you."

"Well, I'm right here." Feeling the alcohol, Sasha started to rock her hips and dance.

"Not you, silly. Sasha, I want you to meet *D. D*, this is Sasha."

Her mouth dropped. "What? Damon is your *D*?"

"You two know each other?"

CHAPTER SIXTEEN

As Sasha stood there, words could not be thought out. This was too much of a shock. *Did Damon plan this? Was this revenge? Lisa—did she know too?* Sasha reasoned with herself. Sasha never introduced them. They only knew him by Damon, not *D*. Still Damon had been to her house many nights. He had to have seen Lisa's picture. This couldn't have been any damn coincidence.

Damon began to explain, but Sasha had already made up her mind.

"Wait a minute, before everyone gets all bent, Lisa, I had no idea the Sasha you knew was the Sasha I knew."

Lisa sucked her teeth.

Damon turned to Sasha. "Now, Sasha, I had no idea Lisa was your girl."

"Yeah right. How could you sit there and lie to my face? You mean to tell me you never once saw Lisa's picture in my house? You never once heard me mention her name? You didn't see Raymond here?"

Damon put his hands up. "I knew when I got here. When I

saw your brother, when I saw your picture on the cake, I knew then. I never knew before."

Lisa cut in, "So why did you insist on me calling you *D*?"

"What? I like you to call me that." He batted his eyes, trying to look and sound sincere.

Damon was one of the smoothest brothers out there. He stood with his Armani suit on, clean-cut, shaved, Rolex blinging on his wrist, manicured fingernails, and the shiniest of shoes. Damon had the smile that would draw a woman's attention. Women got wet when he would start to flirt. His maple-brown smooth skin and bubbled light-brown eyes made him the handsomest of men. Anyone could see how Lisa was smitten with him. Sasha was too, but she let him go.

"Look, I didn't know, Sash, and I didn't know, Lisa, baby. I can see this is awkward, so I will leave." He kissed Lisa on the lips, whispered something in her ear. Then he turned to Sasha. "Happy birthday, Sasha."

As he left Lisa turned her head from his disappearing back. She rolled her eyes and looked dead at Sasha.

"So that was your booty call, Damon? How could I be so naïve to think he only wanted me? Didn't you diss him? He was probably trying to get back at you." Lisa was trying to sound convincing to cover how she really felt.

Sasha knew what Lisa was saying, and she also knew what she really thought. On the forefront, she thought Damon was wrong, but in the back of her mind, she hated her friend. She hated the fact that men were always about Sasha. Sometimes she felt second best when they went out. Men were attracted to Sasha first, then her. Sasha knew she couldn't stand that, so she always flocked them off to her. Lisa was her girl, a true friend, but she knew them green eyes came out once in a while.

Sasha felt like screaming inside. She didn't know what Damon's motives were. *Was he just as crazy as Jason?* Sasha couldn't get Lisa's face out of her head when she introduced them. She looked so happy. Now her face was gloomy, though she tried to hide her true feelings of hurt. Sasha couldn't deal with this. *Where the hell is Montel?*

"Lisa, have you seen Montel?"

"Nah."

Just then, Michelle and T came over. "Where did mystery man go?" T asked.

Quickly, Lisa said, placing blame, "Ask Sasha."

Sasha looked at her reproachfully. "Whatever. Did you guys invite Montel?"

T answered, "Raymond told him about it. He should be here. Maybe he's just late"

"Or maybe he's not coming," Lisa said.

Sasha tried to ignore this girl, but she was beginning to piss her off. "Yo, Lisa, cool it!"

"What's going on, Sash?" Michelle asked. "What did you do?"

"What did I do?"

"Yeah, what happened to *D*?"

"*D* is Damon, Sasha's booty call," Lisa bluntly pointed out, still uneasy about the whole situation.

Mouths dropped, and hands covered them.

"What!" T said. "Men are scandalous."

Michelle asked, "Did he know you were friends, Sasha?"

"He claims he had no idea," Lisa answered.

"Well then, what's the issue?" Michelle asked.

T couldn't help herself. "It's always like you, Michelle, to believe every word that comes out of a man's mouth."

"Fuck you, T. Don't go there with me. I don't see Linc on your arm, just that trifling Richard."

"Well, where is Jamal? Trying to find his next victim?" T could care less what Michelle thought.

"All right, damn it!" Sasha said in frustration. "This is supposed to be my birthday."

"Whatever." Michelle grabbed Lisa by the arm to console her.

T stood by Sasha's side with that same old attitude. "Niggas ain't shit!"

That was how they were, T and Sasha were more alike, and Michelle and Lisa were more alike. Probably because they had kids and had been married. Birds of a feather. That would explain their bond. Nonetheless, Sasha was too aggravated to explain. She just wanted to know where the hell Montel was.

The night went on song after song, hour after hour, and still no sign of Montel.

The girls each gave a speech about Sasha, the friend they knew. Raymond also spoke. Sasha had discussed Raymond's case with Aunt Mimi and Tanya. Sasha cut the cake, drank some more and still no Montel. It was a quarter to two a.m.

Sasha had no one to dance with when they played the last song. She sat holding on to her bottle of Moet.

A tall figure walked through the crowd. It was none other than Detective Perry. He reached his hand out for hers.

She thought, *Why not?* Montel stood her up. He couldn't get mad if he wasn't here for her to dance with. Sasha stood up and let Michael lead her to the floor.

They danced. Sasha even buried her head in his shoulder as Jagged Edge's song played, *I Gotta Be*, the same song her and Montel made love to.

Where is he? Did Raymond give him the right information? Sasha was vexed that he didn't show up. Maybe he would surprise her at home. She lifted her head from Michael's shoulder and looked around. No sign of him.

"Face it," Michael said. "He isn't coming."

Sasha looked at Michael in the weirdest way. "How do you know?"

"Look, Sash, I don't know how to tell you this, but your so-called man is an asshole."

Sasha tried to break away from him.

"Wait before you say anything. I care about you, Sasha Freeman, and I know I always give you a hard time, but I do. Take this from a friend, let him go." Michael lifted her chin when he said that. It was almost as if he wanted to kiss her. Instead he stared at her and said, "Do you know how beautiful you are?"

She broke away successfully and wiped a tear. She didn't want him to see. "Just leave me alone, Michael."

He pulled her into his arms and held her in a bear hug. "Listen, Sasha, I'm only telling you this as a friend. On my way here, I got a call to check out a party in a hotel that was making a lot of noise since I was the nearest officer in the area. When I knocked on the door to the hotel suite, a young brother opened the door. He was throwing a bachelor party for his man. I asked him if he could keep it down. Man to man, I understood what this party meant to his man. I didn't want to kill the party. 'Just keep it under control,' I told him. He understood and was like, 'Cool.' This was a wild party. There were drinks, drugs, everything. Even strippers. Just as I was about to leave, the strippers came out. As a man I wanted a peek, so I did just that. To my surprise, the strippers were advised to start with the groom, who sat in a chair, six-foot two, and light-skinned with chinky eyes. The groom was Montel."

CHAPTER SEVENTEEN

Sasha couldn't move for a second. It was like someone just knocked the wind out of her, and she had to pause. "What are you talking about? Would you go this far, Michael? Leave me alone."

She walked off the dance floor, not knowing where she was going. She needed to catch her breath. *This didn't make any sense. Getting married? What? That couldn't be true. Montel was my man. Married to whom? What the fuck was going on around here?* She needed answers, and Montel was the only one who could give them to her.

Just as she walked inside to talk to Michael, to ask him where this hotel was, he was on her, trying to calm her down, but there was nothing he could say or do.

"Look, Michael, just tell me where the hotel is. I won't believe it unless I see it for myself."

"I'll take you there, but promise me you won't act crazy."

"Done," Sasha said quickly.

She was on fire on the way to the hotel. She felt crazy, out of control. She couldn't be held responsible for her actions. She wasn't thinking about the party, the people, the presents, she left. She wasn't thinking about Raymond's problems with the law. She wasn't thinking about Damon and Lisa. She wasn't even thinking that she might lose her job. Nothing was important. All that mattered were her feelings for Montel. He couldn't have been there. Michael was wrong. He only got one good look at him. This just couldn't be. Sasha was open. Her emotions were on her sleeve. She was vulnerable, driven by what she was feeling inside. She wasn't together. The only thought that crossed her mind was a plea. *Please don't let it be him, please don't let it be him. I couldn't bear the thought of losing him again.* She couldn't grasp her breath. Her anxiety was through the roof.

Michael looked at her in a weird way. "Are you all right? You don't look so good."

"I'm fine. Just keep driving." Sasha started to slowly breathe, so she wouldn't hyperventilate.

"Look, maybe this isn't such—"

"What? A good idea? I have to see for myself, Michael, you don't understand. You just don't understand."

"What? Betrayal? My wife cheated on me when we were married, I cheated on her. We just weren't happy with each other, and we kept hurting each other. Finally, we let it go. That's what you have to do—Let it go."

"Look, Michael, I appreciate your unnecessary advice, but please, you don't know Montel. You think you do. We're happy. We don't want to hurt each other. You just have to be wrong. That's why we're going to the hotel, to prove to you that you are wrong."

"Oh, is that why we're going?"

They reached the parking lot of the hotel. It looked empty.

"Look, Sasha, it was a while ago. He probably isn't even there."

"There's only one way to find out. You wait here. I'll be back."

"No, I'm going with you."

"This is something I have to do on my own. I'm not going to act crazy. Just give me the room number," Sash pleaded.

Michael opened his mouth to argue, but Sasha took her finger and silenced him. He couldn't win with her. She didn't even know why he tried. This was something she had to do on her own.

Sasha heard the words, "Room 224," and was out like a prowler in the night.

The Double Tree was a very classy place that only the ballers and ballettes could afford. One night cost like five hundred or more for a suite.

Room 224, Room 224 was all Sasha kept saying to herself. She hopped on the elevator, pressed button 2. Once she got off the elevator, she could hear the music. It wasn't loud, but you knew a party was going on.

A thought crossed her mind. *What will I say when I knock on the door? Hey, is Montel there?* That wouldn't get her through the door. She kept on walking with no plan in hand. She was just going in there, and no one was going to stop her.

She knocked on the door three times. *Maybe I need to bang it with my foot.* Just before she placed her boots in position to kick, a young, spaced-out brother came to the door.

"Hey. Whazzup!"

It was evident this brother drank up all the available alcohol, probably smoked all the weed, and then some. He smelled like Hennessy and smoke. His platinum teeth blinded Sasha. He was big and burly like a wrestler. So big, Sasha couldn't see past him. He would have to step aside for her to see what was going on.

"Is the bachelor still here?" Sasha asked

"Oh snap! Yo, dawg," he yelled through the room, "you hired another stripper?"

The music was so loud, no one heard, except for one brother, who said, "Nah, I didn't order another, but the more the merrier." He came to the door. "Damn, you fine as hell. What's your name?"

Sasha cleared her throat. "Alize."

"Well, hello, Alize. Where you been all night? The party's almost over."

Sasha didn't recognize any of these men, and it was even better that they didn't recognize her. She played along with this role like she came up with it. She eased her way inside, quickly scanning the room for familiar faces. No sign of Montel. The room looked pretty empty. The party must have been over.

She walked through the room while these two hound dogs chased her tail. The room was dirty—crumbs, blunts, empty glasses, and sofa pillows undone. *These nuccas threw down.* Still no sign of Montel. Sasha turned to the two strays. "Where's the bachelor?"

"Oh, are you just here to dance for him?"

"Yeah, I was hired for a private dance, a special dance, if you know what I mean." She winked at them.

They were so blazed, they had to watch her lips to understand what she was saying. Their eyes were blood red. All the men in there were blazed, drunk, and surely didn't know what the hell was going on. There was even a brother on the sofa asleep, passed out.

The big one with the platinum teeth smiled. "Well, if you're looking for the bachelor, he's in the master bedroom."

The big burly one pointed, and Sasha made her way to the master bedroom.

As she kicked her way through the empty bottles, the crumbs, the garbage, she noticed a torn-down banner at the tip of the so-called bachelor's master bedroom door. Sasha maneuvered it with her foot. It read, *Congrats, Montel!* Her heart stopped just then, before she could open the door.

It didn't matter if she saw him or not. She saw the banner. Still, she set herself up for more torture and entered the room. It was dark, and the only light coming in was from the moon.

Sasha heard a familiar voice.

"Who is it?" He lay on the bed, hurt from all the alcohol and substances he'd abused that night, his face flat down on the bed.

Sasha leaned over. She had to see his face. She took her hand and lifted his chin, still hoping all this was a dream, still hoping there had to be some explanation. There wasn't. The man face down on that bed, the bachelor, her man, the one who claimed he loved her and only her, was getting married.

The instant their eyes met, he jumped up. "Sasha, what are you doing here?"

She silenced him with her finger, the same technique she'd used to silence Michael. Sasha couldn't speak just then. Words couldn't come out. She felt a pause, nothing moved, and nothing made a sound. She could see Montel talking, and moving his lips. She could see his facial expression, the surprise, the amazement, and the fear. But still Sasha said nothing.

She turned her back to him to get out of the room. She felt him on her, at her heels. She moved through the trashy room, still not speaking.

Montel dashed out after her, hot on her trail. She almost made it to the elevator. She felt like a predator was on her tail and she had to make it. She just had to. She reached to push the button. She didn't hear the bell to the elevator ring, she just saw the light.

The elevator doors opened, and Sasha got in. She could still see Montel talking, trying to explain, but she couldn't hear him. She was in shock. As the elevator door closed, Sasha suddenly got back her hearing, and with her hearing came her voice.

"Listen . . . just listen to me, Sasha. Before you say anything, I can explain. I wanted to tell you, but I didn't know how. I just found out myself. I know this looks bad, but trust me, this doesn't change how I feel about you."

Sasha looked at him as her eyebrows rose. She knew then that she was out of control. Before she knew it, her fist balled up and struck Montel in his eye.

He fell back. "What the fuck is wrong with you?!"

"What is wrong with me? You can sit there and try to explain! What are you going to say? How are you going to say it? You are fucking getting married, Montel, married. Not to mention that you are fucking me, not to mention that you said you were in love with me, not to mention that today is my fucking birthday and you are supposed to be at my party dancing with me. What do you think you can say? You tell me you still love me. Does that word just ooze out of you like diarrhea? You are sick, a sick bastard, and I hope shit never goes right in your life, you bastard."

She just started hitting him. All her hurt, all her anger, words couldn't express.

He tried to block her blows, but there was no one there to hold her. It was just them. He finally wrestled her to the ground.

She still kept hitting him, yelling at the top of her lungs. "Where were you when I needed you? Where were you? Married, Montel. I could take you breaking up with me, but this? You didn't even tell me. You pretended everything was cool." Her face was reddening as she kept yelling, "How could you do this? What the fuck is wrong with you? Get off of me! I hate you!"

"Stop hitting me! Just listen."

"Listen to you? That's all I've done for months! 'I love you, Sasha. I want to be with you, Sasha. You and I belong together. I want to marry you, Sasha.' That's all you say. You're a liar! A fucking liar!"

He attempted to hold her down, but she was so full of adrenaline, she pushed him off her, rolled to her side, and got up off the ground.

"Don't touch me!"

Montel stood up too, still trying to plead his case.

The elevator door opened, and Sasha dashed out, Montel still on her heels.

"Sasha, would you wait a minute!"

"Get away from me!"

They caught everyone's attention, but Sasha didn't care who

knew or saw. "Leave me alone!" She walked out, with Montel still following, and ran to the parking lot.

"Look, damn it, Sasha, she's pregnant!" Montel yelled across the starlit parking lot.

That stopped her cold. She turned and looked to him. "What? Is that supposed to be some excuse? Is that supposed to make me feel better? Is that supposed to make it right?"

"It explains this—I was going to tell you, but I didn't know how. I didn't want to ruin what we had. You mean so much to me."

"Shut the fuck up with that shit." Sasha pushed him away from her.

He tried to hold her, but she pulled away again.

"I didn't want it to be this way. It was just one time, one time. That one time changed everything though." Montel shook his head.

She looked at him. *Who are you fooling?* Sasha cleared her throat. "I could see if you and I had problems that couldn't be worked out, but that's not the case. You have the need to be overly loved because you are overly self-indulged. One woman's love isn't enough for you. You can't stand there and tell me this is just a one-time thing. You love this. Through my entire time with you, you always loved the drama. You always loved the conflict. I don't care if it was one month, two months, or three weeks ago, you demolished any chance we had together. Do not call me, write me, or come by my house. We can't be friends. I love you, but I love myself more. I have to move on past this anguish. It's so over. You have no fucking idea how over it is between us!" Sasha couldn't hold back her tears.

"Sasha, wait. I-I-I don't know what to say. I love you, you know that. I could never hurt you intentionally. I don't need two women to love me. I only need you, and I know that now. I know I should have told you what was going on, but I didn't know how. I didn't want to lose you. I wanted to tell you in my own way, not like this. It was months ago, one time with my ex-girlfriend. The week we split up, when you came back from your weekend trip with your girls, I thought we were over. It was one time, a time when I was weak, missing you like crazy. I felt like shit when it was over. I wanted to tell you. I wanted to build this up from the truth and truth only. Please don't walk away from me. I need you. I don't want anyone else but you. I can't sleep without you next to me. You are the missing piece to my soul. I made a mistake, I'm willing to admit that. I never ever wanted to hurt you. That look on your face kills me." Montel tried to hold back his tears. He kneeled down and clasped his hands in prayer. "Please forgive me. I know it's going to take a while to trust me, but I will earn it. I want you in my life."

She turned away because she didn't want to let him in. "I don't know what you are asking me to do."

Montel took a breath. "I'm asking you to wait for me. Don't give up on us. I made a mistake, and now I'm paying for it. I know what it's like to grow up without a father. I don't want that for my child, you know that. Let me do this. Let me make this right. I promise I will do right by you. Know that you are the only one for me. I just have to do this right now." He got up off the ground. "I just hope you can understand." He reached for Sasha's hand.

"Go away. I don't want to hear from you. I can't think clearly with your words. You have to go."

"I'm not going. You are never going to get rid of me because I am part of you. I know you hate me right now, but I'm going to do whatever it takes to make you a part of my life again." He moved closer to her. "Sasha, I love you. Do you hear me?"

Sasha placed her hands over her ears and turned away.

"I need you. I want you. Hear me, baby, please. I—"

"Leave me alone, damn it. I can't take this." She stormed off, crying the whole way to the car.

Montel didn't follow her.

She stopped and fell to the floor. It was as if she was having a nervous breakdown. Sasha began to breathe faster and faster, her heart pounding. She tried to raise her legs, but her knees gave way. She tried to pull out her keys, but her hands were shaking.

I love this man. Why would he hurt me so? I trusted this man. Why would he lie to me? I need this man. I'm empty without him. Could I forgive him? Could I wait for him? No, that's not an option. Pick yourself up, girl. Don't let him do this or see you like this. I love this man. I don't want to be without him.

Don't think that way, Sash. He did it before, he will do it again. Why can't I just let go?

She finally realized that she couldn't find her keys because she didn't drive.

Just then Michael came out of the hotel. "Where were you? I've been looking for you all over."

"Just take me home."

"Are you all right?"

"I'm fine. Just take me home."

Michael put her in the car and closed the door.

On the way home from the hotel, she started putting things together. Montel had lied to her for months. This was no one-night stand with his ex. They had probably been kicking it the same time she and Montel were. Pregnant, married: two things Sasha just couldn't understand. They'd talked about marriage, they'd talked about kids.

When was he going to tell me? He wasn't ever going to tell me. He would rather keep this lie going so he could have his way. Greedy bastard! The audacity to ask me to wait for him. I ain't waiting for shit.

As Sasha followed the yellow and white lines on the highway, she thought, *Now that Montel and I are over, what am I going to do?*

CHAPTER EIGHTEEN

The next morning felt like a hangover. Sasha wasn't drunk, but she was hungover on love. Her everything just went away. It was as if she was in mourning. Everything seemed to move in slow motion. She was angry and sad inside, all at the same time. She thought *Montel loved me; I thought we were building something*. She broke every rule she'd ever made when it came to men. Couldn't anyone tell her shit. She knew what she wanted. She let him in again and experienced the same pain.

That morning was one of her worse ever. It felt worse than the morning after her parents died. She was left alone again. Abandoned. Love left her behind. It was different because then she had Raymond, and they both were going through it together. Now, who did she have? Who knew what she was going through? Raymond had Tasha, T had Ricky, Michelle had Jamal, Lisa had Damon, and Tanya had her husband. She was sure Aunt Mimi had some fella.

Sasha had cleared her life of past acquaintances to be with Montel. Now that he was gone, she was left standing alone, something that hadn't happened to her in a very long time.

This felt like it was going to last forever. *When did it get this bad? When did I lose control of me?* She hated Montel for doing this to her and herself even more for letting him.

It was eleven a.m., and she still was in bed. She didn't want to get out of bed ever. She didn't have to go to work, and had nothing to keep her busy. She wanted to cry, but she was too angry.

She pulled the covers over her head to block out the sun beaming in through the window. Her belly began to growl, but she wouldn't even get out of bed to eat. If she could hold her pee, she wouldn't get out of bed to go to the bathroom either. Life sucked.

Her phone rang.

Who the hell is this? I don't want to talk to anyone. She reluctantly answered the phone after letting it ring twelve times.

"Girl, I've been trying to reach you all morning," T said. "You have to come down to my house. Shit is about to get ugly."

Sasha didn't feel like explaining to T why she wasn't coming. Instead she said, "No."

"Sasha, you don't understand. Linc done put all my stuff on the lawn. He done changed the locks, and he's seriously throwing with me."

Still not in the mood for this, Sasha said, "I thought you let Linc go. You're with Ricky now."

"I was, but I never got around to it."

In other words, T was holding on to her spare tire, just in case things with Ricky didn't work out, something Sasha should have done with Montel. Rule number one in relationships: Never burn all your bridges.

"Well, T, what do you expect? How long do you think Linc was going to take you stringing him along?"

"Whose side are you on?"

Honestly, Sasha was on Linc's side. T had done him so wrong, but how could she explain this to her girl? "T, I'm just trying to tell you the facts. Linc is upset with you and tired of your shit, so just pick up your stuff and go about your business."

"Whatever, Sash. I can't go out like this. He has my clothes in garbage bags, my things boxed up, like he's a fucking mover. I can't get into my own house."

"I thought that was his house?"

"Yeah, he bought it, fine, but still I decorated it. He just put out my clothes and stuff. I want my other things."

"T just move on. Is that stuff that important?"

"Damn right, it is. It's the principle. He can't dump me, I'm dumping him."

"Well, why don't you just call him and straighten things out?"

"That jerk done changed the number," T yelled.

"Damn, T, how long you been gone for him to do all this?"

"Oh, just like two days, but I'm saying, I want my stuff."

Sasha wanted to laugh but had no energy. "T, what would you like me to do? Help you move your stuff?"

"Oh, I can see you got jokes, Ms. Sasha. You better get down here before things start to get out of control and you see me on the news for strangling Linc." T hung up.

She had no motivation at all to go almost forty minutes from her house to T and Linc's crib. She had her own thing that she was going through. Sasha lay in the bed for like twenty minutes.

Oh, hell, it's better than lying here crying about spilled milk. She got up, got dressed, and went down to see what was going on.

As she walked out her front door, Michael was out there. She asked him what he was doing there, but she already knew. He had bagels and juice from Dunkin' Donuts in his hands. *How sweet.* Sasha grabbed him and the bagels and took him to T's house just in case things got out of control.

By the time they got to T's place, Linc was at the first floor window calling T out her name. "You slut! It's women like you who give other women a bad name!"

"That's right, nigga. I played you before you got a chance to play me. Now stop all this dumb shit and open the fucking door."

This scene was similar to a ghetto soap opera series with reverse roles. Linc was the angry wife, and T was the no-remorse husband.

Sasha got out of the car and went over to T. "Girl, stop making a fuss. Get your stuff and go."

"Fuck that! I'm not done with this nigga."

Linc said, "You better get your girl, Sasha, before something happens to her."

"What? Are you threatening me, little man? If you're so tough, open the door. Why did you change the locks? What? You afraid of me?"

Linc didn't even answer that taunt.

Michael flashed his badge. "Sir, can we just calm down and work this out like adults?"

"Yeah, we could, if we were dealing with adults, but you see her right there, she's nothing but a little tramp."

T took off her shoe and threw it at Linc, hitting him in the nose.

He grabbed his nose. "You see, this is what I have to deal with, officer. I want her off my property now."

Michael said, "Do you have proof that this is your house?"

"I sure do." Linc gestured for Michael to come to the door.

T followed Michael, but he turned around and ordered her to stay right there.

Michael went inside and in five minutes came back. "I'm sorry, T, but you're going to have to leave."

T looked astonished, like she couldn't believe it.

Sasha said to Michael, "Well, can she at least have her shoe back?" She couldn't hold in her laughter much longer.

T rolled her eyes at Sasha.

Michael went in to get her shoe, and they helped T put her things in her car.

Sasha then thanked Michael for his help and told him she would call him later, and Sasha and T drove off to her house.

T stayed at Sasha's house for a couple of hours and made reservations to stay at one of her suites. Sasha called Michelle and Lisa over for reinforcements because she couldn't handle T on her own, not today, not after the bullshit she was going through.

T sipped her coffee and began to question Montel's whereabouts. "Where's Montel? I don't want to interrupt anything. Then again, you two don't be sexing anyway, so I guess I'm not interrupting much."

Sasha gave T her cold eyes. T didn't know Montel and Sasha had gotten intimate, nor did she know they were over. "You don't have to worry about Montel. He ain't here, that's for sure."

T looked at Sasha funny. She knew there was more to what Sasha was saying, from the look on her face when she made that last comment.

"What's up? Is everything all right?"

Sasha said sadly, "Yes, it sure is."

Sasha thought of how all of her friends warned her about Montel, told her something was wrong when we they weren't sleeping together, but Sasha didn't listen. She definitely wasn't going to feed them this new information, especially, seeing that they all still had a man.

Sasha began to think maybe that was the reason it took so long for her and Montel to sleep together. He was getting his needs met elsewhere. To think she believed his stories about wanting to wait, wanting it to be special. He had her so good, so nice and snowed. She believed anything that came out of his mouth. *Gullible bitch*. She was so angry at herself.

The doorbell rang.

Michelle and Lisa came in with food and drinks. It wasn't even six o'clock, and they were about to get wasted on a Sunday evening.

They hugged, laughed, drank, and ate.

Sasha began to feel a little upbeat.

T told her story about Linc kicking her to the curb. Sasha thought she was going to bust a gut, when T told the part about the shoe.

The laughter simmered, and the alcohol took effect.

Sasha began to feel confident about telling them about Montel. She cleared her throat. "T isn't the only one here with a story to tell. I found out the truth about Montel last night. Before anyone says, 'I told you so,' understand, you can't tell a woman in love anything. This you all know from experience. Montel is getting married to his ex, who is pregnant, and would like me to wait for him."

Silence took over for an eternity.

T said, "What? Well, at least you know now before he actually tied the knot."

Michelle asked, "Does his fiancée know about you?"

Lisa, T, and Sasha looked at Michelle.

Sasha said, "Duh. Of course, she doesn't." She knew her friend couldn't stop being the wife.

"Never mind," Michelle said.

Lisa added, "Fuck him! You got your girls, you got your job, you got everything going for you. He is just another waste. Chalk it up as a loss."

"I don't have a job either."

"Excuse me?" T said.

"The other day, I was temporarily suspended. I'm waiting for the hearing, when they're going to decide my fate."

"Someone pour this girl another glass of Moet." Lisa poured Sasha another glass of champagne.

"Yeah, no job, no man, just me, myself, and I."

Michelle said, "No, Sash, you got us, you got your family, you are very talented, and you can do anything, M.D. or not."

Michelle was always like that. If there was a brighter side, she knew what it was. Sasha realized that was how she stayed in her marriage. Her kids were her brighter side, even if Jamal wasn't.

Sasha took a good look at Michelle. In a way, she admired her. Sasha always did. She worked hard for her family, for her kids, for herself. Here she was living with HIV, but not letting it destroy her, not letting it end her life, not letting it take control. Where did she get all her strength?

Sasha asked her, "Michelle, how you can stay this positive and this strong?"

"Let's just say, I've had the opportunity to look at life and all that I've done wrong and all that I've done right. It has all brought me to this place. I wouldn't change any of that. I love where I am, and who I'm with. My kids are my world. They keep me going. If I didn't have them, I'd still have you guys. Sasha, I have to tell you what I already told Lisa and T. I wanted to tell you last because I didn't know how to tell you first. I have HIV. Yes, Jamal. Till death do us part, right?

"I know what you're going to say, but listen, I'm dealing with it. I've been dealing with it for some time now, and I won't say that everything is all right, or that everything will be all right, but I have a lot of hope and life in me, that's what I know for sure."

Sasha hugged Michelle because her tears were taking over. True, she already knew this, but she loved Michelle even more for believing in her, to tell her, to tell all of them. Sasha thought before she had nothing, but she was wrong. She had everything right there. Everything happened for a reason. She wasn't quite sure what the reason was, but in time, she'd know.

Michelle asked, "Are you going to wait for him?"

Before Sasha could answer, Lisa yelled, "Hell no."

Sasha exhaled with the insecurity of an eleven-year old. "I really don't know. How can I get over this, see past this?"

"If you let him tell it," T said, "he really is sorry and he wants to be with you."

Lisa jumped in. "Of course, he's sorry. Probably the sorriest muthafucka on earth. Look, Sash, you don't have to go for that. You are pretty, successful, fun, full of life. You don't need any bullshit from Montel. Just chalk it up as a loss."

"I can't. I have this ache in my heart. I never felt like this before. I've broken up with a bunch of boyfriends and it's never felt like this. I was truly into this, and now it seems like the pain is never going away. You know how I feel, Lisa. Remember when Jake got locked up? You were a mess, going up there to see him, bringing clothes, money, anything he needed. Knowing how wrong he did you, knowing how he fucked up your life, you still held on to whatever piece of him you could."

Lisa rolled her eyes back to that time. "I was young and dumb and in love. I would've done anything for Jake. When he went to jail and the judge said life, I almost had a breakdown. Actually I did. I didn't know what to do. I would have twenty dollars in my pocket and put eighteen of it in his canteen, leaving me with enough for bus fare to get home. I didn't have shit.

"After the IRS decided to take all I had, I went to stripping in nightclubs. It wasn't until Social Services tried to take my daughter away that I woke up. I was lucky. I realized my daughter was all I had, and that whatever it took, I was going to make sure she was cared for. I figured if Jake and me were meant to be, we would be. I stopped going to see him because he was so negative and discouraging. 'What are you going to do without me? Who is going to want you?' he kept saying to me. Visit after visit, you knew there was no end to this. He was sentenced for life, I wasn't. It was his life, not mine."

"Whatever happened to his wife in Atlanta?" Sasha asked.

"I heard she's locked up for like twenty-four years for trafficking with him. That could have been me there. Where would my daughter have been? In a foster home somewhere? Living through that made me a stronger person, and I don't regret anything. I haven't been up to see him in over four years, and it feels damn good."

Michelle said, "See, all of us have a plan in life, a purpose that has already been made for us. We may dip in and out, take shortcuts and detours, but no matter what, you are going to end up where you're supposed to be, like Lisa, like Jake. Like you, Sash. I can't tell you what's going to happen with Montel, but know that if you and him don't make it, you are not meant to be."

"So do you think you and Jamal are meant to be?"

"T, if I wasn't certain before, I know now. Till death do us part, right? I have accepted that this is how it was supposed to be. I never once cheated on Jamal. I was a good wife to him. Did I deserve this? Of course, I don't think so, but look where I am. I have HIV, and my husband gave it to me. If that isn't a life sentence, I don't know what is. He can't take all the blame though. I looked the other way when he was having affairs. I chose to stay with him, even marry him, when I knew the kind of man he was."

"Are you angry though?"

"Of course, I'm angry. Of course, I'm afraid. But what can I do? Go on a rampage? I have kids. I can't change my fate. I was so bitter, full of self-hatred, full of denial, but I keep saying to myself, 'What about my kids?' Jamal, I hate him, but I love him at the same time. It's hard to explain."

"I know," T said. "Rick is so for me. I don't know why, but he is. I can't get him away from me. I know that through your eyes, Michelle, I'm doing dirt, but I love him. I'm not sure we belong, I know it. I just need some time to see what my next move is."

"Montel is getting married. How permanent or destined is that?" Sasha interrupted.

"If you don't know now," Michelle said, "you will. You will know, Sasha, you will know. Look at the circumstances, though. Montel is marrying his ex-girlfriend that he got pregnant from a one-night stand. Now to me, that doesn't seem like a blissful, happy marriage. I give it a year."

They laughed, but Sasha knew it would take longer than that for her to get over Montel, or for them to be together.

Changing the subject, Sasha said to Lisa, "So what's up with you and Damon?"

"Please . . . that's over."

"He sure did put a smile on your face."

"I know. He was a fresh breath of air too."

"Look, Lisa, I'm not the one to give advice. I don't know what Damon's motives were, but if shit was good between you and him, you owe it to yourself to find out if he's that special someone or not."

"I know all this. I'm the expert in failed relationships."

"No, I think that would be Sasha," T said.

"Hey, I'm in pain here," Sasha said sadly. "Show some sympathy."

They began laughing.

Sasha felt so lucky to have them, even if she didn't have Montel.

They sat talking about Michelle, re-enforcing that they would stay her girls, no matter what.

Sasha knew all about HIV and how it was transmitted, so she didn't look at Michelle as a walking disease. She was a beautiful person inside and out.

Things got sad in Sasha's house for a while, with talk of what Michelle would like to happen with her kids if anything happened to her.

The ladies cried and laughed. No matter what men entered their lives, no matter what mistakes they'd made in life, no matter what wrong was done to them, they had each other. With no promise that tomorrow would be any better or any worse, or that there would be any tomorrow, they just hung on to hope that there would be.

CHAPTER NINETEEN

The next two months felt like two years. Sasha hadn't spoken to or seen Montel since that night. He still was in her system though, and she still felt for him. The days went by so slowly, and the nights were so lonely. It was such an unfamiliar feeling to her, as if she was with Montel since birth and now he was torn away from her and she didn't know how to live without him. She still couldn't believe he got married.

Where was I when all this happened?

After two months, the hospital still hadn't called her for a hearing. Yep, she hadn't worked in two long months. She wondered if she still knew how to deliver babies.

With no work and no love life, Sasha thought she'd go crazy. The bills started to pile up, and her savings had been almost tapped out by Raymond's case.

The D.A. dragged Raymond's case on for a month, all for him to get a slap on the wrist. He was ordered to do six months of community service and take an anger-management class. That slick-ass lawyer did a very good job of cleaning up the mess, but he wasn't cheap. Sasha got his bill for a whopping thirty thousand in the mail a week after the case.

What did she do? She didn't want to cover it in her savings, so she American Expressed it. Now she was paying that monthly with the interest, a mortgage, plus her car payment, insurance, house taxes, medical, etc. She hadn't seen a mall in two months. She was broke like she was in college, stretching a hundred bucks for a month.

Her pride wouldn't allow her to borrow money from anyone. Besides, Raymond was making contributions. He started paying rent for living upstairs, so that helped out a lot, but she couldn't live like this for long. The bill collectors were calling, and she had no answer for them. *The check is in the mail, buddy. Wait for it.*

Sasha had to do something, if the hospital didn't call her soon. Like, maybe, selling the BMW and everything else that was unaffordable. As anxious as she was about the fate of her future as an obstetrician, she couldn't bear to call to find out what was the holdup with her hearing. *Life just couldn't be better,* she kept thinking to herself.

Lately she'd been seeing more of the ladies, and more of her Aunt Mimi. Since she and Tanya were the ones to clean up Raymond's mess, she took it upon herself to watch them, like they were kids.

It took her Aunt Mimi a long time to realize when they were kids that they needed her. After Sasha's break up with Montel, Aunt Mimi noticed her niece's pain and became a parent again, putting her party life on hold. When Raymond was arrested for illegal possession of a firearm and faced five years, she hated herself for not being around for him like her sister had wanted. Since then, she had tried to make up for the past.

Sasha and Raymond forgave her and let her be a part of their life as adults. Sasha would go over to her house for dinner, and Raymond and Tasha would come too. They would laugh and talk about old times, their parents, and about growing up.

They all knew about Sasha's job status. Sasha thought Aunt

Mimi would scold her, and be so disappointed that she'd fucked up. She was disappointed, Sasha could tell, but was very encouraging.

As they reminisced about when she was a little girl, she told Sasha how everyone knew she was going to be something. Everyone knew she was going to have her name in lights somewhere. She could do anything.

"Sasha Freeman is going to do something special some day, she just doesn't know it, she doesn't realize it. She may try to fight it and hide from it, but she won't be able to." That's how her mother described her, in those exact words.

Of course, Sasha didn't share her enthusiasm, but tried to live up to what she knew Sasha would be. Sasha guessed that's where becoming a doctor rooted from. She chose something respectable and honorable, so obstetrician was the perfect choice. She excelled in high school, college, and even medical school.

The more time she spent away from being an obstetrician, the more she began to question her motives for becoming a doctor. She loved delivering babies, no question. The look on the parents' faces when that newborn's face appeared moved her beyond words. She wasn't fond of the hospital politics and the rules and regulations though. She didn't miss the hospital though, but she did miss her patients and the money, of course. But the more time she'd been away, the less important it seemed.

Sasha was in a weird place, doubting herself in every way. She hadn't been on a date, or even pulled a number from a guy when she went out. She felt like a recluse, an outsider, antisocial even.

Aunt Mimi encouraged her to do something, in the meantime, to at least pay the bills. Teaching popped in her head because she liked to teach her new mothers and enjoyed sharing information when she was a physician, so she decided to renew her Lamaze license.

After college she was a Lamaze instructor. Once she went

into medical school, she didn't have time anymore, but that was something she enjoyed a lot.

Sasha was used to working up to fifty hours per week. Now she had so much time on her hands, she didn't know what to do with herself. Sunday dinners at Aunt Mimi's house turned into three nights a week.

Sasha volunteered to take Tasha to her doctor's appointments, signed her and Michelle for her Lamaze class, their babies being due around the same time. So time was starting to fill in.

Another month went by, and still no word from the hospital board. Bills piled up even more. Her Lamaze classes would have been sufficient to pay her bills, if she didn't live beyond her means. She lived a physician's life, not an instructor's, and that started to catch up on her real fast.

Raymond was doing his community service, working two jobs to prepare for his unborn child. Tasha and Sasha became real close in the months she was pregnant. She really loved Raymond, and Sasha was glad he had Tasha in his life. Sweet, smart and funny, she was no way near as trifling as that Tina. She didn't have much family though. They were from New York, and it was just her and her cousin. So Sasha got with her cousin, Marsha, and they planned a baby shower for her.

Aunt Mimi, Tanya and her husband, Raymond, Tasha's cousin, and Tasha's parents attended. They got mostly everything they needed, with the exception of a crib, which Raymond and Tasha wanted to pick out themselves.

Of course, the shower was at Sasha's house. It was more of a grown-up shower and included more than just the women. Tanya's husband was there, and Aunt Mimi brought a younger man she had been seeing for about five months. Now that was a record. Raymond had Tasha, and Tasha's parents had each other. It was starting to turn into a couples only party, one Sasha knew she had to cut out of.

The doorbell rang. It was Detective Perry. He dropped by

from time to time, so-called checking on Raymond to make sure he was going to his anger management classes and such. Sasha guessed that was his punishment from the D.A. for helping Raymond out—baby-sitting him.

Sasha, under the influence of two Alabama Slamas that she'd made herself, said to Michael. "What are you doing here? Did I forget to pay you, babysitter?"

Michael chuckled. "No. For your information, Ms. Sasha, I was invited." He stepped in the doorway, without her moving or inviting him in, like he owned the place. He yelled out a hello to everyone and turned his attention toward Sasha. He took one look at her, as she swayed left to right, her third cup of Alabama Slama in her hand.

Sasha was about to lash out another smart comment, when he took her cup. "I think you've had enough of that, miss."

Sasha was astonished. Who did he think he was, coming in her home, telling her what to do? "Whatever. I'll just get another. What are you drinking, Detective?"

He leaned in to reach her ear and said in a very sexy voice, "How many times do I have to tell you, Miss Sasha, call me Michael."

Sasha didn't know if it was the drinks or the fact that she hadn't been done in three months, but with those words, she got very hot. She switched her hips in the kitchen to pour herself another cup and cool off.

Of course, giving her no space, Michael came into the kitchen to lecture her on drinking. "You really should slow down on the drinks. It isn't attractive."

"Look, Michael, you may think you know me, but you don't. I'm grown, and very capable of taking care of myself. Oh, and I know what is attractive and what isn't, and trust me, there's no one at this family gathering I'm trying to attract."

Michael bent his head back and rolled his eyes. "You're always taking my concern for something else. I'm not trying to tell you what to do, I am just worried about you."

Sasha looked at him in disgust. "Worried? What do you have to be worried about? This is a party. If you haven't noticed, everyone is drinking and having a good time. Why don't you have a good time and stop being so worried about me?"

"Why are you always pushing me away?"

"Why are you always pushing up on me?"

"Because I . . ." Michael stopped, as if he was about to say something but wasn't sure how to put it.

"Look, do you want something to drink or not?"

"Yeah, pour me whatever you're having."

"That would be an Alabama Slama, Detective. Watch it now. It might creep up on you."

"Yeah, I know how that can happen."

Sasha wasn't sure if he was talking about the drinks or something else. She ignored it, and went to continue her hosting duties.

They laughed, ate, and talked about old times. Aunt Mimi even brought out a baby picture of Raymond, trying to figure out what this baby would look like.

Of course, Tasha's parents proclaimed they had the dominant features in the family, but it was just playful antics, nothing serious. Her parents seemed very cool. They seemed to like Raymond a lot.

Tasha's father, Mr. James Anderson said, "Well, when are you kids getting married? This baby is coming soon, you know."

Tasha said, "We're getting married after the baby is born."

Sasha looked a bit surprised, as did Raymond. She didn't know about this. She didn't even see a ring on Tasha's finger. She would have to question Raymond later.

Raymond just nodded and smiled.

Sasha began to clean up as everyone started leaving. Tanya had to be in court the following day, and her husband was going out of town. Sasha thought of them as the perfect couple. They'd started dating back in high school. Sasha even remembered when they met. The next thing Sasha knew, they were together.

As Aunt Mimi began to leave she said, "Why do you act like that towards that man?"

"What man?"

"That fine detective. He's got it bad for you, and you treat him so wrong."

"What?" Sasha had a look of astonishment, the same look she gave her when she figured out she was lying, trying to go somewhere she was told not to go.

Aunt Mimi put her hands on her shoulder. "Girl, you just don't know when to open your eyes, do you?" She left Sasha with that thought.

Sasha started a fire and turned on the TV to watch a movie. She was no way near tired, and was very much up. The alcohol began to wear off, and she was left thinking about Montel. She also tried to analyze Aunt Mimi's comment. Did that mean she let Montel trick her into loving him and only him? Or she didn't know how to pick men?

After all this time, she still didn't get it right. She was watching a movie all alone. She had dated a ton of men, wasted a lot of fingers, and wasted a lot of time. Sasha counted her sex partners on her fingers but needed more than two hands.

As she devised a new dating plan, her doorbell rang.

Who the hell is this?

The door opened, and Michael entered, saying nothing. He had a peculiar look, like he was on a mission or something.

"Can I help you? Did you lose something, forget something? What?"

He paced her living room floor for about a minute, still saying nothing.

Sasha shut the door. "Hello, do you hear me talking in that thick skull of yours?"

He looked at her and walked up to her swiftly. Before she knew it, he grabbed her face and kissed her.

She felt that kiss forever. It was so sensual and endearing. She wanted more.

He stopped and looked at her in her eyes. "I wanted to do that from the first day I saw you. All this time, I fought what I felt and how I felt because I was afraid. I still am, but I feel like, if I don't kiss you, if I don't tell you this, I will regret it for the rest of my life."

She knew what Michael was saying, what he was feeling. She'd felt it too, but it was so forbidden. She'd been secretly attracted to Michael but hid it with the snide comments and rudeness to him. But she knew what her next step was.

She kissed him back without saying a word. She began to undo his coat, undo his sweater. Then she kicked off her shoes, and he kicked off his shoes. She unbuckled his belt, then his pants.

He pulled off her dress over her head and kissed her neck.

Her nipples rippled, and she felt his hardness against her belly. She grabbed it and caressed it with her hand.

As he sucked on her lips and chin, she moaned. He kissed her neck again, and then moved to suck her breast like a lollypop, pulling her to the floor.

Her body became submissive to him, following his every motion. She licked his belly all the way up to his neck.

He grabbed her hair, turned her over to her back, and licked her, first down, then up.

She kissed him as his fingers ran through her kitty kat, causing her to moan. As her tongue was down his throat, she heard the tearing of a condom packet.

Michael slipped it on and then slid inside of her. He lifted her up and lay her down on the sofa, where he could control the strokes, and kissed her breasts as he thrust himself inside her softly. Then he lifted her legs over his shoulders, moaning and kissing her lips.

She moved up and down, riding him, as the sweat from their bodies soaked her pillows. She grabbed the ends of the sofa, biting her lip, trying not to scream. As she reached her point, she buried her face in his neck.

Just then, he began to thrust faster and harder, pinning her hands down as he came. His body collapsed onto hers, as he kissed her neck and then her lips.

They lay there for a moment in silence. She didn't know what to say and didn't think he did either. As the silence filled up the room, she closed her eyes.

A moment later, she felt Michael lift from her shoulder. He said in a playful voice, "What? I know you're not falling asleep on me."

She smiled and kissed him.

They continued their romp upstairs in her bedroom, with no fear, no regrets. Even though they didn't know where this was going, neither of them wanted it to end. They just carried on like tomorrow didn't matter. This was their time, and that's all that mattered.

CHAPTER TWENTY

The next day, Michael got up and ran Sasha a bath. He scrubbed her back, and she scrubbed his. She asked him, did he want to know where the donut shop was, for breakfast. He asked her, did she know how to turn on a stove. When he told her he'd call later, she just knew he would.

They continued with playful little smart-ass remarks, as if nothing had changed. Always bumping heads and at each other's throat, what were they going to do now? Sasha didn't have the answer, and neither did he, but she was just going with the flow, letting the chips fall. She didn't know if what they had would go any farther and tried to convince herself that this was more than a fling, more than a rebound type thing. She did like Michael. He definitely grew on her.

After pondering and pondering, she just gave up and said to herself, "Fuck it. It will be whatever we make it."

As far as she was concerned, Michael turned her little ass out.

She went to teach that morning and afternoon, feeling good. She was even glowing. She couldn't believe it. She'd been feeling so down, so unwanted lately, it felt good to feel alive again.

When Sasha went home, Michael called, wanting to meet up before she went to her next Lamaze class.

They went out for some buffalo wings at Pizzeria Uno near the center where her class was. The plan now was for him to pick her up after Lamaze class. She must've put it on him, 'cause he couldn't get enough of her.

They started the smart-comment routine over dinner. The atmosphere felt comfortable, almost like she was out having dinner with the ladies.

"What time is your class over?"

"Oh, like around nine."

"That's good. I should be off by then to pick you up. Can't have my lady out too late by herself."

"Your lady?"

"Yeah, you're my lady, my home girl, my buddy."

"I see. Well, as I recall, you refer to me as a man-eater, so why would you want me to be all of this to you if you think of me that way?"

"And, as I recall, you told me that I have nothing better to do than to bother women I can't have."

"So you think you have me now?"

"Look, before this gets into a debate or a heated argument, let me just say that last night wasn't a fling or just some one-night thing. I've been trying to get at you for some time now, but you always seemed preoccupied. When I first met you, I thought you were full of yourself, always having a brother hemmed up, love sick over you, that's why I didn't bother. I didn't want that brother to be me. But it was no coincidence why I kept coming around. I was drawn to you, Sasha, but I didn't want to get hurt by you.

"After my first wife, I was never going to let a pretty face be the basis for any relationship. Some of you women with these faces think you can get a guy to do just about anything, which is true, but I didn't want to be motivated by external beauty. I began to date six- or seven-pieces and left the dimes alone. I let that control my whole thought process on meeting some-one. The pretty women will hurt you, but the not-so-pretty ones will worship you."

When Sasha tried to interrupt, Michael held his hand up. "It wasn't until I met you that I realized that whole thought process was stupid. Not every pretty face will treat a brother like shit, and not every pretty woman sees herself like some sort of goddess that needs to be worshipped. In fact, a lot of pretty women are insecure. Anyway, I tried to deny my feel-ings for you for a very long time, but the more I'm around you, the more I can't keep away from you. You have a big heart and a lot of courage, that's what I like most about you, and I feel like we have a lot to make something between us work. I care a lot about you, Sasha, and I'm trying to be with you, but I don't know what you want. But I'm damn sure going to try because I won't forgive myself if I let you go so easily without letting you know how I feel."

Sasha sat back. *Wow! That sure was an earful.* "Look, Michael, you're right. I'm not so sure that this is the right time for me to be getting involved like that. I do care about you, and I do love it when you're around, no matter how much I try to push you away. But I just don't know if I'm ready for all that, and I don't want to leave you hanging. I don't want to rush into something just because it feels right, you understand what I am saying?"

"Of course, and I'm not trying to push you anywhere you don't want to go. But I feel for you, and that's something I can't ignore. So what do you want to do?"

"I just want to take things super slow. I want to continue being friends with you, no matter what. I'd like to keep you in my life. I'd like to try to see where this is going. How does that sound?"

"If I'm not mistaken, you want to just kick it."

"Exactly. Is that cool with you?"

"Yeah, that's straight with me for now."

There, it was settled. She and Michael were not obligated to one another, meaning they could see other people, but it was understood that they were trying to build something together. Which was different from what she had with Damon because, with them, it was all about sex.

With Michael, it didn't have to be about sex. They could see each other, go hang out, and not just call each other to have sex when they were horny. If sex came into play, it just did, but they both understood that this wasn't just a booty-call relationship. Sasha didn't know how else to describe it, to make it sound good.

Afterwards Michael dropped her off at her Lamaze class. Since she still had some associates at the hospital, they recommended their patients to her, so her little sessions were beginning to pay off. Each class had six to ten mothers in each session. Some came once a week, some twice a week, and other four times a week. It all depended on their bankroll, since health insurance didn't cover Lamaze classes. Sasha charged three hundred for a four-week session, two nights a week. If a person wanted to come four nights instead of just two, she charged two hundred for the extra days for a four-week session. Her prices were pretty good compared to others.

This brand-new class she was conducting had ten clients. If the referrals kept coming in like this, she could do this full time, but then again, it all depended on how many people signed up. She couldn't very well plan her monthly salary if she didn't know how many clients she was having for that month. But it was an idea to keep in mind if her license was actually taken away from her over Doctor Roebuck's trivial accusation.

Michelle and Tasha, of course, received a discount. They were the first two in. Raymond had to work, and Jamal was not around, so Lisa came with Michelle, and Aunt Mimi came with Tasha.

They sat around chatting, waiting for the other eight clients to arrive.

Aunt Mimi said, "You've got a kicker on you, Tasha. Why didn't you guys figure out what the sex of the baby was?"

"Oh, we wanted it to be a surprise. Raymond talks of a boy all the time, but it really doesn't matter to me," Tasha replied.

"Yeah, Raymond has high hopes for a boy," Sasha added. "I'm sure, though, he'll love the baby, no matter what sex it is."

Aunt Mimi said, "Now you have yourself a good, hard-working man. He loves you and this baby a lot, and would do anything for you, just remember that, honey."

"Oh, and this wedding," Sasha said. "Why didn't you tell me, Tasha? I didn't know you guys were getting married."

"That was my fault. I didn't want to walk down the aisle all fat and unattractive."

"Girl, pregnancy is a beautiful thing." Michelle smiled. "I waited after my first son to marry his father though, so it's really up to what you guys want to do. There are no rules."

"Plus, with that case Raymond had, and him starting his new job and all, we just couldn't afford it."

"What about your parents?" Sasha asked.

"Come on, I'm nineteen. I couldn't ask them to pay for my wedding."

"Why not?" Sasha said. "That's what fathers are supposed to do."

"No rules," Michelle said. "Remember."

Sasha said, "I just thought, since your father was pushing marriage so much, he would want to pay for it."

Aunt Mimi said, "Well, it doesn't matter. You two love each other, you are good with each other. A piece of paper isn't going to change that. So if you don't have the money for the wedding now, you will have it one day, and you can get married then."

"Yeah, I know. I just wanted to be married before my child realized his parents didn't have the same last name, that's all."

Sasha got the feeling from Tasha that there was more to it than that. The more she went on, the more it sounded to her like she wanted them to pay for the wedding.

The classroom began to fill up. Sasha checked off her list and noticed there was one missing client, Jennifer Hayes. The class started at seven, and it was seven on the dot. She couldn't let one client make everyone else late, so she started the class, introducing herself and detailing her background.

Sasha went around the room to let them introduce themselves. Most of the clients were twenty-eight to thirty-six-year-old white females, first baby, and naturally very anxious about giving birth. Michelle and Tasha were among the youngest.

Just as she was about to begin the session, her late client arrived. She was about Sasha's height, looked the same age as her, light-skinned like her, with long brown hair and hazel eyes. She wobbled in and began to excuse herself for being late. "I'm so sorry I'm late. My husband has no track of time and claims I don't. He thought the class was over somewhere else and started at six. Come to find out, he doesn't have a sense of direction either, but hey, I still love him."

"Okay. Well, I'm Sasha Freeman, the instructor for the class. Just come right on in."

Sasha quickly went around the room and gave everyone's names. "You said your husband is with you?"

"Yeah, here he comes. He just had to park the car."

Jennifer went to sit on a pillow as her husband came into the doorway. His light skin, chinky eyes, and six-foot frame almost knocked the wind out of Sasha. His face was all too familiar.

Montel stood in the doorway, not so sure he should enter. He looked at Sasha, as she looked at him, and time seemed to have stopped.

Sasha's heart thumped. She stuttered, "Well, come on in and join us, Mr. Hayes."

Montel found his wife Jennifer and sat with her.

The two-hour session seemed to last an eternity. Sasha ran over the material too fast, and the time went nowhere.

After realizing she'd finished the session at five minutes after eight, she let everyone take a break. She went out of the room to grab some water.

Lisa and Michelle came after her.

Michelle hugged Sasha. "Are you going to be all right? I couldn't have done what you just did. I mean, the nerve of that asshole."

"I know, but I'm sure he didn't know I was running this class. I haven't spoken to him in three months."

Lisa said, "Still, he should've thought of some way to get him and that dippy girl out of here."

Sasha laughed. "She is kind of dippy, huh?"

"Yeah, girl," Lisa said. "She's definitely a bad copy of you. I mean, look at her. You are so much cuter, so much prettier."

Shit, how am I going to get though the rest of these eight sessions with them? Oh, this is not going to do.

Lisa added, "Well, she obviously doesn't know about you, or else she wouldn't be so damn cheerful."

They laughed.

"Oh, where's T when I need her? This is her thing to do, dealing with the ex and his new wife."

"No, honey, you should be glad T isn't here. She would have blown up Montel's spot and you don't need that in front of all these clients," Lisa said.

"You're right. Let me just get through the last forty-five minutes and figure out how I'm going to deal with this."

"We got your back, you know that," Lisa said.

"I know. I'm so glad you two are here. I couldn't face this on my own." Sasha hugged them.

Her Aunt Mimi came out. "Is everything all right?"

"Yeah. Let's get this class over with."

"Sasha, is that who I think it is?"

"Yes, Aunt Mimi. Let's just finish this up and talk about it later." Sasha grabbed her by the arm to come inside. She could feel Montel's eyes watching her, wondering what she was going to do next. *The boy has no shame, staring at me while his wife has her back turned.*

Aunt Mimi warned her, "Oh no, you don't need someone like that in your life. No matter how fine he is, he is a dog with a capital *D*. Leave him alone, Sasha. Be the bigger person."

Since Sasha didn't have any more material to discuss for that night, she figured, What better way to pass the time than let the people discuss their concerns and ask any questions they had? Everyone seemed so receptive, seeing they could benefit from her expert information as an obstetrician as well as the Lamaze teaching all in one. She answered question after question, and began to feel a little relaxed because it took her mind off any crap. She loved teaching new mothers, loved the exchange of information.

The session was going really well, and everyone seemed really into it. She felt like they were getting their money's worth.

With five minutes to go, Sasha was about to close up the session, when Jennifer decided to ask the final question of the evening. She hadn't heard anything from her all night, except her husband this, her husband that. That's all that seemed to come out of her mouth. She was really annoying. Her question had something to do with the pain of labor and techniques to soothe the discomfort.

This is why you're taking Lamaze, dumb ass. Anyway, she answered her simple question and ended the session. If she had to go through another night with her and him, she didn't know what would come out of her mouth.

Montel couldn't have gotten out of there faster, dragging poor Jennifer out of there by the arm.

Sasha knew he couldn't stand it, but what could he do? She just hoped he would convince her not to come back to this class with his ass, 'cause she might not be so friendly next time.

Aunt Mimi went home and took Tasha with her, and Sasha and the girls went out for a drink. Lisa called up T to meet them at Uno's for a double dose of Piña Colada and Pearl Harbor, and Sasha called Michael and told him of her plans. He seemed cool about it and asked her to call him later.

"Damn," Lisa said, "you got a new man already?"

"See, that's what I'm talking about. Don't sit around moping. Find you another young, handsome brother."

T and Lisa slapped hands. Those two were just what the doctor ordered.

Michelle asked, "Who is this new fella?"

"Okay, ladies, brace yourselves. Do you remember, Detective Perry?"

"Yeah, girl, I remember him," Lisa answered.

"Well, we're trying to do our thing now."

"What!" Lisa's mouth dropped.

"I knew he had a thing for you," Michelle said. "He's a good brother, seems real nice. Don't let this one go."

"I know. We bicker like cats and dogs, but I guess opposites do attract, and he is fun to be around."

"Oh, stop trying to convince yourself, Sash," T said. "You've been attracted to him from jump. You just be playing yourself with Montel."

"True, but I don't want him to be a rebound type, you know. Besides, I wouldn't know a good guy if he smacked me in the face. I just don't know how to pick them, I think. I know what I don't want, but I don't know what I do want, you know. I like Mike, but I feel closure hasn't happened for Montel and me yet."

"Oh, please! Close that book while you're ahead. Don't play yourself any longer," Lisa advised.

"Enough about me. Did you and Damon make up, Lisa?"

"That man has been ringing my phone for weeks. After not returning one call, he shows up at my daughter's school, knowing I would be picking her up. He has flowers for me, a Barbie doll for her, and some lame excuse, talking about he had to see me and that we needed to talk."

"So did you fall for it?" Sasha asked.

"Of course, she did," T said.

"After hours and hours of discussion, we came to an agreement."

"In other words, you dropped the panties." T smiled.

They started laughing.

"I can't hold out too long. I feel funny talking about Damon around you, Sasha. You two were together and all."

"I know. From now on, just an update on your progress. No details, please."

"I hear that," Lisa said. "It's so funny. I never thought I could talk to someone one of my girls had been with. That was a rule."

Sasha responded, "Yeah, well, one, you didn't know about it, and two, when your feelings are into it like that, the rules don't apply."

"True."

Sasha never would talk to one of her girlfriends' leftovers, but with such a scarce population of good men, who was she to be picky these days. "Just let me know if it gets serious or not, Lisa, and if it doesn't work out, it just doesn't."

"I know, girl, I know."

They sat and talked about new relationships and failed relationships. Their conversations always seemed to be about men, gossip, money, and family. Sasha didn't mind though. Anything to keep her mind off the other things bothering her right now, like Montel. The way he looked, the way he smelled, how jealous she was that he actually got married and was having a baby. That was supposed to be her.

Sasha thought, *How long can he live this lie? How long can he pretend that what he feels for me is just a thing of the past? Can he truly move on, or is he just trying to spare my feelings because he knows he'll hurt me in the end?* She didn't have the answers to these questions, and there was only one way to get the answers and the closure that she needed. She had to call him.

Sasha jumped in the bath and let her body soak. Oils and bubbles were just what she needed. She kept thinking, *This is all for the best. We shouldn't be together. Just move on, sister girl, move on.*

After an hour of relaxation and a pep talk about keeping her distance from Montel and focusing on Michael, she crept downstairs to get a snack before going to bed.

Her living room was dark. The only light filtered in from her porch light. She looked outside, as if she was expecting someone. She noticed Raymond's car in the driveway, so she turned off the porch light.

As she began to walk upstairs, she noticed a flashing red light in her living room. It was the answering machine. She had messages. Too busy pondering about Montel, she must have overlooked over them and went right upstairs. She pressed the button. The first message was at one p.m.

"Hello, Dr. Freeman, this is Dr. Westgate from General Hospital. We've set up a time and date for your hearing. Please give me a call at 617-555-9990, so we can discuss this matter."

The next message was received at eleven-fifty p.m.: "Hey, it's me. It was real awkward seeing you today. I hope I didn't cause you any pain. I honestly didn't know it was you who was teaching the class. I basically don't know what's going on in your life anyhow. I just thought I would call you. I don't even know how it got to this point. Well, look, call me when you get this. I really need to talk with you, all right? Bye."

In the background of that message, she heard a women's voice saying, "Montel," as if his call woke her.

There it was, her future as a physician and her future with Montel, all in the same night, two things she wasn't ready to face.

CHAPTER TWENTY-ONE

Sasha agonized over that phone call for hours. The hours turned to days, and the days turned to weeks. She didn't pick up the phone to call Montel. She couldn't. She didn't know what to say or what would happen if she did. However, she did call Dr. Westgate back. Her hearing was in three weeks.

Dr. Westgate went over all the particulars. Sasha could have co-workers write personal recommendations, anything to make her look good. She could even hire a lawyer if she wanted to, but she didn't feel the need to. Sasha went over her case in her mind, and after all the complaining and moaning she did when she was suspended, she realized that it was her fault, breaking patient confidentiality, overstepping her boundaries. Ready to face her fate, she decided to tell the truth about her actions.

Her hearing was on a Monday morning at eight. She had butterflies in her stomach the entire morning. Of course, she was dressed to impress in her Ann Taylor navy blue pants suit, yellow silk blouse, yellow socks, and navy blue Enzo penny loafers. Her hair, which she'd been wearing straight in a wrap for a while, was down.

Michael stayed over the night before. He really was there for her, like a real friend, making her breakfast and wanting to drive her to the hospital, but Sasha wanted to go alone.

He tried to encourage her during breakfast. "So when you start practicing again, you won't have as much free time as usual, will you?"

"Oh stop. I don't know how this is going to turn out. I appreciate you trying to cheer me up, but I did the dirt, so now I have to face it."

Michael had a very surprised look on his face.

"What's that look all about?"

"Well, I have to tell you that you've changed a lot from the first time I met you. You seemed more defensive and righteous then."

"What can I say, Michael? I have to open my eyes sometimes, especially when I'm looking at myself."

"Wow! I'm growing to like you more and more every day. I admire your strength and courage. You really are woman enough, even at your weakest moment."

"I assume you're talking about Montel."

Michael's eyebrow rose a little. "Whatever happened to him? You don't talk much about him."

"That's because I don't have much to say about him. I've moved on. He got married, and is having a baby."

"I know all that. On the outside you seem over it, you seem through with him, but I don't know how you feel on the inside about him. Talk to me."

Little did Michael know, she was contemplating calling him. *Damn it! Why did he have to go and bring up Montel? No, I'm not over him. I still think about him every day. Oh what can I say to get out of this conversation?* "Look, Michael, there is nothing to talk about. Yes, I was in love with that man for a long time, but I know what type of man he is now, and I don't need that in my life. Besides, you do a pretty good job of occupying my time. Why would I want to think about anyone else?" She placed her hands on his face and gave him a soft kiss to his lips, along with that look that he couldn't resist. He was putty in her hands. At least she thought so.

Anyway, he dropped the subject and proceeded to finish breakfast. He kissed her on her forehead instead of her lips when he left.

Sasha figured that meant he wasn't pleased with her behavior. *Who needs men anyway? They're just driving me crazy. Here I have Montel calling me, then Michael wants to go deeper into our relationship.*

It was all too much for her to handle. Maybe a sane person would know what to do, but she didn't.

Sasha made her way to the hospital. Even though in a few minutes her fate as a doctor was about to be decided, she was kind of nonchalant about the whole thing, as she kept weighing the pros and cons. She just wanted to get this part of her life over with so she could find out what her next move was. She'd decided long before the hearing that she was going to tell her story, and if they decided to welcome her back, she would go back. If they decided to dismiss her, she was going to accept that too.

Sasha arrived one hour early for the hearing, to get her bearings. That hour seemed to drag. As the time came near, she began to see a couple of familiar faces. Tammy, the back-stabbing bitch, went into the room. Dr. Roebuck managed to crawl her creepy self out from her rock and appear as well. The director of the hospital, the Chief of Staff, Dr. Westgate, and the director of occupational affairs all went inside without saying a word to her, just a snobbish look, like such do-rights.

Sasha felt like saying, "Fuck y'all." Why couldn't they have had this trial months ago instead of dragging it on for three and a half months? Why keep her out of work for so long without pay? The more she thought about it, the angrier she got. *These bastards were trying to shaft me!* One mistake, one false move, and they were ready to kick "blackie" out the door.

As her rage began to boil, she thought of all the other things she had going for herself and all the other things she had to be grateful for.

Dr. Westgate came into the corridor where she was sitting and signaled Sasha to come in. She went into the dark room, feeling confident, unafraid, and ready for her fate, and sat down, crossing her legs and hands.

"Dr. Freeman, do you understand the accusations and reasons for this hearing?" Dr. Westgate said.

She nodded.

One of the directors of the hospital board started the hearing with, "Then let's begin. I have here a signed affidavit from Tamela Jones and Dr. Roebuck that you underhandedly broke the policy of patient confidentiality. I also have a form that you signed pertaining to the disclosure of all patient information and how it should be used in this hospital. We've heard from Tamela Jones and Dr. Roebuck. Now we'd like to hear from you."

She cleared her throat and began to tell her side of the story with all sincerity. Sasha started off saying that she did willingly break patient confidentiality, and was sorry for it. She went on to say that she meant no harm and that it would never happen again. That she had no excuse for her actions, except that she was worried about a friend, and took full responsibility for her actions, and was willing to accepting whatever judgment they pass on her.

Whether they bought it or not, suddenly she didn't care, she thought to herself.

They looked at one another and wrote a little something on their papers.

Dr. Westgate then turned to her and said, "We've decided to let you go this time with a warning."

"Thank you."

He then put his hand up. "I'm not finished, Dr. Freeman. Although your actions didn't bring any harm to this hospital, they were still against hospital policy. We would like to reinstate you at this hospital with a few restrictions. First, you will have Dr. Roebuck sign all the prescriptions you write, and you will work with her when admitting, treating, and discharging patients. We've also moved your office to the fifth floor, so Dr. Roebuck and you can work more closely together. And of course there are some other few gray areas about your salary, but you can go over that with Human Resources."

Sasha tried to keep her anger hidden. "Well, as pleasant as that offer sounds, I'll have to decline. I didn't go to four years of college, four years of medical school, and three years of residency to be watched like a neonate. Since my license hasn't been taken away, I'll find work elsewhere because, this, I must say, is unacceptable. I'm not giving Dr. Roebuck the satisfaction of treating me like she did in med school."

"Dr. Freeman, you do understand that you haven't finished your fellowship contract with this hospital and would have to start all over anywhere else."

"I completely understand, Dr. Westgate, but in all this time that I've been away, I had a chance to realize that this wasn't the work I was meant to do. I don't know what that is, but this isn't it. I want to help people, not hinder them. With all these rules and regulations and insurance this and payment that, I'm not so sure I'm helping. I hope you understand."

It was one thing to put up with the politics of how a hospital is run, but to have to put up with Dr. Roebuck was an entirely different story. Sasha just couldn't do it. She left that boardroom not knowing what her future held for her. She thought maybe they wanted her to self-terminate. If so, she would've done it without their help. Sasha had been feeling this way for a while, she just never had the time before to really look at herself and what was going on in her life.

Sasha passed by Tammy's trifling self. She stopped her and said, "What you did, Tammy, just reminds me of what a sneaky little bitch you really are, but, not to worry, unlike yourself, I have no intention of going back on what I said. In the whole scheme of things, people like you always get what they deserve. If you don't know it now, you'll know it soon. You better make peace with all your wrongdoings because your time is definitely near."

Sasha left Tammy and called Michael to meet her for a drink at Cathay Pacific, even though it was still morning. She was in desperate need of a scorpion bowl and some shrimp fried rice. She remembered Montel taking her there a few times. They would drink at least two scorpion bowls and drift off into each other's conversation.

She tried to keep her mind off of things, but she just couldn't. Why would he call her, she hadn't seen him or his wife in her Lamaze class in weeks. *Wonder if he told her about me? Doubt it.*

Anyway, as she reached the door to the restaurant and was about to go in, she heard someone yelling her name. She turned and saw it was Montel. Sasha wanted to escape, but she couldn't. He was already on her.

"Hey, Sasha, wait a minute. You don't have to ignore me. I was hoping I'd run into you sooner than later."

Sasha rolled her eyes and turned her back as if she didn't see or hear him.

"Damn, can you at least give me one minute of your time, Sasha, please?" He grabbed her arm. "Look, I know things aren't how you wanted, and it's my entire fault. But, damn, we can't even talk to each other? We can't even try to be amicable?"

She looked at him as if he was crazy. "Amicable?"

"Jennifer had the baby a couple of weeks ago."

Sasha quickly said, "Congratulations," and tried to go inside.

Once again, he stopped her. "Damn, Sasha, I tried to say the right words, but they all just get mixed up. When I try to call you, you either aren't there or don't return my calls. I've written you a thousand letters, which I can't seem to send to you in fear that I won't get one back. What can I do to make this up to you? What can I do for us to be at least talking again? I miss that so much."

"I'm afraid there is nothing you can do, so just go."

"No, I'm not leaving until you say yes."

"Say yes to what?"

"That you'll try to call me. That you'll try to understand my situation. That you'll consider holding me in your heart."

Sasha tried to let her words come out without crying. "I still hold you in my heart—That's the problem."

Montel looked at her and put his hands on her shoulder. "Can I call you some time?"

"You don't need permission to call me."

"I just want to make sure it's okay with you."

"Call me and say what?"

"I don't know. I'll cross that road when I get to it."

"Whatever, Montel. Look, I have to go. I'm meeting someone."

"Who? Your new man?"

She wanted to tell him but knew it would lead to another discussion, and Michael would come and see her out here with him and things just wouldn't be right. Michael was already asking too many questions about Montel.

"Look, just go."

Montel stood there for a few minutes and gave her his look that sent heat waves through her body. He kissed her on her forehead and walked away, just as he'd walked out of her life before.

Sasha tried not to let his words get to her, but it was too late. She didn't want to think like that. Here she had Michael, a wonderful person and a true friend-lover, and all she could think about was Montel.

Minutes later, Sasha stared down at the scorpion bowl that she and Michael were sipping on, thoughts of Montel ruling her head. She thought about when they first met, when they first kissed, when they made love, how happy he made her. She would give anything to get that feeling back.

"Hello, Sasha, are you with me or what?"

"Yeah, I'm here. Why? What's up?"

"You haven't said a word since we got here. You seem distant. Do you think you made the wrong choice about leaving the hospital?"

"No, I'm getting past that. I think I'll be okay. I just have to tell everyone. They won't be too pleased, but it's my life, right?"

"You got that right. If they really love you, they'll support your decision. Then they have to get over the fact that they won't be able to borrow money from you for a while."

Sasha laughed.

"So, I was thinking . . . I have this weekend off. Let's go somewhere like Las Vegas for the weekend. You gamble?"

"Oh, Montel, I just really don't feel like it." Sasha covered her mouth with her hands.

"I'm so sorry, Michael. I meant Michael, you've got to know that. There is no Montel."

Disgust in his eyes, Michael said, "Yeah, but you wish there were."

"No, I don't."

"Face it, Sasha, you're not over him. How could you be? You never talk about him."

"Hey, I'm trying to get over him, but it takes time, you know that. Look how long it took for you to get over your wife. I was hurt real bad, and I have to move on, I know, but I'm learning how to do that every day. Hey, we're all right, aren't we?"

She stroked his cheek with her hand and smiled, but he pulled away.

"Hey, let's get out of here," she suggested with a "let's-knock-boots" look.

"You can't say things like that and put sex on a platter like it solves everything. It doesn't. Sex only makes it worse, harder to let go, harder to get over."

Sasha felt as if he was accusing her of something she didn't do, something she thought about but didn't do. "I don't think sex is the answer to everything, and I don't think I like what you're implying."

"What am I implying? That you're sleeping with Montel? That's your guilty conscience working. If you're not sleeping together, then you're thinking about it. If you're not thinking about it, then you probably will be soon anyway, if you don't just let go. Face the fact that he is gone."

Michael's words cut through her like a paper shredder.

"Look, you don't have to worry about my issues and me, okay? Don't worry your pretty little head about it. See, that's why I didn't want a relationship, but you keep pushing and pushing, and you just don't seem to understand that these things take time. I can't cut my feelings on and off like the electric company does your lights. I thought you could understand, but you don't. What's the big deal anyway? I haven't committed to any relationship with you. We're just kicking it. If I want to sleep with Montel, I will. You know what your problem is? You're too judgmental. You want everything and everyone to follow your rules and follow your commands. Well, I'm sorry that I don't fit in your academy, officer. Sorry to be such a weak link."

"I think you need to stop there before you make a mistake."

"Too late for that one."

Sasha rolled her eyes at Michael and turned her head as if she wasn't even with him.

"Yeah, I think that sums it all up, Ms. Sasha." Michael threw a couple of dollars to cover the tab and looked like he was going to say something like, "I'll call you later," but instead he said, "Fuck it," and left her there sitting alone.

That was bound to happen. We never got along anyway. I'm just glad I didn't waste too much time on him.

On the way home, she tried to go over what was going on in her life. She tried to convince herself that she and Michael didn't belong. They didn't fit together, and he would always be judging her and making her seem so incorrect. She then thought about Montel, who never corrected her and only thought the world of her. If only Montel could make himself available. She didn't think she would ever be satisfied until she got her way. She always got half of the broomstick, but not the entire broom.

Here she was twenty-eight years old, no man, no career, and no money. She should be swinging from monkey bars with joy. When she was a kid, she always pictured this happy life at this age. She thought she'd be married, have a few kids, and be successful and loved. But she had none of the above. *What a crap of shit! You plan your whole life out and nothing is as it should be. I just thank the Lord for the health and strength to get through all of this disappointment.*

Dressed in her pajamas, and wide awake at midnight, she decided to read a book to shut everything out.

Her phone rang. She was sure it was Michael calling to apologize. He was so predictable. She let it ring four times, so he wouldn't think she was up waiting for him to call. She answered the phone, only to discover it wasn't Michael but Montel.

"It's too late for you to be calling me," she said, really trying to mean it.

"I know," Montel said, "but I had to talk to you again. Look, Sasha, I need to see you. There are some things I didn't tell you today, and some things I need you to know. Since you were so busy shooing me off so you could be with the next man, I didn't get to finish. But I need to talk to you real soon."

No, he didn't say I was too busy with the next man. "What's real soon, Montel?"

"Like tonight."

"What! What about your wife? What about your baby?"

"My wife and son are at her mother's. She's been staying over there for weeks, to get used to motherhood and all. I'm here all alone."

"I know that's not a signal for me to come over."

"No, I was just answering your question. Can I come over there?"

"It's late."

"I know, but I just want to talk, you know."

"No. I don't know, Montel. You can't keep doing this, calling me when you need to, running into me when you need to. This has got to stop."

"I know, Sash, but I do need you. I'll only stay for a little while. Please?"

She heard the desperation in his voice. She tried to speak another no, but the only word that came out of her mouth was, "Whatever."

She crept downstairs like a burglar, ashamed of who was coming over. She wanted to find out whether or not Raymond was home. With a swift look out the window, she saw no car. *Good, No one will see this one.*

She kept trying to convince herself that nothing was going to happen between Montel and her. He was just coming over to talk, nothing else. Sasha checked herself out in the mirror, admiring herself in her pajamas, the ones with the skintight tank top and little booty shorts, Montel's favorite. He said she looked so cute in them. *Oh, here I go. No, damn it, the man is married, he has a child. I'm no home-wrecker. He's just coming over to finish things up with us.*

After saying those words to herself, she wasn't so sure she was ready to finish things up with him. *Damn it, why does it*

*have to be this way? Why is love so damn complicated? If two people
are in love, then they should be together.*

She didn't want to hurt anyone. She would hate for someone to break up her marriage, but what was their marriage
based on? It couldn't have been that strong, if he was calling
her up this late. She was starting to sound like Tammy. She
never wanted to do that to anyone, what Tammy was doing to
Michelle's marriage, and figured she just had to be strong.

Sasha got to thinking about T and Ricky. They were in love.
They were together. T just said, "Later for the wife."

Why couldn't she do that? Why was she reading so much
into this? Whatever, she didn't know why she was beating herself up about this. She hadn't made any calls, hadn't arranged
any secret rendezvous. Montel was the one in control, and she
was just an innocent bystander trying to figure out where she
fit in all of this.

After waiting fifty minutes for Montel to arrive, she came to
the conclusion that whatever happened wasn't her fault. She
didn't ask for any of this. She still loved Montel, and if they
were meant to be together then, like Michelle said, they would.

The house was so silent, Sasha could hear everything. She
heard Tasha walking back and forth upstairs. *She must be waiting up for Raymond.*

The phone upstairs rang, and Tasha answered on the first
ring, as if she was waiting for the call. She answered a loud,
"Hello." She didn't sound too pleased with whoever was on
the phone with her.

"Why did I page you, nigga? I paged you 'cause I needed to
talk to you. I been hearing some stupid shit, you running your
mouth about business that isn't yours. You keep talking and
you'll see what happens to you."

Then there was a little pause.

"What? Test me, nigga, and see what happens. Look, you
need to keep all that nonsense to yourself. I'm doing what's

best for me, not you, for me. You didn't want anything to do with me. Now you hear I'm doing good without you, you want a piece of this pie? It's too late."

Tasha was silent for a moment.

"I'm getting married. You heard about that, huh? What? Yeah, I am pregnant. So? Nigga, fuck you. I know who my baby's father is. No, it ain't you, and if you keep spreading that bullshit, I'm going to put one in you, ya heard. Whatever, nigga. Yeah, see me around." Tasha slammed the phone so hard, Sasha could feel the vibration all the way downstairs.

Sasha had never heard Tasha talk in such language. This wasn't the sweet, innocent girl she'd come to know. She must have been talking to some dude, some no-name cat. And what was this about her getting married? Raymond hadn't set a date. Sasha needed to find out what was really going on real soon. She'd been putting this off too long. Tasha was up to something, and she was going to be the one to find out what.

The time was now two a.m. It shouldn't have taken Montel that long to come over.

As she made her way upstairs, she heard a car pulling up in her driveway. She was certain it was Raymond and didn't want to talk to him about Tasha anyway, so she went to the door to see. *Well, if it isn't Mr. Hayes . . .*

Montel ran up the stairs and quickly into the house to fight the rainy weather. He kissed Sasha's cheek. "Did I take too long?"

"Yeah, you did. I was just about to go to bed."

"Oh well, I don't want to hold you up from getting any sleep."

"So what did you have to discuss with me in person that you couldn't say to me over the phone?"

"Can I take my coat off, get a little comfy first before I begin this?"

"No, 'cause I doubt you'll be here that long. You can have a seat over there."

"Your place looks nice, Sasha. It smells good in here. I remember when you used to dedicate Saturdays as your clean up days."

"I never had time during the week, but now I have all the time in the world."

"With teaching Lamaze and working at the hospital, how can you?"

"No, Montel, FYI, I don't work at the hospital any more. I quit."

"What? I thought your work meant a lot to you. You used to spend more time there than with me."

"What? Montel, you were the one who was always off somewhere, promoting this group and that group."

"I made time for you though."

"Obviously, not enough time, since you went off and got some other girl pregnant and then married her. What's up with that?" Sasha glared at him for a response, but Montel didn't say anything. "Oh, now you're all silent, as if that didn't happen. You make me sick."

"Do I really? I don't mean to. You have to know that. What I felt for you—no, what I still feel for you is right here. This isn't going anywhere. That's what I came to tell you. This is why I had to see you to tell you this. I don't know how long I can live this lie with Jennifer, but I want you to know that you're the only woman for me. I don't care how long it takes, or who you're with at the time. I'm going to make you mine some day. It may not be today, but I will, trust me."

"Trust you, Montel? How can I trust you? Look at what you've done to us. Look at the mess you've made. If I'm the only woman for you, how come you weren't thinking about that when you and Jennifer were one-night standing it? Look at you. Can you honestly look me in the face and say it was only one time? That the whole time me and you were together, it was always about us? Not her, not anyone?"

"Yes. Listen, Sasha, I told you what happened between Jennifer and I was just one night, just one moment. I was weak. I let her in. I should've been trying to figure out what went wrong with us. I know you can't understand it now, but I'm begging you to please try to understand. When she told me she was pregnant, I felt like I had no choice but to marry her."

"Yeah, yeah. 'Cause you grew up without a father. But you still could have been a father. You didn't have to be married to do that."

"Yes, I did. I felt I did."

"And now how do you feel?"

"I feel like I am going to fuck everyone's life up, yours, hers, my son's life, and mine. I thought I was doing what needed to be done, but now I see what a mistake I made."

"How long before the wedding did you decide to marry her, after she told you she was pregnant?"

"About a month."

"So in one month's time, you still didn't feel the need to tell me? When did you plan on telling me?"

"The bachelor's party was a surprise. I didn't know about that. I had planned on telling you before the wedding. I just didn't know what I was going to say."

"I see."

"How'd you find out about the party anyway?"

"Detective Perry came across it on his way to my birthday party."

"Oh, my number one fan, huh? I bet he's been around more now, huh?"

"I thought you were here to talk about us?"

"I know. Just the thought of you with another man, you just don't know what it does to me."

"How do you think I feel? I had to sit there while you and your wife played house. Do you have any idea how unimportant that made me feel?"

"I know, but, look, I'm trying to do right by you, and I just need you to stop shutting me out. You said I make you sick. Give me the chance to make you feel better, that's all I ask."

Sasha wanted to give him that chance. She needed to know what was going to become of them, in order for her to truly move on. "Look, Montel, I don't know. I can't be sneaking around with you like that, and I wouldn't feel right."

"What? You think this is about sex? Come on, Sasha, you know better. I'm trying to stay in your life, that's all. Will you give me that chance?"

Montel started his stares at her with his chinky eyes, the ones that heated her up. Damn, she loved this man so much, how could she let him go so easy? She tried not to show her weakness.

"Can I call you later?"

"I just can't answer that right now. I need to work some things out on my own, see what I want to do."

"I understand, Sash. Just don't forget about me. I won't let you."

Sasha gave him a soft hug that seemed to last forever. *How could I let him back in my life?* "If I do decide to let you back in my life, it will be just as friends, that's it. I'm not about to break up a happy home, ya heard."

"I feel you. I'll take whatever I can get from you. I need you in my life, Sasha, for real."

With those last words, she fell asleep on the sofa with Montel. She didn't want to send him out in the rain, and it was late too.

Sasha kept saying to herself, "Friends." That's all she needed from him. But she was lying to herself. She knew that she was always going to want more, want him to herself.

So there they slept, with no easy road to take, no easy way to love each other without hurting someone, but still with the understanding that one day they would be together.

CHAPTER TWENTY-TWO

"Sasha, what do you think of this table?"

Sasha didn't know why Lisa brought her all the way down here at eight in the morning to go furniture shopping. Her place was fine. She guessed Lisa wanted something different.

"Lisa, everything you've shown me is nice. Why are you redecorating your house? Christmas is like in two weeks. Do you honestly think this is the time for redecorations?"

"Yeah, girl. There's no time like the present. Besides, I've gotten all of Jasmine's toys and everyone else's presents, so I thought I'd fix up the place."

"Okay, fix up the place, not buy an entire room or two."

"Do you think it's too much?"

"Well, look at this bedroom set you've picked out. It doesn't look too dainty for a woman's bedroom set. And this table looks more neutral, masculine even. This doesn't look like single-mom-and-one-child furniture. You're picking out family, mom-and-dad-and-children furniture."

"It's that obvious, huh?" Lisa smiled.

What's this girl talking about?

Sasha had her own issues to deal with. She still didn't know what she was going to do about her career, hadn't figured out what Tasha was up to, and didn't know what the hell Montel and her were doing.

Since the night they'd talked, that fool had been calling her every day. They'd met every day this week for lunch. *When did he spend time with his wife?*

This so-called friendship had gone on for like a month now. Not to mention the fact that she was still stringing Michael along. He'd called her the next day after their fight, and they'd both agreed to take things slow, not rush each other.

Sasha had already made up her mind that she and Montel would be together. Jennifer and Michael were just little obstacles that they had to bypass in time.

Tasha had a couple of false alarms, all this month. Every night, she'd think it was time. That's all that came out of her mouth, besides questions about marriage.

Sasha's question was when and if Raymond was going to marry this girl? If he was, it didn't look like he was in any rush. Sasha barely saw Raymond. He worked at the fire station late, and his second job, construction, was early in the morning. That boy must've been saving a fortune, but as long as he kept up his payment for the rent, she wasn't too concerned.

Then again, when was I ever around? Between Michael and Montel, it seemed like Sasha had been working two jobs. Oh well, she tried to avoid Montel, but he was always in her face, always making it seem like they were meant to be together. She tried to make him focus on his wife and son, but when he was with her, it was like he was in another world. She couldn't call it. She was trying to keep things on the friendly tip, so she couldn't be blamed for whatever happened.

Michael pretended to be clueless about her feelings for Montel. Oh, everything was such a mess. Anyway, Sasha kept telling herself that she wasn't responsible. As long as Michael played along, she would play with him, and as long as Montel was married, they were just going to be friends. That's right, no sex, no kissing, no nothing, no matter how she felt about him. That rule lasted a hot minute. Temptation couldn't be ignored, and Sasha's feelings couldn't be hushed.

As Lisa rambled on to the next table, she looked at Sasha for approval.

Sasha nodded like she did at all the other tables. Lisa was really starting to bug her. Sasha had to meet Michael to help him pick out a present for his mother. She'd made plans to meet with Ray to discuss Tasha finally, and she still hadn't finished her Christmas shopping. Lisa needed to come on.

After they reached the last set of tables, Sasha snapped. "Lisa, you've dragged me through this entire store. We have looked at every table in here, and you still haven't picked one out yet. Would you come on? I have some things to do today."

Lisa looked at her like she had to tell her something very important.

"What, girl? What's up?" Sasha said.

"Okay, I didn't bring you down here to help me shop. I brought you down here because I needed to tell you something. I figured that if I kind of hinted at what was going on with Damon and me, you would guess, but seeing how you're clueless, I'll just tell you. Damon and I are moving in together." She took one breath and put her hand on top of Sasha's as if she were bracing her.

So you and Damon are moving in together, woopty doo! I have my own issues. "How nice." Sasha didn't see the point of Lisa trying to be subtle about this. "You know, Lisa, that's really good. Does this mean this time next year I'll have a wedding to go to?"

"I don't know. We're just going to try this moving in together first, see how things work out. Then who knows, anything is possible." Lisa smiled.

"My thoughts exactly."

"I just wanted to make sure things were okay with us first before I told everyone else."

"You don't need my stamp of approval when it comes to you and Damon. I'm over him, and I don't even look at him the same. If you two are happy together, that's all that matters. Do your thang, ma."

Lisa smiled.

Sasha was never in love with Damon, and she definitely wasn't holding any feelings for him. Granted, she didn't like the idea of him dating one of her girls, but by the time she'd found out, it was too late. Lisa had already fallen for him. Who was Sasha to interfere with that?

After Sasha finally left the store with Lisa, she met up with Michael to pick up a few things for his mother and her laundry list of presents she had to buy. But by the time they got to the overcrowded South Mall, everything was sold out and there was nothing good left on the racks. Macy's was like a mob house.

Sasha suggested to Michael he buy his mother an expensive scarf or some perfume. He couldn't go wrong with that. She made her way to the jewelry counter.

Sasha, Aunt Mimi, and Tanya made it a point to buy each other jewelry each Christmas. She just wondered what she was going to get. She hoped it was that gold bangle she had her eye on. Anyway, she picked up a pretty set of gold earrings for Tanya and a bracelet for Aunt Mimi, two items she would've loved to see on herself.

Sasha found herself staring at the diamond engagement rings and started fantasizing. She pictured herself and Montel shopping together during Christmas. She would be eyeing platinum diamond rings, and he would pretend not to see her staring at it. On Christmas Day he would surprise her with it and ask her to marry him. She smiled at the thought. Wouldn't that just be grand?

The sales woman asked her, "Do you need anything?" interrupting her fantasy.

Sasha reluctantly declined and made her way back to find Michael. She passed the scarf section. No Michael. She figured he must've made his way to the men's section and started shopping for himself. They were alike in that way, trying to do for other people but never forgetting about themselves. He was probably in the shoe section. Michael loved his shoes.

As she passed the jackets and trousers, she found the shoe section, and sure enough, he was there. Sasha crept up on him while he was at the register and put her hands in his pocket. "Hey, Santa, this doesn't look like the scarf section," she whispered in his ear.

Michael turned around and gave her a kiss on her lips.

"What are you buying, Santa?"

"Just a little bit of this and a little bit of that," he replied.

"Anything in the bag for Mrs. Claus?"

"Yeah, I bought my mother a nice scarf."

"I was referring to myself."

Michael knew that. He gave Sasha a kiss on her forehead and put his arm around her.

Sasha was trying to walk one way when he was persuading her to go another, as if he knew something she didn't. Just as they played tug-of-war, Sasha saw why Michael wanted her to go his way instead of hers. Montel was shopping for shoes as well, not alone. Of course, he was with his wife and baby. Sasha tried to glance away before he saw her, but it was too late. He saw her, and his wife's eyes were not too far behind his.

Sasha didn't know if she should wave or just pretend she didn't know them. As she walked by, Jennifer said, "Hey, didn't you teach Lamaze class at the YMCA?"

"Yeah. Isn't your name, Janet?"

"Jennifer. You remember my husband Montel?" Jennifer gestured her hand toward Montel.

Sasha said her hello, as if she didn't know this man. "Well, I see you had your baby. Labor wasn't too hard for you, was it?"

"No, one day of your class really helped. I still had an epidural, but the pain wasn't that bad. I recommended a few friends to your class. They should be calling you."

Great! Why did she have to be so damn nice? "Well, it was nice seeing you again. Congratulations. You have yourself a beautiful baby."

Jennifer smiled. "Thank you."

Sasha gave Montel the stares that said all she was feeling inside. She couldn't have walked out of Macy's fast enough, as Michael trailed her, not saying a word. All that went through her head was how could she be so cold, so nonchalant. That just tore her up inside. She saw the man that she wanted to marry with his wife and child and pretended like she didn't even know him. She knew this wouldn't work. She knew she couldn't just remain neutral, go on with her life as if she didn't want to have any part of his.

By the time they reached the car, her brain was fried.

"I see you're still holding a candle for that one, huh?"

Sasha wasn't in the mood for small talk or interrogation by Michael. *Here we go.* "I knew you weren't going to let this opportunity go by."

"All I am saying is, I could see what was going on back there. The tension between you two was obvious."

"What tension?"

"As if something is going on with you two."

Michael's insecure comments really pissed her off. But he was right. What pissed her off was that she couldn't fool him. Every chance he got, he would drill her about Montel. "When was the last time you spoke? If he wasn't married, would you still be with him?" He would go on and on, like he was trying to get a confession.

"Michael, for the umpteenth time, there is nothing going

on between Montel and me. We're friends." *Oops, how did that slip out? Last I told Michael, Montel and I didn't even speak.*

Michael had a confused look on his face. "Friends since when?"

"Since I don't know. Since I met him."

"Sasha, is there something you'd like to tell me?"

"Michael, we're all right, right?"

"I used to think so until lately. I feel like you're holding back on me because you're waiting for someone else to come along."

"I like us, Michael. I do. I just . . . I don't know. Everything seemed to move so fast when we said it would move slowly. I haven't had a chance to figure everything out."

"You mean you haven't had a chance to realize that I'm the one for you, not Montel?"

What? Where did that come from? If Michael knew this whole time that she still was in love with Montel, why did he even bother with her? "Michael, you don't understand."

"I understand more than you know, but I'm not going to sit around and watch you make an ass out of me and an ass out of yourself. You and Montel have some unfinished business, and we can't move forward unless you face that."

What? Was Michael testing me to see if I would fall for that one? "Montel is married. There is no business between us. We are over."

"I wish that was true, Sasha. I wish that was true."

Michael didn't say much to Sasha on the way to her house. He dropped her off, thanked her for helping him find something for his mother, and drove off.

Sasha couldn't understand it. On one hand, she thought he was testing her to see what she'd do if she had the chance to be with Montel. On the other, she thought he was trying to flip it on her by pretending he didn't care, so she wouldn't think his feelings were into this.

Michael shouldn't play so many mind games. He should just say what he feels.

Anyways, Sasha dropped off her shopping bags and met Ray for lunch to warn him about Tasha and to see what was going on with this marriage thing. She met him downtown at this place their mother used to take them called Aunt Bernie's Grill. She couldn't wait to eat.

"Hey, sis. I haven't seen you in a minute. Michael keeping you busy?"

Sasha looked at Raymond. *I thought I was playing this friendship role pretty good. How do you know anything is going on with Michael and me?*

"Big sis, don't front. I know the brother's got a thing for you, and you got something for him too."

"Look, Ray, big sis can handle hers. I want to talk to you about Tasha. What's up? You two getting married? She's about to set a date if you don't say anything. She's about to drop that load any day now, so if you plan on marrying her, I suggest you do so soon."

"I know. That's why I work two jobs." Raymond smiled and pulled out a black box. Inside the box was a gold band with a 1-carat Marquise diamond.

"Oh, Raymond, you two really are getting married. I thought this was all in her head?"

"At first, I wanted to see how things were going to go with us. I met her right after I broke up with Tina. In a week we slept together. Six weeks later, she tells me she's pregnant, so I wasn't really sure about her. But in all this time we've spent together, she's grown on me, and I'm ready to make that step. For real, Tasha is the one, and I didn't even know it. I was messing with this chick and that for a minute, but ever since she came along and put it on me, all I want is her."

"Wow! How do you know what love is at twenty-three?"

"Hey, this is what I feel love is. Therefore this is what it's going to be—me, Tasha, and the baby forever."

"I see. Well, when did you meet her? In like February, pregnant in April, due in December?"

"I know where you're going, Sasha. Don't. I thought you liked her?"

"I did, but something is off about her. I heard her on the phone talking to some dude."

"Some dude? When?"

"Like a month ago. At least I thought it was a dude. She said something like she has moved on, getting married, having a baby, no, not yours. I don't know. I'm not trying to place doubt in your head, but something doesn't seem right."

"Sasha, I'm a grown man. Let me worry about Tasha. If she's playing me for a fool, she will feel it. She's carrying my seed, and I don't want to hear anything more about it."

"Fine. I just wanted to give you a heads-up."

"Yeah? Well, don't worry."

That love-sick look in Ray's eyes let her know how snowed he was on Tasha. It never dawned on him that Tasha would lie about her pregnancy. Why would she? For her sake, she hoped she was telling the truth, because Ray's temper was unpredictable. Sasha didn't want to go through another court case, which is why she wanted to prepare him for the upset.

"Well, Raymond, I trust you can handle your business. I just want to remind you that women take care of women in their own way, just like men take care of men in theirs."

"Enough, Sasha. I got this. I know how scandalous woman can be."

She backed off.

"Men can be just as scandalous."

"Yeah, well, um, what up with Montel? Tasha told me she saw him coming out of your place the other night."

Sasha almost choked on her water. "What?"

Raymond laughed. "No need to deny it, big sis. I see your game—You're playing Michael close, but you got yourself a spare if you need it."

More like the other way around. Michael was the spare. Sasha nodded like that's what was really going on.

"You don't have to explain. You know what you're doing." Raymond responded.

How could Ray be so sure that she did?

"See you haven't reached that level yet with someone special, someone you can trust. Because if you did, you wouldn't need a spare, ya heard."

That's what she thought she was doing with Montel. She didn't think she needed a spare when they were together. She also thought she could trust him. Boy, was she wrong. "Yeah, Raymond, I know what I'm doing. Let's just leave it at that."

"Say no more, Sasha."

Raymond paid for lunch and went on about his merry little way.

All day she thought about Montel. How easy Lisa found trust in Damon. How easy Raymond found trust in Tasha. Why wasn't it so easy for her? T and Ricky even hooked back up, how crazy was that? And after all Jamal's dirt, Michelle still clung on to him. Tanya and Larry kept it going strong for years. What was her problem?

As she let her thoughts take over, her phone rang. It was Montel. It was late, of course, twelve in the morning, his regular time for calling.

"Hey, baby girl? What's up?"

"Nothing. Just sitting here thinking."

"You want some company?"

Yeah, but not you. Sasha was sick of the sneaking around together. "Montel, I think I need some distance between us."

"What? Why?"

"Because you're making me crazy. We can toy along with the idea that we're just friends, but you and I both know the real deal. You're married. I can't live like this."

"Oh, you and my man getting serious or something?"

"No, Montel. I just don't think you're giving your marriage a try, if you're always calling me."

"You're not making sense. You know what my marriage is based on. You know who I wanted to marry, you. So why are you trying to flip the script on me?"

"Because you're married, and it isn't to me. The longer I hold on to you, the harder it is for me to let go."

"I thought you didn't want to let go?"

"I didn't, but things are so complicated. I try to be friends with you, but when we're alone, I can't help my feelings. One of these days things are going to get out of control. Then where will we end up? A lot of people are going to get hurt if we keep carrying on this way, Montel."

"So what are you saying? You don't want to be with me?"

Sasha paused, trying to get her words right, trying to make it come out right. "I can't be with you, is what I'm saying, Montel, I can't."

Montel was silent for a long time.

"Hello, are you still there?"

"Yeah, all right, Ms. Sasha. I'll see you around." Montel hung up.

She tried to sleep, but couldn't. She didn't know what just came over her. How could she end things with Montel when she swore they'd be together? Trying to flip the script on Montel, like Michael was trying to do to her, make it seem like she didn't want him, so he would want her.

In the middle of her thoughts, the doorbell rang. To no surprise, it was Montel.

She went to the door. "What are you doing here?"

Montel busted through her front door and kissed her hard. He started to undo her robe.

Sasha stopped him. "Montel, I can't. What about your wife?"

Montel looked at her. "What about us? You don't know how much I wish things were different. You don't know how much I want to be with you. Every day I wake up to her, and I wish it were you I was holding. Sasha, you know why I'm here. I'm not letting you go. You can't let me go, you know that." Montel began to kiss her, a crazy look on his face. He was determined to break her, to make her see things his way.

She tried to fight, Lord knows, she did.

He began to undress her, sliding his fingers in her.

Sasha moaned as she tried to pull away. "Montel, this is wrong."

He silenced her with his kisses, tonguing her down. She tried to fight him some more. Her defenses were becoming weary.

"Montel, do you love me?"

"If you don't know the answer to that, why are we here? This isn't lust I feel, this is love. I can't breathe without you, I can't think without you. Don't turn me loose, please." Montel kissed her again, undid his clothes, undid her clothes, and slid inside her.

A half an hour later, the deed was done. The line was crossed. There was no turning back.

CHAPTER TWENTY-THREE

The doorbell rang, then the knocking started. The knock was crazy, like the police were at the door. Sasha tried to get up but couldn't. Something was wearing her down, and she couldn't move.

The knock got louder and louder. Then she heard footsteps. She had this sick, terrifying feeling in her stomach. She tried to find out what was holding her down so heavy that she couldn't get up.

The footsteps got louder and louder, and her bedroom door opened.

The shadow from this figure was dark. So dark, Sasha couldn't see the person's face.

The doorbell was still ringing, and someone was yelling. "Sasha, Sasha, you better get out of there!"

She tried to get up, tried to move, and still couldn't. She realized that a body was holding her down. Montel's dead body.

She looked up as a woman with a knife stood over her, blood dripping from the knife.

"Aaahh!" Sasha screamed, kicked, but still couldn't move.

Then the face became clear. It was Tammy.

* * *

Sasha woke up to the knocking on her door, sweat pouring from her forehead.

"Sash, she's going to have the baby!" Raymond yelled.

Sasha rushed out of her bed. It was three in the morning. She could hear the sirens from the ambulance.

"Sasha, she doesn't look too good. She's bleeding. I called the ambulance, and Tasha said she can't breathe."

Sasha rushed downstairs and threw her robe on. She opened the door. "Where is she, Raymond? Where is she?"

"Upstairs."

Raymond pulled her arm and dragged her upstairs.

Sasha yelled, "Tasha, honey, breathe. You have to breathe."

A hyperventilating Tasha was turning blue. She needed oxygen.

Sasha found an empty Burger King bag on the floor and told her to breathe through it. "How long has she been like this? Have you been counting the contractions?"

"Yeah, they're like seven, maybe eight minutes apart," Raymond shouted.

Tasha looked very puffy in the face, and her ankles were swollen.

"Okay. Looks like she has pre-eclampsia."

"Eclamp-who?" Raymond questioned.

"High blood pressure. It isn't good for her or the baby. Tasha, I need you to keep breathing slowly into this bag. You're going to be okay. I can hear the ambulance."

A squad car got to her house before the ambulance.

Sasha ran into her house to put on some clothes to go with Raymond and Tasha to the hospital.

A frantic Michael came through the door. "Sasha, are you all right?"

Sasha was surprised and terrified all at the same time. "Yeah, it's okay. Tasha's in labor." She tried to steer him away from the bedroom, so he couldn't see who was lying in the bed, but wasn't fast enough.

Michael could see the trail of men's clothes on the floor, leading to Montel's yellow back. He didn't say a word. He just looked at her with disgust, like he wished he didn't even know her name.

Raymond yelled, "She's getting worse, Sasha."

She grabbed her black medical bag engraved *Dr. S. Freeman*, a graduation gift from her Aunt Mimi, and ran to Tasha. She took her blood pressure. It was 200/100. She definitely was pre-eclamptic.

When the ambulance came, Sasha explained the situation, and they proceeded to give her oxygen.

Sasha tried to reassure Raymond that everything was going to be okay. "Just stay with her, Raymond," she said when the ambulance door closed. "I'm right behind you."

She turned and Michael was still there. He looked at her, but said nothing. She didn't say anything either. What could she say? Michael now saw all of her, even her darkest side.

"I have to follow the ambulance," she said in a monotone voice.

"You have to do what you have to do."

Sasha went inside her house and quickly threw on a sweat suit and grabbed her keys.

Montel was up and at the door. "Is everything all right? You need me to go to the hospital with you?"

Michael said, "Don't you have a wife, no, excuse me, a family to go home to?"

Montel looked at Michael, Michael looked at Montel in a nose-to-nose, chest-to-chest stand-off.

She looked at both of them. One who brought her so much joy and, at the same time, so much pain. The other who only wanted to make her happy, and protect her from harm, even if that harm was self-inflicted. Sasha couldn't choose sides, fearing neither side was right at that time.

Montel and Michael walked around each other, still saying nothing. Montel, who was now on the outside of the door, backed off and left Michael standing beside her. He smiled. "Call me later, Sash, and let me know if everything is all right."

Michael said with fire in his voice, "Good night," and waved goodbye to Montel.

Michael turned to Sasha and still said nothing. She eased by him and locked the door. She tried to walk away before he got the chance to say anything to her.

"So this is what you want? Him? It has always been him?"

Sasha started crying. "Michael, I don't know what I want. Can't you see I'm torn and confused right now?"

"Ms. Freeman, you don't want to know what I see."

Sasha turned and got into her car and drove off. She stopped crying on the way to the hospital. She kept saying to herself, "It isn't my fault. It isn't my fault."

Meanwhile, on the other side of town, Michelle, eight months pregnant, paced her kitchen back and forth. She wasn't trying to let her husband's newest antics upset her, but she just couldn't get over the balls he had.

Jamal had told her that he needed some space, and that her HIV condition with a baby on the way was stressing him out. He needed some alone time, so he was going to stay at his brother's house for a few days.

Michelle sympathized with him at first, but then wanted to spit nails at the thought of her selfish husband. Her hormones made her mood unstable, and she found herself happy, angry, or sad. There was no in-between. She was terrified because she didn't know if the medication she was taking was going to protect her unborn child from contracting HIV, or whether she'd be around when her kids grew up. She was the one who needed a break, not this asshole who she thought about killing almost every other day.

Angry as she was, she went over to Jamal's brother's house that same night, wanting to set things straight with her bull-shit husband.

His brother Tony came to the door with a surprised look on his face. "Hey, Michelle. What are you doing here?"

"Where's Jamal?"

"I dunno." Tony shrugged his shoulders, clearly lying.

Michelle pushed past him and made her way to Tony's base-ment, where she knew Jamal stayed from time to time. She could smell the reefer coming from the basement and could hear Marvin Gaye's "Sexual Healing" playing. She just knew what she was about to walk in on.

She yelled, "Jamal!"

"Michelle?" Jamal's voice heightened. "Wait. I'm not dressed."

How many times have I seen your naked ass? Michelle ignored her husband's silly request and pushed the closed but unlocked door.

"Oh shit!" Tammy hid her face under the covers, as if Michelle didn't see her.

Jamal blew out a cloud of smoke. "I can explain."

Michelle put up her hand. "Fuck you and your tired excuses. You needed some alone time. Well, that's exactly what you can have. Don't bother coming home, you spineless muthafucka." A hormonal Michelle stormed off but stopped herself and turned back around and said to Tammy, "Oh and, you under the covers, I hope you made Jamal strap up because he's got HIV."

"What?" Tammy jumped up from under the covers and started cussing. She instantly jumped on Jamal, swinging her arms. She was like a wild hyena.

Michelle grabbed Tammy by her long blond hair and wres-tled her to the ground. She directed all her hurt and anger and beat it out of Tammy. "Get off him, you lousy bitch!" Michelle straddled her naked body, all two hundred and fifteen pregnant pounds of her, and gripped Tammy's hair tight and punched away like a title contender, drawing blood from Tammy's nose and mouth.

When Jamal got a possessed Michelle off Tammy, he said, "Baby, chill. You need to calm down."

Michelle broke free of Jamal. She turned around and punched him then grabbed his exposed penis. "I'm gong to rip that poisonous son of a bitch off."

Jamal hunched over in agony. For a second, he was sorry for all he had done and afraid he'd turned his wife crazy. He barely could speak through the pain. "Michelle, please," he said, gritting his teeth, but she wasn't letting go.

"Oh no!" Michelle shouted in fear, as fluid dripped down her leg. "My water just broke." She snapped back to reality, leaving her rage at the door and releasing her husband's jewels. "Get dressed, and take me to the hospital NOW! I'm going to have the baby." She was so afraid.

"Oh Lord, it's too early. Oh NO!" Rage came back as she heard Tammy crying in pain and shame on the floor and still bleeding from her attack.

Jamal got dressed and grabbed Michelle by the arm. "Let's go, baby."

Michelle turned around and looked at her husband's pathetic excuse for a mistress and said, "You're lucky my water broke, bitch!" and kicked her in the stomach.

"Aaaaaah!" Tammy cried in agony as she curled up in a fetal position.

Jamal pulled at his mistress-beating wife.

"Don't pull me, muthafucka." She pursed her lips and tried to breathe the way she'd been taught at her Lamaze classes. "Lord, please let the baby be okay."

By the time Sasha got to the hospital, Tasha was on the operating table. She found Raymond hunched over, his hands buried in his face. She sat next to him and lay her head on his shoulder.

Raymond began to cry. "She has got to make it. She has to."

After sitting in the waiting room for an hour. The doctor came out and congratulated Raymond on a healthy baby boy.

Raymond jumped up. "What about Tasha?"

Dr. Walters smiled. "Everything is all right. Is this your sister?"

"Yeah, this is li'l Ray's auntie, Sasha."

Sasha wiped her tears of joy. "You already have a name for him?"

The doctor patted Sasha on the back. "They wouldn't have made it without your fast thinking."

"I'm just glad to see everything is all right. Thank you, Dr. . . . ?"

"Dr. Walters."

Sasha went home to get some items for Tasha. She had a few messages on her phone. The most important one was from T, telling her that Michelle had gone into labor and delivered a girl. Sasha had to sit down. All this in one night. It was too much for her to grasp.

On her way back to the hospital, she stopped by Boston General, where Michelle had delivered, to check out this new addition to her family. Lisa and T were already there, arguing about who'd be the godmother.

"Damn, can I know the little one's name first?" Sasha busted in.

"Sasha, where have you been?" Lisa demanded.

"Long story. Didn't come here to talk about me. Let me hold my new godchild."

Sasha made the goo-goo and ga-ga noises at the precious little thing.

"Michelle, honey, you look worn out. Where is Jamal?" Sasha asked.

"Probably with his girlfriend."

Silence entered the room.

"Excuse me, his what?"

Michelle took a breath. "I was due two weeks from now, but that asshole made me go into labor."

"What happened?" Sasha asked.

Michelle went on to tell them how she'd found Jamal in bed with Tammy and how she beat her ass.

Their mouths dropped, then they started laughing.

T said, "Chelle, why are you even with this fool?"

"Lord only knows, T, Lord only knows."

"You know what you need to do," T told her.

"I know, but I feel like, who else is going to want me?"

Sasha said, "My Aunt Mimi told me you don't know what is in front of you until you open your eyes and, Michelle, you've had your blinders on for years."

"I know."

"Well, if you know, then why can't you dig your head out of the snow and stop this madness?"

"I will some day, ladies, I will. I just don't know when."

"How about now?" T asked.

Michelle took a hard look in the mirror, a real good look, like she never saw herself before. "I always thought 'til death do us part, but do I really want to die like this?"

Sasha told her, "Only you know the answer to that, Michelle. You think you'll lose something, when you're the one who will be found."

They hugged for a little bit.

Lisa told everyone about Damon and her moving in together, and Sasha told them about Raymond and Tasha. She also told them about her drama.

Raised eyebrows, but no surprised looks came across their faces. They had all been there, going back to those they should've left behind.

T began to tell them about her drama. "Ricky's wife is trying to hold on. She still hasn't signed the divorce papers."

Lisa added, "That is if Ricky even filed them."

A bunch of, "Hmms," and grunts took over the room.

"Don't go there with me," T said. "I will be the first to admit that I didn't think things would go this way with Ricky and I, but hey, love is something you can't help. Now Ricky and her are through. He realized he'd made a mistake and it's time to correct it."

"How can you be this forward about it, T?" Michelle asked. "Do I have to remind you of the damage you've done? Look at Jamal and me. You want to be that self-serving bitch?"

"Too late for that," Sasha said.

T put her hands on her hip and began to break it down for them as to why Ricky and her were the right thing. "Look, first off, Ricky got with her when he was supposed to be marrying me. She was a rebound. She had no business with him in the first place. After years of living with this woman, he realized where he went wrong and who he should be with. Me. We've had a dozen conversations about this. Ricky knows what I want from him, and he's prepared to give it to me. I'm giving him a second chance, and so far, things have worked out. He lives in my suite at the hotel, and his wife lives in an apartment on Beacon Street. They don't even share the same space anymore. If you really look at it, I'm doing Ricky's wife a favor. She would have set herself up for a lifetime of pain and disappointment by staying married to him. I'm the woman for him, not her, and he's made that painfully obvious to her."

"How so, T?" Sasha asked.

"For one, he doesn't live there. Two, he spends all his time with me. Three, when he does go by their house to pick things up, I'm either with him, or I call him to make sure he's on his way to my place."

"So she knows about you?" Lisa asked.

"Trust me, she knows. If she doesn't, shame on her."

"Well, I guess you've made up your mind. Are you making plans for a wedding again?" Sasha asked.

"Hell no! I've come to realize that marriage isn't a part of me. I was just trying to follow along with every other normal couple. The truth is, we can be together and love each other without some marriage certificate."

"I see. So you two are going to be together forever, with no bands?" Michelle questioned.

"Look, I don't need a ceremony to validate our relationship. We love each other, and we know how to make it work with us."

"I see. Well, I guess your only obstacle is the divorce then," Sasha said.

"Happily ever after, huh?" Lisa added.

"Yeah, just don't marry him, and you two will be fine," Michelle said.

T's attitude shifted. "See, that's why I can't tell you anything, Michelle. The way I live my life has nothing to do with Jamal and you. Frankly, Jamal and Ricky are two different people with two different circumstances."

"Yeah, right. Ricky dogged you out while y'all were dating. You even admitted that you knew he saw other women," Michelle reminded her.

"Okay. We were like, what, eighteen, nineteen?"

Sasha said, "No, T. You said you knew the type of man Ricky was and you were happy with him as long as that shit didn't creep up on your front door."

"I said that? Well, that was then, this is now. Ricky and I are older, more mature, and know what we want from each other."

Sasha said, "Well, look, T's mind is made up, so nothing we say or do will convince her otherwise. My question to you, T, is, What do you think about my situation with Montel?"

"Honestly, honey, I think you should've left him alone a very long time ago. You're messing up. I understand that he's married and is in that situation because of a child. I know you think if there were no baby you and he would still be together. The fact of the matter is, Montel has never been persuaded to do anything. He looks out for himself. I still don't think he married her because of a baby. There's more to that story. If he's trying to be such a family man, then why is he knocking down your front door every chance he gets? As for Michael, he's a decent brother, but if you're not feeling him, you just aren't feeling him. Don't waste your time on him like I did with Linc. In the end, someone gets hurt, and you end up feeling worse."

Sasha took in T's advice. She still was going to make her own decision, but needed another's point of view. She didn't know how she felt about Michael. He was always there for her, and would do anything for her. She messed up with him, that was for sure. She didn't know why, though. She always complained about men being dogs and there being no good men around, and the first real man she got, she treated him so bad. Maybe she just didn't deserve a good man.

Anyways, she cut her thoughts off and changed the subject. "So, Michelle, what are you going to name this little one? Sasha maybe?"

Michelle laughed. "The doctors told me that, since I took the medications during my entire pregnancy, there's only a two to five percent chance she'll be infected, and that her HIV test isn't going to come back for at least three weeks."

Shouts of glee bounced out of their voices.

"I'm so happy and thankful that her weakness and lack of sense for staying with Jamal hasn't affected her children. This little one represents hope that everything is going to be okay. Yeah, Hope, that'll be her name. Hope Janeya."

They each held Hope in their hands and made silly faces.

Sasha was so happy that things turned out good for Michelle and the baby. She just hoped that their conversation had given her the strength to let that lowlife Jamal go.

Back at home, Sasha gathered her thoughts and tried to get her life together, making a list of all the goals she had for the new year. First on her list was to find a job or career, whichever came first. She hadn't decided what she wanted to do.

When Tasha went into labor like that, everything came back to her, like riding a bike, but she still didn't have a passion for that kind of work, still didn't have that fever. She thought of how she enjoyed teaching and how she loved to bring joy to people's lives. She just had to figure out a lucrative career that would allow her to do that, one that she would be happy in.

Her professional woes switched, and she began to think of her personal problems. How could she have allowed herself to become so vulnerable? She hurt Michael, and she hurt herself. Where did her rules go? Where did her stability go? She thought about how she threw everything away for Montel, how she had jeopardized everything. For what? Montel was still married, and she was still alone.

After hours of pondering her mistakes, she built up enough courage to call him. She left a message on his voicemail: "Montel, it's me. What happened tonight was a huge mistake, one that I will forever regret. Tonight I realized how much hurt and pain loving you has caused, and I just can't do it any more. I can't see you any more. As long as you're married, there's no chance of us, so please hear me when I say this—Good-bye."

CHAPTER TWENTY-FOUR

Christmas rolled around, and Sasha hadn't heard from Montel or Michael. New Year's Eve came around and still nothing, so she ended up spending the holidays with family. She hadn't seen either of them since the night little Raymond was born.

Valentine's Day crept up on her, and still neither one had called her. In fact, months went by, and still no calls from either Montel or Michael.

She was helping out Tasha with the baby because, when it came to babies, she was clueless. Tasha started wedding plans for them of course. She was so excited.

Sasha had made some New Year's resolutions, of course, that she wanted to stick by—start her own business, lose like ten pounds, and get over Montel—but not a day went by that she didn't think about him. Every lonely night she reminisced on what they had.

She thought about how she'd hurt Michael and wished he was still around. Nonetheless, she hadn't been serviced in three months, and her well was running dry.

Sasha spent all her time trying to figure out how to start her new business. She figured out that during those Lamaze classes, she really enjoyed the teaching and positive responses. Her classes started to fill up, and before she knew it, instead of four times a week, she was teaching classes six times a week, with all the positive responses from mothers who had given birth and referred her to friends and family.

One woman wrote Sasha a thank you card: *Sasha, I just want to say thank you so much. My labor was twenty-three hours and you would think my pain was unbearable. I did the relaxation techniques you taught us, and it was like I was in a trance. My mind, body, and soul felt like they were one and the pain was shut out. I'm not saying there wasn't any pain, but your relaxation methods got me through it. I hope I didn't write too much. Thank you again. Lena Richards. P.S. You should really think about broadening your classes. They would benefit so many women.*

With that note, the inspiration came.

T helped her a lot, since she was a successful business-woman. She was so excited for Sasha, and so proud too.

Sasha created her own web page and made some business cards. And with the good referrals from her former colleagues at Boston General, she was on a roll.

At first it started off slow. Then after three months the volume picked up. Her classes fit ten couples, three hundred bucks a pop, two nights a week for four weeks of training. Her business started booming when she put the thank-you letters people sent her on the web and in the newspaper. She was booked through June. If business continued this way, she'd need to lease out a building to teach the class, instead of using the YMCA, which a friend of a friend let her use.

Financially, things were looking up. It wasn't a physician's salary, but it was something to pay the bills and leave her plenty to spare. She cut down her living expenses, sold her BMW, did a few yard sales, and pawned some unnecessary jewelry.

She was happier than she'd ever been, even though she didn't have a man in her life. She met a fella here and there but nothing that led to more than one phone call. Sasha was getting used to the idea that she might end up alone. She had to learn how to cope if she was going to make it. She got so tired of hearing family and even strangers say, "A pretty girl like you should have a man in her life. Where's all the romance, Sasha? Where's your man?"

Damn it, people, I don't have one. It's not my fault that men are dickheads.

For instance, she went to the movies alone, something she never did. After the movies, she walked down Newbury Street to window shop and passed some guy leaning on a silver 2002 Lexus GS400 with tinted windows.

He stopped Sasha. "Hey. How you doing?"

"Fine."

They proceeded to talk and exchanged numbers. The next day he called with the when-you-coming-over routine.

First off, she couldn't stand a man whose first words were, "When you coming over?" To her, that meant, "When you letting me hit that?" So from there, Sasha knew what Sean was after. She contemplated it though, seeing that she hadn't been serviced in a while.

Finally, after two weeks of conversation, she met him on Michelle's street, not wanting him to know where she lived. He could be another psycho, like Jason.

She parked her car, jumped in his, and they drove off. To her surprise they went to pick up his friend.

Sasha thought to herself, *Is this a date?*

His friend jumped in the car, and Sean introduced them to each other.

As they were driving down Washington Street, Earl asked Sasha, "Do you smoke weed?"

Sasha said, "Occasionally, and this could be one of those oc-casions."

They went to Malcolm X Park, smoked two blizzes, and talked for a while. Sasha felt like she was hanging out with her girls. It was good because she didn't feel the pressures of dating, but at her age she was used to the royal treatment, not this high-school shit.

As she thought about it, high school times were so much simpler. The dude you wanted to talk to was a couple of classrooms over, and seeing him in the hall was like heaven. And at lunchtime you could always put on a show, just in case he was watching. You would ride the train to the movies, play video games at his house, smoke trees together, chill, and try to explore each other's body. Damn, she missed those days. Things were just too complicated now.

Anyways, Sasha got hungry, so she asked Sean could they go get something to eat. Sasha asked Sean, not Earl. It was time for Earl to go home.

When they got in the car, Sean had the nerve to ask Earl what he was going to do.

Earl said, "I don't know. I'm kind of hungry too."

"Sean, let's go get something to eat. Where you live, Earl?" If Sean didn't get that hint, she might just have to be blunt.

Sean dropped Earl off at his house, and they went to Boston House of Pizza.

While ordering, Sean's pager went off. "I'd be right back."

Sean was still on the phone, so Sasha paid the $17.98 for the food. She sat down started to eat.

After about a good fifteen minutes, Sean came back into the shop. "Oh damn! The food is ready. Let's go."

Sasha was eating, stuffing her face. She looked at him like he was crazy.

"How much did the food come up to?"

"Seventeen ninety-eight. I've just started eating. Why don't you sit down and join me?"

Sean was still persistent, like he had to be somewhere. "Nah, I'd rather eat mines on the way."

The way where? "Who were you talking to all that time?"

"Oh, it was my little sister's birthday."

Please, the smile that man had on his face when he came back from the phone was no smile from talking to a sibling. It was a smile that he was getting up with someone else tonight. She brushed off his lie and continued to eat her food.

"Well, I'll be in the car."

Sasha was so disgusted, she lost her appetite, but she stayed in the pizza shop, just for spite. *See, this is why I don't even deal with dudes the same age as me. They're so immature.* How rude was this dude to leave her alone twice in the pizza shop after she paid for their food? This night was over.

After spending another fifteen minutes or so in the pizza shop, she went outside and got in Sean's Lexus, not saying a word.

"You wanna chill at my crib?"

"Negative. And bring me to my car."

He was silent for a minute.

"Why are you silent all of a sudden? I know you aren't sweating me over any punk eighteen dollars."

Nigga, please. Do you see these shoes I am wearing? Prada? Do you see the matching bag, one and a half platinum diamond earrings, and Movado watch with diamonds bezels on me? Do I look like I'm worried about eighteen punk dollars? Hell, I could buy a nigga if I wanted to. Sasha said nothing though, thinking the silence would kill him even more.

Sean just kept sighing all the way to Michelle's house. When he pulled up to her car, he said, "Yo, if it's the money you're worried about, I got you."

I haven't been worried about such a small debt since I used to spot one of my girls for a forty ounce of Olde English and three bottles of Boone's Farm. Sasha quietly got out of his car.

"Damn! Is it like that? What you going to do tonight? You want to come to my house?"

I can't even fathom the idea of your cheap-ass, no-class, low-life dick in me. She said nothing, got in her car, slammed the door, and started her engine.

As she peeled off, he had the nerve to say, "Thanks for dinner."

If she had a bottle, she would have thrown it. Sasha just counted her blessings that she didn't have to deal with this shit on a regular basis any more. To her, it seemed like men just didn't know what she wanted. They didn't have the *je ne sais quoi* quality she was looking for. Who was she kidding? None of them could hold a candle to Montel, her standard for all men. To date anything less would be a crime.

It was Saturday. In two weeks Raymond and Tasha would be getting married. Sasha was happy for Raymond, and scared for him at the same time. She didn't trust Tasha ever since that night she heard her on the phone with some no-name person. She'd kept that to herself though, not wanting Raymond to think she was jealous or envious of his relationship. If Tasha was doing wrong, she'd be found out, one way or another. More and more, to Sasha, it seemed like she was all about the money.

Sasha and Raymond had fronted the bill for this wedding. Tasha's father was supposed to chip in, but they were still waiting for that check. Sasha knew one thing—If that check didn't come, there'd be no photographer or video man. It would just be her with her disposable camera and camcorder.

It was a small wedding though, about a hundred guests, and the cost was under five thousand, so it wasn't that bad. Through these months, Sasha had learned how to budget, and this was definitely going to be a low-budget shotgun wedding.

Tasha asked her to pick up her dress because she was busy doing little last-minute things.

Sasha faked like she liked her, waiting for her slip-up, because liars always do. She should have felt bad about her feelings towards Tasha, but she didn't. Maybe she was jealous and envious. Maybe if she was planning her own wedding, she wouldn't be so harsh.

Sasha picked up Tasha's dress at David's Bridal in Dedham.

She hadn't been out there in a while. She and Montel used to go to the movies out there, shop, and then eat.

As memories crept up on her, she wandered into the restaurant Montel used to take her to for brunch on Saturdays. She missed him, but would never tell him that. She sat down by herself and ordered.

Feeling empty, she left the restaurant. On her way to the car, she heard someone shouting her name. She didn't want to turn around. She knew the voice.

Montel came up on her like a speeding car. "Sasha, you didn't hear me calling you? Yeah, you did. What's up? How have you been?"

"I'm fine, and yourself?"

"Doing good, real good. I miss you."

Oh here we go. She had to fight her emotions, try to stick by everything she'd been saying. She couldn't though. So happy to see him, she was dancing inside and didn't want to let him go. "Who you out here with? Your wife?"

Montel shook his head. "No, I'm just chilling, enjoying this nice spring day. What about yourself?"

"I'm picking up Tasha's dress. Raymond and her are getting married."

"Oh really? They in love?"

"They appear to be."

Montel's face turned serious. "Well, I hope so, because a marriage without love is doomed."

Sasha felt he wanted her to go deeper into his comment, but she didn't. She herself wanted to know what he meant by that, but she left it alone. "Well, nice seeing you." She proceeded to walk away.

He grabbed her arm. "Can I call you some time?"

Sasha wanted so bad to say sure. "Call me for what? Our lives are in two different directions. The past is the past. Let's just leave it at that."

Sasha couldn't get out of there fast enough. She felt like crying but managed to hold back the tears.

Sasha reached home to find a series of messages on her answering machine: Lisa left her a message to go see Michelle; T left her a message saying it was important that they talk; a few sign-ups for her Lamaze class; Aunt Mimi wanted to go over last-minute preparations for the wedding; and finally, a message from Tasha asking if Sasha could watch little Raymond for her because she needed to go over a few things with her cousin for the wedding.

Sasha called Raymond, who was upstairs with the baby, and told him she would baby-sit so he could go to work and Tasha could do whatever. Sasha was about to go upstairs when something dawned on her. She looked at her caller ID again, Sean Moss. Sean's number was on her caller ID, 617-555-3876. She never gave that boy her number. He only had her cell phone number. Could he have been the one calling and hanging up?

She sat and thought things out. The last number on her caller ID was his. The last message on her answering machine was from Tasha, same time. Her imagination started running wild.

She decided to call Sean.

A girl's voice picked up. It sounded like Tasha, but she wasn't sure.

Can't make accusations if I'm not sure. Sasha tried to disguise her voice and began, "Who is this? Is Sean there?"

"No! Who the fuck is this calling my man?"

That was Tasha for sure. Sasha decided to play along. "Where's Sean? This is Lisa."

"Lisa who?"

"Lisa who wants to speak to Sean."

"Whatever. Don't be calling here for my man, bitch!" Tasha hung up.

Sasha called back, blocking her number.

Tasha yelled out, "Fuck you, bitch!" and hung up again.

Finally, after Sasha had called back like five times, Sean answered the phone, "Who is this?"

"What's up, Sean? This is Sasha."

"I thought you weren't going to call me any more."

Sasha could hear Tasha yelling in the background. "I changed my mind, but I guess I should've kept it simple because I see you are with the next chick."

"Well, you were acting funky about your loot, so I left it at that."

"I see. Can you do me a favor, Sean?"

"What?"

"Put Tasha on the phone. Tell her it's Sasha Freeman, Raymond's sister. She'll know."

Sean shut up like he knew Raymond and the whole situation.

Tasha jumped on the phone, still thinking Sasha was the other woman.

"Tasha, do you know who this is?"

"Yeah, the bitch that keeps calling my man."

"No, honey, this is your soon-to-be sister-in-law, Sasha. I just have one question for you—Are you coming to get your things, or should Raymond throw them out?"

Tasha hung up.

Sasha called Raymond down right away and told him what happened.

Of course, he didn't believe her, so she had him call the number. No answer. She figured as much.

"Call her cousin, see if she's there."

No answer there either.

Sasha tried to convince Raymond, but he wouldn't hear it. He kept asking, "Are you sure it was her?"

If only she knew where Sean lived, they could go over there. She recalled Sean saying something about Maywood Street in one of their conversations. She didn't know the house, but she knew where the street was. If Tasha's car was parked out front, then Raymond would know.

Raymond called into work sick, and they dropped off the baby at Aunt Mimi's house.

"What's going on?" Aunt Mimi asked.

"I'll tell you later," Sasha said.

When they reached Maywood Street, Tasha's car wasn't parked on the street, but her cousin's was.

"See, her cousin is probably over there, and they were just fooling with you, you know how you girls do."

Sasha shook her head. "I know what I'm talking about."

Raymond was ready to go, but Sasha wasn't. They argued for ten minutes. Then, just as they were about to pull off, Tasha came out, got into her cousin's car, and drove off.

Sasha asked Raymond, "Do you want to go inside?"

"Hell yeah!"

Sean answered his bell, not looking the least bit surprised. He said with a smirk, "Your girl just left."

Raymond balled his fist.

"Are you seeing Tasha, Sean?"

"Yeah, I been seeing her for a minute. Yo, money, if you ask me, she is just a trick-ass bitch, no one to fight over."

Raymond's was ready to crush Sean into little pieces, and his face was on fire.

Sasha pulled his elbow. "Let it go, Raymond."

"Hey, Sasha, call me some time."

"I don't think so."

Raymond was silent on the way home. He'd tricked around with so many women, it was ironic his love would trick on him.

"Raymond, I know how you feel. Trust me, I been there. It takes time. Just don't do anything crazy."

Raymond huffed. "Crazy? You haven't seen crazy. Pass me your phone." He called Aunt Mimi and asked her to watch the baby for a little while longer.

Sasha called the locksmith to change some locks.

When they got home, Tasha still wasn't there. Sasha helped Raymond pack up her things as the locksmith changed the locks.

The phone rang, and Raymond answered. It was Tasha. He was calm at first, then all of a sudden, he started wailing on her.

Sasha could hear her cursing through the phone, so she started yelling, "The locks are changed, you trifling bitch. Don't bother coming by to pick up your things 'cause I'm going to drop them off at your cousin."

Tasha was stilling yelling and cursing through the phone.

"Little Raymond ain't your concern right now. I've parked him at my aunt's house, and he's going to stay there until this drama me and you got dies down."

Tasha didn't sound like she was going for that and yelled some more.

Raymond hung up on her, looking even more upset than when he'd picked up the phone.

"Raymond, what's wrong?"

"That chick had the nerve to tell me little Raymond isn't mine. What kind of shit is that? You get caught up, and then try to throw more salt to the wound. She's sick. Fuck her! That baby is mine."

Sasha tried to reason with him, but he wouldn't listen. She tried to convince him to let her drop off Tasha's stuff, but he wanted to go by himself.

"Raymond, please don't do anything stupid."

"Okay."

Even though he'd promised not to do anything stupid, Sasha was still worried.

As soon as he left, she called the only person who could help her, Michael. It had been months since they'd spoken. She thought time would heal some of that, or so she hoped anyway.

She got his answering machine. "Michael, this is Sasha. I know we haven't spoken since, well, you know . . . I'm not calling for me, though, I'm calling for Raymond. He just found out some disturbing things about Tasha, and he's dropping her stuff off at her cousin's house. He wouldn't let me go with him, so I was wondering if—Oh never mind, I can't keep running to you with my problems. Sorry. Forget it. Just erase this message."

Hours went by and no word from Raymond.

The phone rang. Sasha was hoping it was Raymond with good news, but it wasn't. It was Montel with old news.

Sasha asked, "Why are you calling?"

"You know."

"Don't play games, Montel. What do you want? I thought we settled this."

"You told me not to call you unless I wasn't married, so I'm calling you."

There was a long moment of silence.

"Montel, what are you saying?"

"I'm out, I'm done. Jennifer and I are divorced. I tried to make it work, but it just isn't. I needed a friend to talk to. Aren't we still friends?"

Sasha thought for a moment. "Yeah, we're still friends." She bounced back on her sofa, like weights had been lifted off her feet.

Montel asked about Raymond and Tasha. She went into detail, as if they'd never stopped talking.

As they made small talk, she hoped that this time would be different, that they could be together finally. All her doubts stayed present, as well as her fears. She knew, though, that if she never got the chance to see what they were really made of she would never know if he really was the one, so Sasha kept on talking and hoping.

CHAPTER TWENTY-FIVE

Once again, Sasha and Montel were back on. The first week, dinner and a movie. The second week, dinner and a movie at her place. The third week, Montel was back in her bed for the third time around. They spent all possible time together. They were doing their love thing. He helped her out with some business ideas.

On nights that he would stay at her place, he would get up early in the morning to take his son to day care. Sasha never once complained about that. If anything, she encouraged him to do right by his son. Since he was still a baby, it was easier and Montel didn't have to explain now. She looked forward to meeting his son one day, whenever Montel was ready. Sasha planned to be in Montel's life forever, so that meant loving his son as much as she could and didn't have a problem with that at all.

Sometimes, Sasha thought about Jennifer and what she was going through. It dawned on her that she'd slept with him when she knew he was with her. Sasha didn't have much sympathy for her after that. She didn't seem like that type of woman though, the sneaky kind of woman who will get what she wants, when she wants, no matter who gets hurt. That kind of woman didn't

fit the person she met in Jennifer. Nonetheless, Sasha didn't
let her marital woes stop her from being happy. She was on
cloud ninety-nine. Montel and her were in love, and loving
every moment of it.

At the end of July, Sasha and Montel wanted to take a trip
together to Hawaii during a one-week break between Lamaze
classes. Montel planned the trip down to the very last detail.
When he showed her the brochure, she was impressed. Things
were going good in her life. Too good. She held on to whatever happiness she had because who knew when this would
stop and when, or if happiness like this would ever return to
her door? She tried not to be snowed under Montel's spell, but
it was so easy. Loving him was too easy.

Sasha's phone rang. She answered another hang up. This
was like the fifth hang up for the week. She'd been having hang
ups like this for a month now. She thought it was Tasha, or Sean,
since he had her number now, but when she thought about it,
these hang ups started before that shit went down with Tasha.
If this continued, she would have to change her number.

Speaking of Tasha, Raymond still wouldn't agree to a blood
test. As far as he was concerned, little Raymond was his son.
Sasha tried to talk some sense in him, but he wouldn't listen.
Tasha was going to take him to the cleaners on child support.
Raymond worked two jobs, and under the court's eyes, lived
rent-free, and had trouble with the law. The court would
gladly grant Tasha full custody and give her half of Raymond's
paycheck. Sasha tried explaining that to Raymond, but he said
he was going to do right by his son, even if that meant dealing
with Tasha. So Tasha's money-hungry ass put in a request to
garnish Raymond's wages for a child he wasn't even sure was
his. Sasha wanted to wring her neck and would have, if Raymond didn't personally ask her to stay out of it. He was his
own man and would take care of his affairs. Sasha didn't know
what got into him. She planned to go over this one more time,
because he couldn't be serious about this shit, no way, no how.

Her phone rang again.

"Girl, where have you been?" Michelle said. "I've been leaving message after message for weeks."

"I tried to reach you too, but you're never home. No one comes by to see me. What's up?"

"I need you to come by my house. We need to talk pronto."

"All right, I just have to make a few calls. I'll be over in a minute."

Sasha made it to Michelle's house in like half an hour. She met her sitting on her porch drinking a cup of lemonade.

Sasha hugged her and said, "What up, girlfriend? Long time no see."

"Yeah, you've been missing in action for a while now."

"I haven't been avoiding anyone. I just was keeping to myself, that's all."

"Who are you kidding, Sasha? I know what's going on."

Damn it! I was going to get around to telling you guys about Montel. I just didn't know how.

"You feel left out because you're the only one without a man?" Michelle said, catching Sasha off guard.

"We're still your girls, Sasha. Just because we have men doesn't mean we can't spend time with you and kick it like we used to."

You are so way off base. Little do you know my love life is better than it could ever be. Sasha just nodded her head and went along with whatever she thought was the reason she hadn't been around much. The real reason was, between Raymond's drama, her new business, and Montel, she just didn't have the time to shoot the breeze.

"I called you over here for two reasons. One was to tell you that I miss you, and I'm sure Lisa and T do too. The other reason was, I need your cousin Tanya's number, so she can hook me up with a good lawyer."

"Lawyer?"

"Oh, so you don't know? Jamal and I are getting a divorce."

Sasha was shocked and gleeful at the same time. "A divorce? What happened?"

Michelle shook her head. "What didn't happen?" She laughed a bit, but it wasn't a cheerful laugh. It was a sad one. She began to tell Sasha her story. "After all this time I've been with Jamal, and all the drama he brought my way, I never thought he would bring it to our home. I never thought he would bring it to my children. Jamal doesn't respect himself, so he can't possibly respect anyone else."

Michelle was feeling so good from her three-day spa weekend with her mother that she decided to cut her trip early one day. She'd left Jamal with the kids and checked on them almost every hour to make sure they were all right. She was relaxed, refreshed, and renewed already but worried about Jamal's parenting capabilities. She didn't call Jamal to tell him she was coming home, since she wanted to surprise him. And that she did.

Michelle opened her front door and found nothing out of the ordinary.

Jamal greeted her like the perfect husband he pretended to be. "Let me get your coat, baby. Damn, you look good. You should go away more often."

What's gotten into him? "You sure are full of compliments. Where are the kids?"

"They're asleep. Tell me about your trip."

"It was nice. I'll have to make it a regular routine." Michelle made her way down the hallway to check on the kids.

Jamal hurried behind her. "Where are you going? I told you they were sleeping."

"I missed them and want to kiss them. What's your problem?"

He stood in her way. "Oh, well don't wake them. It took me forever to get them all asleep, especially Hope."

Michelle pushed him out of the way. "Now you see what I go through."

He tried to stop her, but there was no use.

She checked on Hope first. She was sound asleep in her crib. Then she made her way into the boys' room, Jamal still on her heels. She went in the boys' room and kissed them on their cheeks. As Michelle was leaving she noticed a shadow that wasn't hers or Jamal's. She jumped back and screamed, thinking it was the boogeyman or something.

"Ssssh! You're going to wake them."

Michelle thought she was being silly, but as she walked out of their room past the closet, she thought she was seeing a ghost. Only, it wasn't a ghost or the boogeyman, just another one of Jamal's whores hiding in their sons' closet. "Son of a bitch."

"Michelle, don't go in there," Jamal said, like he was trying to spare her.

But it was too late, Michelle had already found her. "Who the fuck are you?" Michelle was beyond hot and ready to kill.

The half-naked girl, who looked no older than twenty, dashed out of the closet, the rest of her clothes in her hand. "I'm sorry, I didn't know. He said you guys were separated."

"Get the fuck out!"

The young girl raced out of the house with just her bra and panties on. Lawd only knew how she planned on getting home.

"I can explain." Jamal guarded his loins, thinking crazy Michelle was going to come back.

"It's okay," she said calmly.

Jamal quickly scanned their bedroom to see if there was anything Michelle could use as a weapon to kill him with.

But Michelle was still calm. "It's okay, Jamal. You just do what you do best—Fuck people."

As she walked toward him, and he walked backwards cautiously, afraid of what she was going to do. *Crazy Michelle is back.*

"I've let you fuck me for years, so I'm not mad at you for just being you."

Jamal started to feel relieved, at ease thinking he was going to get by again.

"I'm mad at myself. But not any more." She backed him up in a corner, like the mouse that he was. "You've disrespected me for years and I've let you, but to bring one of your whores to our house while our children are sleeping . . ." Michelle shook her head in disgust.

Jamal flinched as Michelle raised her hand and pointed her finger in his face. "God forgave me for the murderous thoughts that ran through my mind when you told me you had HIV. I doubt I will be forgiven for the murderous thoughts I'll have tonight while you sleep." She poked his temple with her index finger.

"Baby—"

"Shut the fuck up!" Michelle pointed toward the door. "Get your shit and get out!" Michelle's entire body shook with anger.

Jamal slid by her slowly, praying she was going to let him go.

"And don't ever come back, because if you do, you'll regret it for the rest of your life!" Michelle's eyes were filled with pain as she spat her words like venom. That was the last time she ever saw her husband. Love me not, she was free.

"Did you know the girl?" Sasha asked.

"No. Probably some random affair. She had these innocent eyes. Her eyes reminded me of mine when I first met Jamal. Excited, naive, and happy. Now look at my eyes. Tired, weary, and sad. I can only blame myself for letting him get the best of my years, but I won't be taken any more. I have a higher purpose now, and Jamal and I don't have any purpose at all. It took me a long time to realize that I can do bad all by myself. I may end up alone without a man in my life, but when I think about it, I've been doing that for the past ten years. I envy you, Sasha."

"Why? I don't have a man either."

"True, but you do fine without them, and you know that. You left Montel alone, which had to be hard. You chose you over him. That's why I envy you."

Sasha felt like a fake. She didn't want to spoil all of Michelle's empowerment, so she pretended and went along with whatever she was saying.

After their conversation, she was about to leave when Michelle stopped her and told her the second thing she had to talk to her was about T.

"I thought you already told me what you had to say?"

"Oh yeah, I must have snuck something extra in. Have you spoken with T?"

Sasha shook her head. "She left me a message, but every time I call her she's never there."

"You have to find her. I think she's in trouble."

"Why do you say that?"

"Well, a couple of weeks ago Ricky got divorced from his wife."

"Isn't that a good thing?"

"Yeah, it would've been good, if Ricky was doing it for T, but he was doing it for himself."

Sasha was confused.

"Look, Sasha, you need to find T and talk some sense into her before she does something crazy."

As Sasha was leaving, Michelle said, "Oh yeah, I saw Montel the other day."

Sasha turned around and tried to show no interest. "Oh yeah? Where?"

"He was at the supermarket with his wife."

Sasha started to correct Michelle and tell her that they weren't married any more, but she would have to explain how she knew. Since she wasn't in the mood for confession, she brushed it off and went on her mission to find T.

After eight phone messages and some information from T's parents, Sasha found her on Martha's Vineyard, at one of her hotels. Sasha caught the next ferry to the Vineyard to find out what was going on with her friend. She got to the hotel and asked for Tamieka Williams.

The staff looked at her like she was crazy.

"Look, I know she's here. Just tell me where she is, please."

The staff still looked at her like she was speaking French.

"Should I do a room-to-room search for Ms. Williams or what?"

"She doesn't wish to be disturbed," this feminine fellow said to Sasha.

"Oh well, she's going to be disturbed and you are too, if I don't get some satisfaction in this place."

He-she rolled his eyes and pointed to the door for Sasha to leave, but she stood her ground.

He-she said, "Look, let's not have to call security, girlfriend. Just leave quietly, and I will forget this."

"I dare you to call security. I'm not leaving until I talk to Tamieka."

He-she rolled his eyes and sucked his teeth and proceeded to call security.

The other desk clerk stopped him and motioned for Sasha to follow her. She whispered, "You're Sasha, right? T's friend? Just go outside around the back and I'll let you into her room. I was getting worried about her and glad to see you here."

The room was dark, curtains closed, and messy with empty pizza boxes covering the glass coffee table. Sasha still didn't see T. The bathroom door was closed. The room was so quiet, so still.

She opened the bathroom door. A trail of clothes, empty champagne bottles, and a blunt that burned a hole in the bathroom rug led to T's body in a tub full of water. Frantic, Sasha ran up to her to find her entire head submerged. Sasha quickly lifted her head from under the cold water. She was heavy, dead weight. Sasha struggled to get her to the floor and yelled her name, screaming for her to wake up and say she was all right.

Sasha yelled, "Somebody, help me!" She checked her pulse. Weak. She wasn't breathing. Sasha flipped her over to pump water from her lungs, then turned her on her back and began mouth-to-mouth resuscitation. Tears rolled down her face as she tried to revive her and yell for help, at the same time. A million thoughts raced through her head. *How? Why? What did she do to herself?*

By now, no one had heard her cry, and Sasha felt like she'd exhaled a hundred breaths into T's lifeless body. She smacked her face and yelled, "Wake up, wake up! You better wake up, or I will kill you!" Sasha gave her two more breaths, crying the whole time.

Just when all was silent and all was still, Sasha heard choking. T threw up in her face. She was awake, breathing, and in a daze. Sasha lost a liter of tears as she hugged her.

After Sasha got T something to wear, some food, and something to drink, they didn't talk for hours. They sat in the hotel room not saying a word. T turned on the TV and started flipping channels.

By now Sasha was getting annoyed and had a list of questions for her, but didn't know where to start. Sasha knew one thing— She wasn't leaving her alone, and she wasn't leaving without her.

T continued to flip through the channels.

Sasha sipped her tea. "So you want to talk about it or what? I'm not leaving here until we do, so you might as well start explaining yourself."

With an attitude T said, "Talk about what?"

Sasha looked at her like she'd lost it. "I don't know. We can talk about why you are here, and why I found you in your bathroom half dead."

T smirked. "I wasn't half nothing. I don't know what you're talking about. I don't even know why you're here, personally."

"Whatever, T. You can zigzag around the issue all you want, but I need to know what's going on. Where's Ricky?"

T laughed. "Don't know, don't care."

"Well, obviously something is wrong, or you wouldn't be trying to kill yourself."

"What! I don't know what you're talking about."

"So are you trying to tell me that I just didn't find you unconscious in a tub full of water?"

"I must have fell asleep in the tub."

"Yeah, right. You were drunk, high, and out of control. You tried to hurt yourself, didn't you?"

T was silent.

"Should I call Ricky and find out from him what the deal is?"

T let out another laugh. "If you can find him."

"What's that supposed to mean? Did you do something to Ricky?"

"Oh, now you're worried about Ricky?"

"I'm worried about you. Now what happened?"

T let out a long huff. "It's over."

"You tried to kill yourself over some nigga?"

T was silent. She began to roll a blunt.

"Don't you think you've had enough for one day?"

"I've had enough for a lifetime."

"T, what's up?"

T sparked the blunt and began to tell her melancholy story. "Ricky got divorced. I thought, after the divorce, I was going to be with him forever. He put up the front like it was going to be that way. Well, two weeks ago the divorce was finalized. I was jumping up and down, but he was calm and silent. He asked me if I could give him some space, you know, to work out what he was feeling emotionally. I gave him hell, but eventually I saw his point and caved in.

"A week went by and I didn't hear from him. Just when I was about to lose it, he called me at midnight for a booty call. After the deed was done, his pager went off. He checked his message and came back to bed. I asked him who would be paging him so late, and he brushed it off, telling me it was his wife. The next morning he got up real early and told me he had a meeting or something and would call me later. By now I'm feeling real insecure, real insignificant in his life. I started tripping, talking to myself, and trying to make sense of his recent attitude change toward me.

"I picked up the phone to call you and get my head straight.

I looked on the phone's display screen and noticed that Ricky left his pager code on the display box. Now I had his code. I fought trying to check his messages, but I couldn't. I started dialing, something I wished I hadn't done."

T ticked off on her fingers. " 'First saved message: Ricky, baby, where are you? I miss you. Call me when you get home. Jocelyn. The next saved message: Ricky, you know you wrong. Call me when you get in. I have to talk to you about something. Angel. The next saved message: Boo, for real, I don't like the way things are going with us. You haven't called me since your divorce, and I'm trying to see you. I thought it was going to be me and you. Call Daria when you get a chance.' There were like ten saved messages, all from ten different women. Ricky was playing his wife and me the whole time. I thought I knew what he needed. I thought I knew him, all the plans we'd made, all the promises, promises he didn't have to make. I let Linc go, I let my life go, all for him. I just knew it was going to be him and me.

"One girl left some message late last night, the message he said his wife left. LIAR! I was dating a gigolo. I couldn't think. I lost it. I changed the code to his beeper, so he couldn't retrieve any more messages. I paged him to my house several times, but he didn't return one page. The least he could do was face me.

"After not hearing from him, I started tripping. I drank and I drank. I smoked and I smoked. Nothing helped, nothing kept me unfeeling. I tried to call you guys, but I couldn't. I couldn't face the embarrassment, the I-told-you-so. I came out here last week to think and try to sort things out. I don't know what happened to me. I don't know where I went wrong."

Sasha asked, "So where's Ricky now?"

"I don't know."

"Well, he isn't going to get away with this shit, no way, no how. Call him now to my phone."

"Why?"

"Just call him and tell him you have a surprise waiting for him out here. Tell him you've been busy. Don't even act like you're mad."

T paged him.

Surprised, he called back hesitantly, and agreed to meet her there. T sounded so sweet, so loving over the phone, no man could resist.

Two hours later, the desk called and said he was there.

After cleaning up the room, Sasha got something sexy for T to wear, popped open some champagne, threw rose petals on the bed, and prepared a bubble bath. Then she hid in the closet with a tape recorder.

When Ricky entered, T started working her magic, getting him undressed and in the tub. She then tied him to each knob in the tub. Ricky looked so erotic, so vulnerable, and pleased with T's performance. Just when he thought all was good, T slapped him, "illed" on him, and told him what she knew, but he denied it.

She turned on the hair dryer and threatened to throw it in the tub if he didn't tell her the truth. He confessed about all his women, his ex-wife, and his new fiancée, Nyesha.

Sasha thought that last confession would send that hair dryer straight in the tub and shock his butt.

T held on strong, and said with a long breath, "Did you get all that, Sasha?"

Ricky looked confused.

Sasha came out of hiding. "Yup."

T threatened to throw the dryer in the tub as Ricky begged for forgiveness. The man was crying. T let out a vengeful laugh.

Sasha let out a couple of giggles too, but was uneasy because she didn't know if T was going to electrocute him or what.

T looked at Sasha, looked at herself in the mirror, then looked at Ricky.

"This is what you made me do. Know that you brought this on yourself. Look at what you've done to me, reduced me to a murderer."

Ricky begged for his life, crying and pleading that he was so sorry.

T leaned over to drop the dryer in the tub and said in a soft whisper, "But you know what, Ricky? You aren't even worth murdering. Ending your life like this would be too easy for you. You would never know your wrongs, and you would never suffer like you should."

She turned off the hair dryer as Ricky began his many thank-yous and left him in the bathroom. She hugged Sasha and thanked her for being here.

"What do you want to do with the tape?"

"Let's make copies and send them to all the women Ricky knows."

On that note, they searched his pockets and found his little address book. Mostly all of the women's telephone numbers and addresses were in there. His precious Nyesha's was the first address they searched for.

They cleaned up the room, took Ricky's clothes, and threw them out. Then they left, leaving him there with no clothes, no money, and no way to get back to Boston. T put a do not disturb sign on the door and that was that. That would be the last time she'd see Ricky.

As the weeks went by, Sasha spent most of her time with friends, making sure T and Michelle had the support they needed to move past their love hardships. She was happy with Montel. Their trip to Hawaii was on the following Saturday. This was going to be seven days of paradise. Just Montel, the islands, and her, that was all Sasha wanted. She felt kind of guilty though, seeing how mostly everyone around her was so sad, and could only share her joy with Lisa, who she'd told about Montel. No one else knew. She gave Sasha her reservations about him, but still tried to support her decision to continue to see him.

After packing her clothes, she checked on everyone before she left. Raymond had the weekend off and was going to spend time with his son. She stopped trying to win that battle with Raymond. He believed that was his son, and that was the end of it. Tasha, of course, was contented, as long as the checks kept coming. Sasha was disgusted by the whole situation, but she was a firm believer that those who do wrong, get done wrong eventually. So Tasha was gonna get hers eventually, just like Ricky and Jamal got theirs. Sasha wasn't worried. She was too happy to be worried about anything.

Sasha showed her ID to the clerk, who looked her up and proceeded to give Sasha her ticket. She smiled, and Sasha smiled back at her. She was feeling so good that day, feeling on top of the world.

Sasha waited for Montel at the gate. He had agreed to meet her at the airport. Their flight was supposed to leave at ten, and it was already nine-fifteen. No sign of Montel. *He must be running a little late*. Sasha began to read her *Vibe* magazine to pass the time.

Fifteen minutes later, passengers began to board the plan. Still no sign of Montel. Sasha began to get worried. *What if something happened to him?* The plane left on time, and Montel was still not there, and Sasha was left there, still wondering what was going on.

She walked out of that airport, without the smile she came in with. She didn't even have enough energy to tell the clerk her luggage was on board. She pulled out her cell phone, and paged Montel. She didn't hear from him, no call back, and no message. She wanted to cry as she sat on that curb, waiting for her call back. Instead, she flagged a cab, as she held her cell phone in her hand, still waiting for her call back.

CHAPTER TWENTY-SIX

Sasha made her way through the packed mall. She needed a new dress, a new pair of shoes, a bag, and a makeover from Mac's counter at Macy's. Yes, it was a good day. She was so surprised when the show called her. Sasha thought highly of herself, but still she felt like a regular Joe, not a celebrity. Wow! Someone actually wanted to meet her, and give her a surprise on the Vicki Rake show. Sasha normally didn't watch talk shows, but ever since the show called her, she'd been watching it every day, trying to get a feel for the audience and the topics.

The day before, the show was about deadbeat dads, and the day before that it was about meeting a long-lost relative. The topics weren't too scandalous, so it seemed like a respectable show. She was just hyped up about being on TV. She'd never been on TV, except in middle school when the news decided to do a story about inner city youth performing Shakespeare. That was only for a second, though, no close-ups or nothing.

Anyway, she had to be dressed to the nines for her debut. Who knows how many phone numbers she would get after this show?

Her personal life had been on shaky ground since Hawaii. It

had been three months and she hadn't heard a word from Montel. She checked the newspapers every day to make sure nothing had happened to him. She'd paged him several times. No returns. His cell phone was off, and his home number was disconnected. She'd even started to write him a letter but didn't know where to send it.

After a while she finally accepted that she'd been stood up, but had no idea why. Things were good between them. He had his divorce, and they were making progress. She'd accepted his son and even wanted to meet him one day. Montel didn't like that idea, but she knew it would grow on him. She just didn't understand. What the fuck happened to them? She blamed herself for days, which turned into weeks. She was just hoping that he was all right, wherever he was, so she could get the chance to kill him when she saw him.

Anyway, the show's taping was in two days. She invited Lisa, Michelle, and T to come along with her. The show was flying her in free, so she flew the ladies in with her. She had a hookup on airline tickets via a new friend. That day when she was at the airport waiting for Montel's sorry ass, one of the attendants took pity on her and tried to talk to her. He wrote down his number, and Sasha called after a week. Paul was cool, but so not her type.

After weeks and weeks of phone conversations and lunches, they decided to just be friends. He was pretty cool about it. That was the first male friend she'd made since Michael, who she'd really messed things up with. She didn't even try to redeem herself and didn't call or write. But, hey, she was in love with Montel. Michael knew that and should've just kept it simple, instead of complicating things. Oh well, another of life's lessons. She still wished Michael would call her, though.

Lisa was afraid to fly and grabbed Sasha's arm every time the plane hit a little turbulence. Sasha needed cocoa butter to smooth away the bruises on her arm. They were sitting in first-class seats, sipping on champagne at ten in the morning, like true queens. They hadn't hung out like this in a while. Michelle was busy trying to pick her life back up after the divorce, and T was trying to recover from her addiction to love.

Lisa was sitting pretty in her relationship with Damon. They were so in love, it was disgusting. He drove them to the airport, helped Lisa with the bags, walked with them to the check-in booth, and even waited with them at the gate. They hugged and kissed as the ladies were leaving.

Damn, could the brother give her some room? Sasha couldn't lie. She was jealous as hell. Sasha was happy for her, though.

But when Sasha thought of what she did have, rather than what she didn't, she held on to the thought that, after all this heartache, her good times would come.

After three glasses of wine, she started to settle in and start talking. The ladies also started running their mouths about whatever came to mind.

T lifted up Lisa's arm and smirked. "Hey, Lisa, where's Damon?"

Lisa grabbed her arm from T. "Don't hate, bitch."

They all started laughing.

"It's cool, Lisa," T said. "You and Damon are doing y'all's love thing. That is peace, that's what's up."

"Yeah, girl, hang on to him," Michelle said.

Sasha said, "Lisa, you deserve some happiness, so take it while it's here."

"I'll drink to that." Lisa held up her glass of wine and motioned for everyone to toast with her.

"So, Sasha, who do you think wants to meet you?" Lisa asked.

"Well, I think it's probably someone who visited my website and is very impressed with my business. Or maybe it's an ex-flame who really would love to get back with me."

"Oh, someone like Michael?" Michelle smiled.

Sasha almost choked on her wine. "Michael is so through

with me, it isn't even funny. I screwed things up with him, I snowed him, and then did him wrong, like Montel did me."

T said, "Please. Michael knew what he was working with. He should've seen that one coming."

"True, but still, I could have prevented it from happening by just being honest with myself and with him."

"Whatever. No use crying over spilled milk, Sash," Lisa said. "What's done is done. If it's meant to be, it'll happen. I'm so happy you gave up on Montel. He was such a loser."

Sasha wanted to come clean, but thought, *What for?* She would just tell the same old story and hear the same old thing. It just didn't matter any more. Some things were better left unsaid.

When they arrived at the studio, security escorted her girls to the audience. The producer came over to meet Sasha and went over how things were going to go on the show. Next, the director came in to discuss other things with her, such as rules and regulations. Sasha had to sign a release form stating that she agreed to the taping.

The makeup artist came in next. Sasha explained to her that she didn't want a lot of makeup because she was already done up. Then wardrobe came in, but Sasha wasn't interested in their outfits either. After all the preparations and such, she was led to the room with some other guests who were going to be on the show as well.

Finally, Vicki came in to meet the guests and thanked them for agreeing to be on the show. Vicki was much smaller in person and seemed like a happy-go-lucky person, making them feel relaxed as she coached them on how to behave on the show. She explained that the person who wanted to meet them would go out first, and then they would be signaled to come out and meet that person. They would be blindfolded until they sat down next to the person.

Sasha was feeling kind of nervous at first, but one sip of wine from in the show's waiting room relaxed her again. Vicki left them with that information then thanked them again for being on her show. She was really nice and down-to-earth. She didn't seem like the queen of scum that newspapers and critics made her out to be. There were three other people waiting with Sasha, who was first up. *Good. I can get this over with and go home.*

She tried to make small talk with the two young ladies who were waiting with her. The other fella seemed kind of distant and slow. Sasha said, "Where are you girls from?"

The chubby black female with a gold tooth said, "I'm from Miami. What about you?"

"I'm from Boston."

"Boston? There are black folks in Boston?"

Here we go again. She got so tired of explaining to folks from the south that Boston is full of African Americans, more than they knew. She kept her composure though, telling the gold-toothed diva, "Yeah, there are plenty of African Americans in Boston. As a matter of fact, I brought my girls with me, and they're all black."

After that, Sasha tried not to converse. The girl seemed kind of slow too. Sasha could hear the audience clapping as well as their "Oohs" and "Ahs," as whoever wanted to meet her was out on stage. Sasha was so excited, she couldn't imagine who it was. She just hoped it was some tall, handsome brother who saw her somewhere but didn't have the courage to say anything to her. That would be so romantic. To bring her all the way out here in New York to meet her would be so sweet. She smiled at the thought.

The producer came into the room and signaled her to follow him. She blindfolded Sasha and led her onto the stage. Her heart racing, Sasha could feel the energy in the crowd. She heard voices shouting, but they were muffled. She couldn't make out what they were saying. It sounded like, "Watch out, girl!"

Sasha sat down and waited for her cue to take off her blind-fold.

Vicki said, "Hello, Sasha. You know that you're being brought to the show because someone wants to meet you."

"Yes, Vicki. I'm very anxious to find out who it is."

"Okay, I'll let our guest begin. Go ahead. Say hello."

"Hello, Sasha."

The voice sounded familiar. It was a female's voice. *No male, no cutie.*

"Do you recognize the voice?" Vicki asked her.

"Kind of. I don't know who it is, though."

The female guest said, "You know me, Sasha, just as I know you."

The squeaky voice sent chills to Sasha's spine. She swallowed as she began to undo her blindfold. She took her blindfold off only to discover it was Jennifer, Montel's ex-wife.

As the audience roared, a million thoughts went through her head. *Why did she want to meet me? Did she know about Montel and me? Maybe she just wanted to thank me publicly for all I did for her.* But that couldn't be. The look on Jennifer's face meant war.

Sasha was hoping that Vicki had hired extra security, because Jennifer looked like she was after her blood and wouldn't be satisfied until Sasha wasn't breathing.

Trying to control the conversation, Vicki said, "Do you know each other, Sasha?"

"Yes, I know Jennifer."

"How do you know her, Sasha?"

"She attended one of my Lamaze classes."

"Is that all?"

"Yes," Sasha said, playing it safe.

Someone from the audience yelled, "Liar!"

Sasha started scanning the crowd, looking for three familiar faces. Just then, she saw Lisa waving her hand. She exhaled. If she was going to go down, at least she had her girls to back her up.

Vicki calmed the crowd down. "Sasha, Jennifer tells us you know her husband."

"I know her *ex*-husband, Montel."

The audience roared.

"Wait." Sasha put her hands up in an effort to explain. "Montel and I go way back. Yes, I know Jennifer because she and Montel came to my Lamaze class, but I dated him before that."

Jennifer barked, "Ex-husband, what do you mean, *ex*? He's still my husband."

Sasha was dumbfounded. *This girl is delusional.*

The audience was taking over the show, it seemed, and no one could hear Sasha's side of the story.

"You are nothing but a two-dollar tramp," Jennifer shouted. "You had an affair with my husband, so don't try to deny it. You were sleeping with my man since we had our son."

The audience roared some more.

Sasha felt like she was cornered. Jennifer didn't have her facts straight. Sasha tried to explain, but the audience drowned her out.

Vicki tried to take control back. "Sasha, what do you have to say about this?"

"Vicki, first off, I want to say that I don't appreciate being dragged all the way to New York for this bullshit. This could've been handled between just you and me, Jennifer, over lunch."

The crowd snickered.

"Second of all, Jennifer, Montel was with me before you. You got pregnant while we were dating. He didn't even tell me he was getting married. I found out after the fact. As far as an affair going on between us, we were together one time during your marriage. We hooked up after your divorce." Sasha crossed her arms as if she was through with this conversation.

Jennifer snapped back, "But we're still married, so what the fuck are you talking about?"

The crowd roared in Jennifer's defense.

"Well, you know what, Ms. Jennifer, Montel assured me that you and him were finished, done, *finis*. I told him I wasn't going to see him as long as he was married. If he lied to me, then he lied to you too." Sasha rolled her eyes.

"Was this before or after you dropped your panties?"

The audience roared again.

Sasha stood up. Jennifer was about to catch the serious smackdown. No one was going to embarrass her on TV. "Look, bitch, you have the audacity to come up on this stage trying to look like Ms. Innocent. The truth of the matter is, you slept with my man on a one-night stand, got yourself pregnant, then trapped him into marriage. Now you want to come on TV and cry about being done wrong when you did yourself wrong. You're the slut. You're the sidekick who threw your panties at my man when we were on the outs."

"What are you talking about?"

"Montel and I were together at the beginning of last year until the spring. We got into an argument, and I didn't hear from him for a week. In that week, you found your way into his bed, got yourself pregnant and forced him to marry you. He didn't want to marry you, he just wanted to do what was right. Montel loved me but was torn between right and wrong, so there."

"That's bullshit. Montel and I been together for the past ten years."

Sasha was caught off guard with that one. "Excuse me?"

"I've known Montel since we were teenagers. We hooked up when I was seventeen, broke up when he went to college, got back together when he moved to New York, and have been together ever since, so what are you talking about?"

Sasha couldn't take this new information standing up. She had to sit down. "You're lying. I've known Montel since I was fifteen. We were together when he went to college, and we broke up after I found him with some chick when I went to visit him in North Carolina. We got back together last year."

"You must be confused because"—Jennifer flashed her wedding ring in Sasha's face—"I'm the one wearing the ring, not you."

The audience was loving it.

Sasha was speechless. She wanted to jab Jennifer in the jaw. If what she was telling her was true, then Montel had been playing her the whole time. She wanted to kill him.

Vicki asked Sasha, "Are you all right?"

Sasha nodded. Jennifer sat there with the look of victory on her face. All Sasha could do was fight back. She started shouting out dates, and other personal things that they'd shared. If Montel played her, he was playing her too, and she was the bigger idiot because she married the fool.

"Well, you know what, Jennifer, that was your mistake. You married a dog who's been lying to me and is obviously still lying to you. I was with him, so just get over it."

Vicki tried to take control of the rowdy audience, which disapproved of Sasha's adultery. "So, Jennifer, how did you find out about Sasha?"

"She left a message on his pager back in December about how she couldn't do this anymore and that she was going to stop seeing him. I asked him about it, and he denied it. As the months went by, we argued every day. I didn't know who she was to confront her, so I just went by what he said. He told me how she wanted him to leave me and start a family with her. He told me how he and she were just friends and she wanted it to be more, but he wasn't having it. So a couple of months ago, I found reservations to Hawaii for two. When I asked him about it, he told me it was a surprise for him and me. After the trip, his credit card bill came, and there were three tickets to Hawaii charged, so I called to clear things up, to explain that only two people went. The representative assured me that three tickets were purchased. I called his travel agent, and she told me that Montel had purchased two tickets, one for him, and the other for Sasha Freeman. He later purchased one for me. I realized that she was the same person who'd taught the Lamaze classes and just took it from there."

The audience roared.

Sasha wanted to cry but was too damn angry.

Vicki turned to her. "So you and Montel had plans to go to Hawaii?"

"Yes, we did, but he never showed at the airport, and I haven't heard from him since."

"I see," Vicki said. "Well, audience, I think it's time we meet Montel."

When Montel came out with a blindfold on, the audience booed him. He took off his blindfold and turned to his left and saw Sasha. Then he turned to his right and saw Jennifer. He sank deeper in his chair.

Vicki said, "So, Montel, do you know these women?"

He nodded.

"Jennifer tells us you two were happily married until Sasha came along and broke up your family. Sasha tells us, you and she were happy until Jennifer came along and broke up your relationship. What's your story?"

"I'm married to Jennifer, that says it all, right, Vicki?"

The audience booed.

Sasha tried to keep her composure. *This muthafucka came all the way out here lying, lying to me for months, and had the audacity to disrespect me.* Sasha smacked him.

Then Jennifer tried to throw a blow at Sasha, but she ducked and smacked Montel again.

Sasha stood up ready for war, but security flooded the stage and held Jennifer back, like little miss housewife was going to do something.

"We don't tolerate violence on the show," Vicki said. Then she took a commercial break.

God knows, Sasha needed a break from this mess. She couldn't believe it. The man she'd loved for so long had faked all his feelings for her, fronting all this time, making Sasha think they were so happy, so meant-to-be. The entire time they'd spent together was a lie. Montel was just another sorry-ass excuse for a man, trying to get in where he fit in. Well, she wasn't going down like this. If her ship was sinking, so was everyone else's. If she didn't know anything else, she knew the only winner leaving here was going to be her.

When the show resumed, Sasha was calm and quiet, not even looking the happy couple's way. *What bullshit! Montel didn't deserve anyone, not even a pet dog.*

Vicki reiterated the fact that there could be no violence on the show, to which Sasha agreed. After all, she already got some licks in. Now she was ready to throw verbal blows.

Vicki now decided to hear from the audience.

Sasha knew things would be going her way now, because she had her girls in the audience, and they knew just what to do.

Vicki walked through the audience. "Does anybody have a question or a comment?"

One lady, who looked about twenty, stood up and raised her hand. "If I were you, girl, I'd beat her ass for sleeping with your husband, and then I'd kick his ass for sleeping with her."

The audience roared again.

Vicki started egging people, as if she wanted to keep those comments coming.

Another girl, who looked about twelve, stood up and said, "Sister girl, she isn't even worth all that. Just kick him to the curb."

Another middle-aged woman said, "See, this is the problem with the institution of marriage these days amongst young people—Y'all don't have any respect for each other. What about the child y'all have together?"

Sasha felt like saying to that lady, "Look around, sister. The institution of marriage isn't just fucked up in young people. Where's your husband?"

One heavyset brother raised his hand. He said, "Montel is a dog and deserves no one."

Another man said, "Jennifer was stupid for marrying him."

Another man from the audience snatched the mike from Vicki. "Yo, Sasha, if it's okay with you, I'd like to meet you after the show. I think you're the shit."

Vicki said, "Please, audience, no obscene language."

A wannabe diva said, "If he was with her, obviously something isn't right in your marriage. Take a closer look."

Finally, Lisa stood up. "Vicki, I'm going to tell you something right now. I know Sasha, and I know Montel. The bottom line is the relationship they had was real. He continued to come around after he was married, despite his commitment to Jennifer. Sasha didn't even know the brother was getting married until someone told her. Montel has stayed over Sasha's house, they've gone to L.A. together, and had other trips and so forth, so if Jennifer even believes one word that lying sonofabitch has to say, that's on her."

The audience applauded Lisa's contribution.

Vicki looked at Sasha. "Is that true, Sasha, that you and Montel had a serious relationship?"

"Yes, Vicki, that's true."

"And you thought it was just you and him going to Hawaii?"

"Yep." Sasha turned to Jennifer. "Look, girlfriend, I could care less what you do with your life, but don't you ever come to me with this bullshit again. The fact of the matter is, Montel is dogging you, and you're an idiot to defend him. It's okay because, Lord knows, he has snowed me too. You can keep your husband. Just keep him the hell away from me!"

The crowd applauded again.

"And another thing, if you're so secure in your marriage and Montel is so faithful, why is there a me at all?"

"Look, Sasha, I came out here today upset. I needed someone else to blame. I needed something else to be true, besides the fact that my husband isn't the man I thought he was. I wanted answers, and I got them." Then she turned to Montel. "I hope you brought enough money with you because the locks are being changed as we speak, and I want your lying, cheating, no-good, pitiful-excuse-for-a-husbandself out of my house. Goodbye!"

This time the audience seemed to explode.

Montel didn't say anything. He just sat there looking as if Jennifer's words weren't true and he could talk his way out of this one.

Jennifer's eyes seemed familiar. They were that similar to Lisa's when she was finished with Jake. To Michelle's when she threw Jamal out. To T's when she gave up on Ricky. To Sasha's when she'd looked in the mirror and realized that she'd been snowed.

After the show, Sasha left quickly. She didn't want to see or hear another word. She gathered the ladies together and dashed to the airport to find the first available flight to Boston.

On the plane ride back, the ladies filled Sasha in on what had happened before she came on the show. Jennifer was bad-mouthing her, making it seem like she stole her husband. They were so shocked and tried to get backstage to warn her, but security wouldn't let them through.

Sasha held her head high. "I did do wrong on my part by sleeping with Montel when I knew he was married. Damn, he was lying from jump." That made Sasha wonder about her judgment. "I don't think I can pick them. Oh well, what next?"

Sasha couldn't reach her house porch fast enough. She was so tired. The plane ride was so exhausting. She couldn't wait to get in her bed and go to sleep. Her porch light was out. *Great. Another thing to fix besides my personal life.*

Well, one good thing came out of this. She finally got some closure. She wouldn't waste her time on loving Montel any more.

Sasha didn't see Raymond's car in the driveway. It was late. *Where could he be?* Anyway, she struggled with the keyhole to the door in the darkness, as the cool fall breeze crept up on her shoulder.

She suddenly got this eerie feeling, like someone was watching her. She turned around, and no one was there. When she finally got the door open, she heard quick steps coming up her stairway.

It was Jason, the lunatic. "Hi, Sasha. How you doing?"

A frightened Sasha tried to keep her composure, so he didn't see how scared she was. "What the fuck are you doing here? I have a restraining order on you."

"Yeah, but that ended months ago."

"Whatever. You're not wanted here, so leave."

"I'm not trying to cause you harm. I just wanted to . . ." He paused as tremors took over his hands. "I just wanted to apologize first for my behavior. Secondly, I want to thank you for your help. I know now that it was you who referred me to those psychiatrists. They really helped me. I been trying to call you, but I never have the nerve to say anything."

The hang-ups. Shit, I never did change my number. Has he been waiting to get me alone, to make his move? What the fuck does he want? "Look, Jason, I appreciate the apology, and I saw that you needed help. I just was trying to do my part, that's all."

"Well, you did, and I am better now."

"That's good to know. Well, I have to be going, so if you don't mind—"

"I know, Sasha. You probably have a laundry list of men trying to get at you, so I won't waste your time. I just wanted to know one thing first."

Sasha knew she would regret asking the question. "What?"

"Why was it never me? All these dudes I've seen you with, all these relationships, how come you never gave us a chance?"

"You're not my type."

Jason's hands started to tremble again, his voice changing from calm to erratic. "Well, why didn't you give me a chance?

Oh, that's right, I'm not your type." He continued talking to himself, freaking her out.

Sasha reached for her can of Mace, but Jason grabbed her arm as if he knew what she was up to.

"Sasha, all I wanted was a chance, a chance for us."

"Let go of my fucking arm, all right," Sasha yelled, trying to sound like she was in control.

Jason held her wrist real tight with one hand and pulled out a knife with the other.

Sasha was hysterical. "What the hell are you doing?"

"I just wanted you to listen. I just wanted you to see that you and me should be together."

"What! By holding a knife to my throat? You are crazy."

"Open your door, Sasha," Jason demanded.

"No!"

"Open the door and let me in!"

"No!"

He pressed his pelvis against her, slamming her back to the door, and tried to snatch the house keys out of her hand, but she threw them in the yard.

Jason pointed the knife in her face. "You're going to pay for that one, bitch!" Craziness in his eyes, he ripped open her coat and began to kiss her neck and fondle her breasts, his knife up against her throat.

Sasha had to think fast. Before she could get her knee up to kick him where it hurt most, somebody snatched him and tossed him to the ground. She thought it was Raymond, but to her surprise and joy, it was Michael . . . to her rescue once again.

Turned out, Jason was diagnosed with schizophrenia and had been in a mental institution for the for the past year. As luck would have it, Michael knew he had escaped and figured the first place he would go would be to Sasha's house. Michael didn't say anything to Sasha, making it seem as if he was only after the bad guy. In fact, he had some other officer take her statement.

Sasha wanted to thank him but feared she wouldn't get the chance. All these months of getting over hurt had silenced him. Now he was cold and reminded her of T, when Ricky left her standing at the altar. Sasha just knew he hated her, but she had to let him know how thankful she was that he'd showed up when he did.

As she was leaving the police precinct, Michael and a couple of other "doughnut lovers" were sitting around laughing. When she walked by him, he had his back turned toward her. Sasha wanted to hug him, wanted to kiss him, but was afraid of being rejected, and walked out of the station alone.

CHAPTER TWENTY-SEVEN

So months later, and then years later, Sasha still knew what was true. It's like making a bowl of rice pudding. You know what ingredients to use to make this fabulous dish. You know how to prepare for it, cook it, cool it, and eat it. To your sweet delight, it could taste just right, or it could need a few things to make it just right. Nonetheless, you can do two things with the rice: eat it, and keep adding ingredients, so it eventually tastes right, or you can throw the rice pudding away and make a new batch.

Lisa chose to keep her rice pudding—Damon. Honestly, she couldn't say she wasn't happier than ever. Although, Damon was the finest thing that ever walked this earth, he had his faults and weaknesses, things that would've made Sasha throw him away and start a new batch, but not, Lisa. To her, he was just right. What they felt for each other was real, and no one was playing any games. No one was pretending to feel one way, when they really didn't feel that way at all. No one was controlling the other's feelings and, at the same time, masking theirs so that the other person couldn't really see what was going on.

Both Lisa and Damon's eyes and heads were clear, and they knew what they had found in each other. That's why they were still together today and in love more than anyone could know.

There was a knock on Sasha's door. She wanted to get this speech down pat before the reception, not wanting to let her girl down. The knocking got louder and louder.

"Damn it, I'm coming. Hold on, I'll be there in a minute."

It was Raymond. He was wearing his tuxedo, and shiny black shoes. She thought it was nice of Lisa to want him in the wedding. After all, he was like a second brother to her, since they were so close. It was Raymond's responsibility to make sure the bridesmaids and groomsmen got to the wedding on time. He and his son, now five, were looking too handsome.

Sasha snapped a picture of the two most important men in her life, her brother and her nephew. Sometimes, it seemed like the only men. Sasha'd had her share though. Sasha thought she would never get it together. There were days when she didn't think she would ever get this relationship crap right. Here she was thirty-four and going to another wedding, but nowhere near getting married.

Montel, someone she hadn't thought about in years, changed something in her. He'd made her lose her trust in men, and gain more trust in herself. She didn't regret anything and was grateful that she got out before it was too late. She never spoke to him again after that day on the show. The last she'd heard of him, he and Jennifer were still married, working on their third child, and Montel was the stay-at-home dad. Sasha had to wonder what went through Jennifer's head. Maybe one day she would see, like Michelle did after child and tribulation number three.

It wasn't too late for Michelle, another bridesmaid. Once a bride, she got through a long, hard storm, and was enjoying the cool spring breeze. She dated here and there, but never gave of herself completely, letting men know of her issues up front. And if they couldn't handle it, cool. They can just be friends.

Tamieka had done a lot of that through the years, just keeping it simple. She'd met this man named Ron when she flew off to Jamaica one year. He lived in D.C., so their relationship was a long-distance one. Their friendship/courtship had been going on for three years now, a record for her.

The limo was going too fast for Sasha to jot her speech down in her head. She wanted to say so much about Lisa and Damon and just didn't know where to start. They had surpassed a lot of obstacles and still remained together. Damon was such a ladies man. How could Lisa fall for him? Sasha guessed Damon saw in Lisa what she saw in him, hope.

"Damn it, if this limo goes over one more bump, I'm going to throw my pumps at him," Sasha said.

"Stop your moaning, Sasha. We're almost there," Lisa said in a calm voice. She was so nervous about her wedding. Her dress was a white, halter-top design by Vera Wang. "Sasha, you can't keep complaining like this. It's my day, not Sash's day to bitch and moan."

"Fine," Sasha said, with an attitude.

Lisa grabbed her hand. "I need you today, girl. I can't do this alone."

"Need who?" T said in a burst. "If I recall correctly, we are all in this together."

"The wedding, yes, not the honeymoon." Michelle giggled.

T wanted to toast of course, but three drunken bridesmaids and one bride didn't quite look right.

Lisa took a deep breath and decided to say a speech before they got to the church. "Ladies, hear me when I say this. I couldn't have gotten here without you. You were there when I was weak, there when I was dumb, and there when I was lost. Now, I have stumbled across something so wonderful, I can't help but be thankful. I found happiness in life, and I owe that to you." Lisa's eyes started to water, as did those of her three closest friends. She looked at Sasha. "Sasha, don't worry about your speech. Just let it flow like that from the heart."

When the limo pulled up to the church, not all the guests were inside yet.

The groomsman went in first, and the bride and her party sat in the limo and waited for everyone to go inside.

Sasha searched thought after thought, trying to come up with something that said Damon and Lisa belonged together. Thoughts just didn't flow into words. She was missing something. As she looked out the tinted window, she saw a familiar face. He was six feet tall, dark skinned, and had pearl-white teeth.

He smiled at her, as if he could see her, and she smiled back at him as if he could see her. Michael always knew how to make Sasha feel happy again, feel like herself, no bullshit, and no games. He'd stayed around just as a friend though. Michael was one of the best friends Sasha had. They could shoot pool together, watch movies, eat out, talk shit, and still call each other the next day. It was like they were old friends from childhood.

Michael would never get intimate with her like that ever again though. She had a lot of work to do if she ever wanted to earn his trust again. He'd loved her and she hurt him. So friends it was, and had been ever since that night he'd saved her from Jason. He'd show up at her house, and they'd talk. Somehow they'd stayed in touch and became close friends rather than lovers.

So there he was, this man who probably would be the only

man to love her like this, probably the only man who could, and she let him go.

Suddenly, what Sasha said at Lisa's reception didn't seem to matter so much any more. Their getting married said it all. When you get right down to it, you just have to know when to keep a good man and when to throw the bad one away.